Buster's Cube

Also by Ben Slotover

The Last Machine

Mr. Thomas

The Low

With Paul Elliott

Captain V

Mick

With Peter Waldeck

Jim and Heinz

Buster's Cube

Ben Slotover

Blunt Productions Ltd

First published in Great Britain by Blunt Productions Ltd 2014

55 Lady Somerset road London NW5 1TY

www.bluntproductions.com

ISBN 978-0-9927349-0-9

Copyright © 2014 Ben Slotover

All rights reserved. This book or any portion thereof
may not be reproduced or used in any manner whatsoever without the express
written permission of the publisher except for the use of brief quotations
in a book review.

This book is sold subject to the condition that it shall not, by way of trade or
otherwise, be lent, resold, hired out, or otherwise circulated without the
publisher's prior consent in any form of binding or cover other than that in
which it is published and without a similar condition including this condition
being imposed on the subsequent publisher.

The moral right of Ben Slotover has been asserted.

For Sissi

Acknowledgements

Although this is the work of one person, there are many people without whose help this would be a vastly inferior book. They have been the buffers that have stopped me going off the hard shoulder into the literary ditch, the mirrors that have shown me what I've been writing from a reader's standpoint and the chorus that have warned me away from overblown prose and hacky metaphor. Asking someone to appraise a painting may only be requesting a minute or two of their time, to watch your film a couple of hours, but a novel takes days, sometimes weeks, and I am eternally grateful to those who have donated their time to do it.

Peter Kravitz went beyond any expectation I had and delivered what amounted to a full on edit job purely out of the kindness of his heart. Kate Slotover provided invaluable advice on content and cover design. Paul Elliott, Peter Waldeck and Ben Rowlinson all suffered through early drafts and bestowed solid wisdom and encouragement. Sissi my wife and Lily, Sam and Amy my kids put up with my tapping away in the corner and occasional requests for advice on some arcane point of grammar- advice that I would often ignore. Finally I'd like to thank (though not name, for reasons of tact) all those who couldn't help because they never managed to finish the book. Your silence told me louder than anything that it wasn't ready. Hopefully you'll give it another go.

B.S.

Chapter one

I heard him long before I saw him. That is I heard the furious clanking of his car after what he'd done to it. Buster had sawn off the whole left side: doors, windows, back wing, the whole lot, then welded everything in one piece and re-attached it on two giant hinges at the bottom. This allowed him to open up the entire side of the car and load it with more stuff than the guys at Peugeot had ever designed it for.

The car turned the corner and came down the narrow alley toward me, its welded-together side flap pushed partly open by what looked like some large boxes on the back seat. The irregular shape of the car and its load was clearly having an effect on the vehicle's steering. If Buster took his hands off the wheel the car would immediately veer left. It did a lot of this as it approached because he was holding the hinged flap closed with one hand and waving madly at me with the other, grabbing the steering wheel occasionally to keep the car from scraping the wall of the alley.

Benson's my name, by the way. Philip Benson. I'm what you'd call an entrepreneur. I look for commercial opportunities and try to exploit them before anyone else beats me to it. I'm OK at it. I've made a bit of dough in my time, had a couple of disasters (of which more later), I'm a straight thinker and a straight talker and have only one proper talent: I can see money.

Go into a McDonalds. What do you look at? The pictures of the burgers above the servers' heads? I look at the cash registers, I look at people fingering their wallets as they decide what to eat. I see a hundred streams of money coming together into a big red river and flowing into the McDonalds account. I see pipes coming out of the river and watering the accounts of ketchup packet manufacturers and potato farmers. I see money flowing through the air from people to companies and back to people. A boy on the bus downloads a tune and plays it out of his phone. Money goes to T-Mobile and Yoko Ono.

So what I do is look for ripples in the money flow, currents below the surface and dry patches which shouldn't be dry. If you've got the right eyes you can jump in and divert the flow in your direction. It all sounds very abstract but for all my fancy talk about seeing money what it really entails is being on the phone all day and adding up long lists of numbers. Today I spent half an hour trying to get an employee of an airline to quote me a price for twenty one seats on a jumbo jet. No, I'm not taking a football team on tour, it's a little scheme I'm working on.

I might as well tell you about it: I want to open a hotel. On a plane. Imagine you're on a long haul jet, in Economy. Like any sane person without unlimited funds you didn't fancy paying silly money for a seat in First, Business or god help you, Premium Economy. However you're dead tired and could really do with a lie-down. So you wander down to the back of the plane to my closed-off section where you pay a reasonable price for a few hours in a bed. When I say 'bed' it's really not much more than a wide shelf and an inflatable mattress but I'm working on a way to stack them up from floor to ceiling in fours. In fact I'm convinced it's possible to get more people lying down than sitting on a 747 or an A380.

The problem is the Airlines: they aren't too keen on the idea. Something about safety but really I ask you. If that monster of a plane takes a dive does it really matter if you're lying down or sitting up when they scrape you off the ground? It's all about their profits of course. Who's going to pay a fortune for canapés and champagne in first class when they can lie down flat in my inflight hotel for a fraction of the price?

Anyway, back to my friend Buster Ames. You could call him a Scientist but any scientific training he's had has ended in disaster or just fizzled out. You could call him an Artist but only as a catch-all label for someone who's created a bunch of stuff that has no apparent use. You could call him a 'Natural Philosopher' like the ancient Greeks which is a nice label, better than the one I came up with which was 'Sciartist'. The Greeks were after the same thing as us anyway. Some of them needed to make sense of the world and others were looking to take those findings and make a bit of cash out of them.

Which is where I come in. You see, I'm convinced that for all his digressions and stubborn refusal to follow a straight path anywhere, Buster is a gold mine. Maybe not so much a gold mine as a badger's tunnel that occasionally yields diamonds. Unlike others who have failed to capitalize on Buster's peculiar genius I can stay the course for two reasons. One is that I don't get distracted. I can look at his ideas and all the chaos that follows them and judge it all purely in terms of whether we're going to be able to make money out of it or not. It doesn't mean I'm not interested in his mental processes, but you don't have to learn how to farm tomatoes to sell a pizza.

The other reason I can handle Buster is I've learned how to handle Buster and the best way to do this is not handle him at all. Just follow in his wake, admire the scenery and jump on any gems that fall out of the badger hole. You'll see what I mean.

Chapter two

I stood in Buster's alley watching his car clank and grind its way toward me. The alley was a canyon that cut through a city block. Open at each end, it was the only way to reach Buster's place and barely wider than his car. Other motorists were never a problem as he had placed No Entry signs at both ends of the alley and painted one way markings that always pointed against you. Buster's door was the only thing in the alley, which was five storeys of featureless brick on both sides.

Buster lived nowhere. When he came to London he looked at some aerial photos to decide where to base himself. This was before Google Earth, you understand. Even before Google in fact. It was a long time ago but the photos Buster looked at were even older and showed all this World War Two bomb damage.

"So what's the point of that?" you're asking. Why not go to an estate agency or even thumb through an A-Z map? Well here's how Buster's mind works. On one photo he found a massive bombsite in the City of London and it was right in the middle of a block that had been built around 1900. Then he went down there and found the buildings had been repaired after the war but not completely rebuilt. Now to look at them from the front you'd not notice anything about them but Buster knew that a giant bomb had fallen right in the middle of that block all those years ago. He found the alley and halfway down it was a door. The door was locked but after a couple of tugs on the handle the ancient lock fell apart and the door opened.

Behind the door was a dark passage that opened out into a courtyard. It wasn't really a courtyard, more a square shaft. What had happened was this: after the bomb made a big hole in this block, all the backs of the buildings surrounding the hole were patched up in a hurry, leaving this open bit in the middle that no one looked out onto and had forgotten even existed. It was a square five metres on each side and surrounded by fifty metres of vertical brick wall, the bottom of which was covered in dead pigeons.

Buster fell in love with the place. It had no address or official presence but that suited him fine. He enlarged the door, repaired the lock and quietly moved in. Naturally he built his home himself. Seeing as the only view was directly up he put all the windows in the ceiling. Then when he ran out of space he replaced the ceiling with a floor and build another level on top. There were now three levels to his home- the top level was the one he lived on, the two below being his workshop (middle) and storage (ground). He paid no rent, his water he tapped from pipes in the ground and his power… well I was never sure how he'd hooked up his electricity but it always went off when there was a tube strike.

The car finally came to a halt beside me and Buster squeezed out of the drivers side door, which could only open a few inches due to the tightness of the alley.

"Euurgh," he groaned with the effort of leaving his vehicle. "Help me with these boxes will you?".

I knew to stand back when he released the car's side-flap. The flap crashed to the ground, pivoting on its hinges. The big boxes somehow stayed in place.

"One each," said Buster, somewhat unnecessarily.

The two boxes were cubes a bit less than a metre along each side. They were bulky and heavy and I was curious to see what was inside them as we hauled them inside and onto a table. Packages and weird stuff were always turning up for Buster at my address as he couldn't get the Royal Mail or Fedex to recognise his own. More than once I discovered I had been holding onto something profoundly dangerous.

Buster grabbed a short bladed knife and very carefully opened the flaps of the first box. There was a second box inside this one, a smooth sided cardboard cube unblemished by tape or sticky labels, unlike its outer shell. Buster cooed in awe and carefully slid the top off.

We leaned forward and found a piece of equipment of baffling intricacy. It had motors and wires, valves and control panels, switches and tanks. If someone had told me it was part of a NASA Mars spaceship life support system I would have believed them. Carefully we lifted it out and opened the other one. Its contents were identical, another of the amazing contraptions in a smooth cardboard cube. We laid the two machines next to each other on the table.

"What are they?" I asked.

"They're crap," replied Buster. "Absolute garbage."

He took one machine off the table and over to the mountain of smashed-up electronics in the corner of the storage room, dumping it in a pile of flatbed scanners which if they weren't broken before, now were.

"Wha… what's wrong with them?"

"There's nothing wrong with them, they're just shit, that's all." Buster jerked the other one off the table and took it to its final resting place. "And no, before you ask, they're not worth any money. I wouldn't sell them anyway, it would ruin my good standing on eBay."

"Then why even bother bringing them here?"

"This is why."

Buster cleared the table of everything except the two boxes that the machines had come in.

"Best cardboard boxes on the market. Actually not even on the market. You can't get hold of these boxes any other way than to buy something from that company to put in the box. These are

Buster's Cube

really good boxes, and they are cubical as well. That's very important. There are almost no boxes that are perfect cubes. It's not a popular shape. No one wants them or makes them. Sometimes an alarm clock will come in a cubic box but that's too small for what I want to do."

"OK," I said, pinching the bridge of my nose to stop the buzzing that would sometimes start up in my brain when trying to follow Buster. "What is it you want to do?"

"I'll draw it for you."

Buster took the knife and sliced open one of the outer boxes, laying it flat on the table in a T shape. He whipped a sharpie pen out of nowhere and leaned over the cardboard.

This is what he drew:

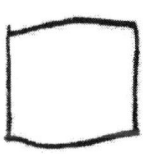

"There. What's that?"

"A square."

"Correct."

He drew some more:

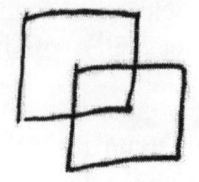

"Now, what's that?"

I paused, trying to sift through my brain to come up with a proper name for the shape, but quickly gave up and stated the obvious.

"Two squares."

"Very good. Notice that they are intersecting."

"I noticed."

"And that the top left corner of the lower square is right in the middle of the upper square."

"And," I said, feeling rather clever, "the bottom right corner of the upper square is in the middle of the lower square."

"Exactly! Remember that, that's very important. Now what are these?"

"Some lines."

"Excellent, now..."

"Parallel lines!" I added, all my school geometry coming back.

"It doesn't matter that they're parallel. I just put them like that. Now this is where it gets complicated. Suppose I took one of these lines and added it to the squares like this:"

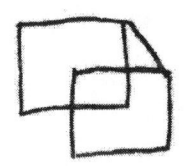

"Can you see it?"

"Of course I can see it."

"Yes, but can you <u>see</u> it?"

I used to hate it when Buster went on like this. He'd always be demanding that I see the world through his own eyes, to...intuit things the way he did. Of course I wouldn't know until he explained, but I've learned to be patient. I don't expect Buster to see streams of money the way I do, it's the brain that's doing the seeing and we've all got different brains. Buster especially so.

"OK, what am I supposed to be seeing?"

"Maybe this will help." he said, drawing again. He drew three more lines on the picture:

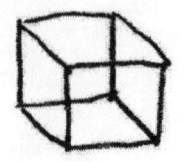

"OK," I said, "It's a cube."

A look of pure delight crossed Buster's face.

"Yes! It's a cube!"

"Well…"

"And no! It's not a cube!"

The buzzing in the bridge of my nose started again. I knew it would do no good to say anything so I just waited for Buster to carry on.

"Look, do you know the work of Rene Magritte?"

"An artist?"

"Yes, he did the man with a bowler hat and an apple in front of his face."

"Yeah, so what?"

"He also did a painting of a pipe and wrote under it in French 'This is not a pipe.'"

"Yeah, very surreal. Never really got that one."

"It's very simple. What he was saying was it looked like a pipe but you couldn't use it or smoke it because in the end it's just a picture of a pipe."

"Oh!. OK, I see. And you're saying that's not a cube because it's just a picture of a cube, right?"

Buster nodded, smiling.

"Well, that was fun," I said. "Shall we have lunch?"

Buster's smile flicked off.

"Look at the first square again. What's the difference between that and the drawing of the cube?"

"Well, I suppose a square is two-dimensional and a cube is three-dimensional."

"And yet you called that drawing a cube when it's just pen marks on a flat piece of cardboard!"

"All right, so sue me! I called it a cube because it looked like a bloody cube!"

Sometimes entire days with Buster would go by like this. What he considered important research and development I saw as wasting time on silly games. I think he sensed my impatience and took it up a notch.

"Let's recap, because the next part is important and I don't want to lose you," he said, pointing at each picture with the sharpie. "This first picture of the square is two dimensional. The two squares intersecting, they're two dimensional as well. Can we agree on that?"

"OK."

"And these lines, they're one dimensional, right?"

I had to think about that for a moment. No one really talks about one-dimensional these days except for describing the performances in three-dimensional films.

"Just take it from me," said Buster. "A single straight line is one dimensional, because there's only one thing to measure, and that's the length of the line, right? Whereas a square or any other shape on a flat surface is two dimensional because there's two things to measure, height and width."

"OK, I'm with you so far."

"Cool. Now when we add one to two, what does that make?"

"Three."

"And when I take these one dimensional lines and use them to connect up the four corners of the two dimensional squares, what does it make?"

"A cube. Well, a picture of a cube."

"That's right, a two dimensional picture of a three dimensional cube, with height, width, and now a sense of depth."

"Great. Now what?"

"Now…" said Buster, sweeping the flat cardboard off the table and putting one of the boxes in its place. "What's this?"

"A cardboard cube."

"Yes, a real life cube in three real life dimensions. You know what's coming next, right?"

"Lunch?"

"Just answer me this: What would happen if I intersect these two cubes the same way I did with the two squares?"

"How can you intersect solid objects?"

"Oh, I'll just cut them up a bit with the knife. That's the easy part, and where before I had two-dimensional squares intersecting, now I have three-dimensional cubes intersecting. And then it will be finished."

I felt very close to the edge of the chasm that separated my mental abilities from his.

"What will be finished?"

"My four dimensional cube!"

"Now wait a minute," I said. "Whatever you're planning to make here, it's only going to be three-dimensional because we live in a three-dimensional world. It's like that drawing of a cube you made, or that pipe painting. It'll only be a model, a 3D depiction of what a 4D object looks like, not the real thing."

"True, but when you saw the 2D picture of the cube you called it a cube, and when people see a picture of a pipe they call it a pipe. Wouldn't you like to see a model of something that is a gateway to another dimension?"

"I suppose so, but what use will it be?"

I regretted the words as soon as I had said them. Buster doesn't see the practical or commercial use of anything he does which is why he needs someone like me around.

"Let's just make it, then we'll see." he said.

Chapter three

As it happened, making a four dimensional cube was quite fun. I was happy to help fetch glue and tape and spare bits of cardboard while Buster did the cutting and sticking. It made a change from the office and allowed me to take a break from the latest crisis that had engulfed my company Benson Enterprises Ltd. It's a pretty dull name but I ran out of cool names with the first six companies I formed which are now defunct. I haven't grown too attached to the name as I know it will probably go the way of the first six before long.

The problem I was avoiding while hiding out with Buster was related to a fantastic idea I'd had while eating some toast. It was an unevenly toasted piece of bread, one strip of it about three quarters the way down completely untoasted. It had been partially toasted by my old toaster, a battered relic which I had owned since my student days. At some point in the late 80s a bagel had got stuck in it and in digging it out with a butter knife I had damaged one of the filaments. Ever since then the toaster had left a raw strip across everything I had put into it.

So why didn't I just get a new toaster? Well, I did. I got four new toasters over the next twenty years, all different brands and prices, and they all broke almost immediately. During this time I kept the old toaster as I needed something to make my toast while I got round to chucking out the latest broken toaster and buying a new one. I eventually gave up buying new toasters and went back to using the half-broken toaster fulltime which has been turning out endless slices of toast with raw strips across them for over thirty years.

When things properly break they stay broken, but when they half-break they seem to last forever. A quick survey of my flat turned up more evidence to confirm this. I have a DVD player that needs to be held shut with a pencil jammed against the carpet.

It's been working since 2000. A dishwasher that vomits a little hot water during its dry cycle: running for eleven years past its warranty. My Hi-Fi (yes, I still have a Hi-Fi) crackles like crazy when you turn any knob on it unless you twiddle the knobs back and forth a bit first. What the world needs, I realised, was not another expert in fixing things but an expert in breaking things.

This revelation led to my setting up the Appliance Longevity Service, a sort of preventative medicine for household objects. People would pay me to send over one of my experts to break their stuff just enough to make it last forever. The problems came from the quality of the people I got to do the breaking. Most of them were ex-cons with anger management problems and the latest did not know the difference between half-breaking something and smashing it to pieces. In a couple of cases my customers hadn't complained, in fact they had even sent me extra money if I promised not to send the guy round again. The money was useful but it wasn't how I wanted to run this scheme. My customers were asking for replacements for their half or fully broken appliances and I was getting sick of the whole idea. Making four dimensional cubes with Buster was a nice holiday from all that.

Buster chopped out a corner of one of the cubes. He then got the other cube and wedged it into the hole he had made. I held it in place while he taped it up. I saw what he was getting at with the two cubes being merged together like the two intersecting squares he had drawn earlier.

We then cut out some cardboard flaps and fixed them between the two cubes so the flaps connected the cubes edge to edge, kind of like the lines had connected the squares in the 2D drawing. This gave the whole structure a strange appearance of two cubes held to each other by webbing. Buster stepped back to examine his handiwork.

"Hmmm," he hummed quietly. "What do you think?"

"Well to be honest I'm not sure what we've got here," I

replied. "Is that really what a four dimensional cube looks like?"

"It's a hint of what four dimensions looks like, an illusion, a clue, as good an idea as the drawing of the cube on paper gives you an idea of a 3D cube."

"Is that it, then? Can we draw a line under the four dimensional cube project?"

"Not yet, I want to see what it looks like inside."

Buster ambled down the length of his toolbench. I call it a toolbench but really it was several tables laid end to end along the whole length of the wall. There was every tool you could think of. I've had to drive Buster to numerous godforsaken districts of outer London looking for the last industrial estate that makes ball-bearing extruders. There were tools for making other tools on that bench, that's how serious it was. If only the tools were in some sort of order it would have been even more impressive but Buster Ames' toolbench was the most disorganized and cluttered one I have ever seen, though I haven't seen many. I'd love to tell you that despite the clutter Buster could lay his hands on any tool he desired within ten seconds but sadly that isn't the case. Whole projects have gone tits-up because Buster can't find one of his tools. The worst is he grumbles and scolds himself while he's looking for stuff while all you can do is stand there or read a book if you've brought one.

"Torch…" said Buster. "Hmmmm…."

He shifted a giant spanner to one side, releasing several ball bearings which rolled to the floor.

"Dammit…"

He ignored the ball bearings, wandered over to the other end and stared in silence at pile of every Allen key ever made. Time passed.

"Oh!" he said suddenly and dug into his pocket, drawing

out a cheap plastic lighter. "This'll do."

Buster went back to the 4D cube and opened up one end. Luckily it was the end that had previously been the top of a box so it had a flap for easy access. It was just big enough to accommodate his head and shoulders. Flicking the lighter on he lit up the interior and peered inside. I had a look over his shoulder. It looked almost how I'd expected it to: the bottom of a cardboard box. Except one thing: one corner of the box was taken up by a smaller box, which I realised was the corner of the other cube sticking in. It looked a bit like a little cardboard room with a cube in the corner. Buster clicked off his lighter and stuck his head in. He was in there for some time before he withdrew his head.

"Wow."

Of all the things to say 'Wow' about, I would never put 'sticking your head in a box' on that list, but when Buster said 'Wow' about something he wasn't messing about.

"You've got to try this." he said.

He stepped aside and I bent over and stuck my head in the box. As I expected it was dark and there was little to do.

"Take a deep breath in through your nose." I heard Buster say from outside the box. I tentatively inhaled.

"What can you smell?" he asked.

"Cardboard."

"Oh, come on. Sniff deeper!"

"I'm sniffing! If I sniff any deeper I'll start inhaling my own nose."

"Let me have another go."

"Fine."

I was just about to withdraw from the box when the smell hit me. It wasn't so much a smell as a memory of a smell. Hard to describe, but if you imagine a memory very intense but only the smell part of it and no other attached senses or other memories, that was what it was like. The strange part of it was it couldn't have been a memory as I had never, ever smelled that smell before. It was an entirely new smell. There was gunpowder and metal and raspberries and rum in it. I took my head out of the box.

"Wow." I said.

"What did you just think happened?" asked Buster.

"Well, the people who made these boxes must have been using some pretty strong glue."

"How long do you think you had your head in there?"

"Thirty seconds?"

"You were in there for an hour and twenty one minutes."

"Don't be silly."

"I'm not being silly. An hour twenty one minutes. I timed it."

"And you just let me stand there?"

"I wanted to see what would happen."

"I don't believe this," I said, checking my watch. "I'm supposed to be… Jesus, it's five o'clock!"

"You see?" said Buster gleefully. "There's something going on with this cube!"

"What's going on," I said, "Is that that box has some kind of toxic glue in it that made me pass out and inhale God knows how much chemical vapour and you just stood there and let it happen."

Buster's Cube

"I didn't just stand here!" Buster protested. "I timed you!"

"Fine." I snapped, picking up my coat. "I'll be sure to mention that to my Doctor."

"Wait!" said Buster, "Let's give it one more test."

"I'm not putting my head back in there."

"I'll do it."

Buster leaned over in front of the box without putting his head in. He held up his lighter to his wristwatch.

"I'm going to put my head in and time how long I'm in. Meanwhile you time how long I'm in there from the outside. If the times are the same we'll know that nothing weird is going on, OK?"

"Go on, then." I said, opening a stopwatch app on my phone.

"Ok, start your timer…. Now!"

Buster flicked on his lighter and put his head into the box. After a while he called out.

"How long have you got?"

"Twenty seconds"

"Me too."

We waited for a while.

"Forty five seconds." he said.

"Me too. Can you smell anything?"

"A bit. Smells different this time. Like toast."

Toast. It reminded me of the nonsense back at the office,

all the complaints that would be waiting on the Appliance Longevity Service Helpline when I got back. What the hell was I doing here timing how long Buster has his head stuck in the fourth dimension? What was worse, anyway, wasting an afternoon doing something serious or wasting an afternoon doing something silly? I could smell the toast now. Maybe it was coming from the outside of the box. I looked at my watch: coming up to two minutes. Buster hadn't done a time check for a while.

"Two minutes." I said. Buster didn't reply.

"Buster?"

He stood motionless with his head in the box. The smell was getting stronger. It was definitely not the same smell as last time. This I had definitely smelled before: Burning.

"Buster!"

A black spot grew on top of the cardboard and at the same time a stream of smoke came out past Buster's shoulders. I grabbed the tops of his arms and pulled his head out of the cube just before it puffed into flame. Buster shook himself awake.

"How long…?" he said

"Never mind how long, the cube is on fire!".

Without a word or a moment of panic Buster reached over to his extinguisher hose. This was probably the smartest invention he had ever devised as it had saved his life twenty times over and my own at least twice. Inspired by one of those soft drink guns you see in pubs, he had rigged up some gas, foam and water tanks to the ceiling and had them dispensing through a dangling hose which could reach any part of the room. With a quick flip of the switch to 'Water' Buster sprayed the burning cardboard boxes until the blaze was out.

We both looked at the soggy pile of charred cardboard.

"Maybe I should build another one." said Buster finally.

"Maybe you should build one that won't catch fire when you stick your head in it with a naked flame."

"Maybe I should have found my torch."

"I'm going." I said. "It's been fun as ever Buster, and good luck with it all but I think I'm done for today."

Buster didn't reply. When I left he was still looking thoughtfully at the wreckage of his day's work.

Chapter four

After that I didn't see Buster for a few days. Then out of the blue I got a call from him. Luckily it wasn't in the middle of the night. Buster may live in a different world but at least his world has the same conventions about not waking people in the night with phone calls. He sounded perfectly normal and, dare I say it, cheerful.

"Hey, come on over. I want to show you something."

A number of situations have followed those innocent words.

"OK, I'll be along after work. Listen Buster, are you OK?"

"Yeah, I'm fine, why should I not be?"

"It's just that after last week I went home and looked up multi dimensional cubes on Google. What the hell's a Runcinated Tesseract?"

"That's just a Convex Uniform Polychoron. You don't have to worry about that."

"Poly-what? What are you getting mixed up in, Buster?"

"Come round and see."

Buster had made good on his plan to build another 4D cube. This one was fireproof. It had been welded together out of sheet metal and was slightly bigger than the cardboard one. When Buster was done with his extra-dimensional obsession it might fetch a few quid. That is, if it didn't end up a pile of ash like the last one.

I looked at it closely. The welding job was excellent, I had to say. Buster won't admit it, but his welding abilities are first rate. It's the one marketable skill he could fall back on if everything else went to shit. Everything's gone to shit ten times for him, and worse, but he's never been keen on using his skills to earn normal money.

"Note that each of the square faces now has a removable side," Said Buster. "So you can access the centre of the cube from any of six different directions."

"Is there any toxic gas in there this time?" I said, rueful of my previous experience.

"There wasn't any toxic gas in it last time." Buster replied, coldly.

"Then why did I smell something funny and then pass out?"

"You didn't, you went into a fugue state."

"What the hell's a fugue state?"

"It's when your perception skips time. You pass through time, in your case an hour and twenty one minutes, while you were only aware of passing through thirty seconds."

"In other words I passed out."

"No, if you had passed out you would have collapsed but you didn't, you stayed standing."

"Haven't you seen 'Blue Velvet'? It was a blackout!"

"Fugue state!"

"Whatever."

"Look, remember when it was my go to put my head in?"

"When you set fire to the cube?"

"Yes, did I act funny before that happened?"

I had to laugh at that. There were so many instances of Buster 'acting funny' by conventional standards I couldn't even take the question seriously. For his sake I skipped the more cynical responses and tried to cast my mind back to when he was standing there and we were both timing him.

"Well," I said, "There was a minute when you stopped calling out the times. You just sort of stood there motionless."

"And yet I had no memory of stopping calling out the times. I believe I would have stood there for longer had you not pulled me out of the box"

"Your head would have caught fire if I hadn't pulled you out of the box."

"Which is why I've made a few improvements. Check it out."

Buster opened closest face of the metal cube and flicked a switch on top. The interior was instantly lit up by dozens of tiny but very bright lights which were secreted in the corners. Not only that, the inside walls were all mirrored, causing so many reflections of reflections it was impossible to see where the actual sides of the cube were.

"Nice, eh?" he said proudly. "The lights are super-bright LEDs and the mirrors are from an Iranian nightclub that was shut down because they found a dope farm in the basement. So many mirrors…"

"You went to Iran for them?"

"No, they were right here in London. In a skip on Queensway as it happens."

Typical Buster. He couldn't just go down Homebase. Half the stuff he makes started life in a skip. OK, to be accurate it ended life in a skip then was given a new life by Buster.

"Stick your head in it." he said.

"After what happened last time?"

"That's the whole reason for making prototypes. This is the real thing. Go on, it's just a box with a few mirrors in it."

"You mean a four dimensional cube."

"That too. Go on, you're going to do it so just do it."

I leaned over and peered into the cube.

"Don't let me black out in there like last time."

"Fugue state."

"No Toccata, Fugue or any other nonsense, OK?"

Buster didn't reply. It's no use getting him to promise anything anyway because, as he says, a promise made under circumstances that are likely to change will be instantly invalidated and circumstances are always changing in his world. I stuck my head into the cube.

I have to say despite my reservations it was pretty cool in there. As you'd expect, I saw my own face reflected a million times but unlike just putting two mirrors together the reflections weren't all in a straight line. The complex geometry of the inside of the four dimensional cube sent my reflection into hundreds of different directions. The result was a view of my head shown on all sides in a thousand different sizes and angles. I pulled my head out of the box.

"Please don't tell me I was in there for five hours."

"You weren't. Did you like it?"

"Very nice. You could build a big one of those and tour the festival circuit."

"I've got plans for a big one, don't you worry. There's plenty of mirrors left over."

"So is that it then?"

"No, that was just to get you started. Put your head in there again."

I leaned over again but Buster stopped me at the last minute.

"Hang on, I forgot to give you these." He held out a pair of sunglasses.

"That's OK, it was bright in there but it wasn't too bad."

"They're not sunglasses. They're polarizing lenses."

"Aren't they the kind that go dark when the sun comes out?"

"No, that's Polaroid lenses. All these do is only let light in in one direction."

"And how're they going to make any difference?"

"They won't. Not on their own."

It was then that I saw what Buster was holding in his right hand. It looked like a remote control for a model car with some extra knobs and switches taped to it.

"What's that?" I asked.

"This is for controlling the inside of the cube. I can raise and lower the lighting, change the angles of the mirrors, that sort of thing."

"And that plus the glasses is supposed to do something?"

Buster nodded, unable to keep a gleam from his eyes. The last person I saw with this kind of look on his face was off his head on Crystal Meth, and no, it wasn't Buster. Buster has no need for Meth or any other drugs. His brain makes all the chemicals he'll ever need plus several he could do without. With a sigh I put the glasses on and went back into the box.

At first it was pretty much the same as last time. Then I noticed the light flickering. It wasn't random flickering, more like a slow strobe. I assumed Buster was controlling it with the remote.

"Can you see the lights flashing?"

"Yeah."

"OK, tell me when you can't see the flashing any more."

The flickering of the lights sped up until they were a continuous blur. It was like before but the reflections of myself looked kind of odd, like they were rippling very slowly.

"I can't see the lights flashing any more, Buster."

"OK, now hold onto your hat."

"I'm not wearing a haaaaaaaoow."

I couldn't finish the sentence because of the shock I got. Not an electric shock but a shock to the brain. All the reflections of my face started moving. Some grew bigger, some smaller, some rotated in place. For a second they all lined up perfectly then diverged again and danced around me.

"What the hell's going on, Buster? Are you doing that?"

"Yep."

"I don't know how much more of this I can take."

"Then come out."

I pulled my head out of the box but the room was still spinning. Removing the glasses I leaned against the table and stared at the floor until reality reorganized itself under familiar lines.

"What the hell happened in there?"

"Do you want the long answer or the short one?"

"Short as possible."

"I was changing the angle and frequency of the light."

"You were giving me a headache is what you were doing,"

"That couldn't be helped. Our brains aren't geared toward seeing quantum potentials. I'll explain."

I sighed. Any explanation involving 'quantum potentials' was going to be hard going, so he gave me as simple an explanation as he could. In all likelihood I've got half of it wrong so if you're a Physicist don't come complaining to me. I'll give you Buster's number and you can confront him yourself. He loves arguing with Physicists.

"Can I assume you've heard of alternate realities?" he began.

"You can assume I've watched a few episodes of Star Trek."

"OK, that's a start. It's very common in Science Fiction. Writers are always banging on about worlds where people evolved from dinosaurs and not from apes, or where the Nazis won the war, or the Nazis lost the war but the apes then developed their own nuclear bombs. It's a popular concept, and do you know why?"

"Because people like books about Nazis?"

"Because people are always examining their own lives and wondering how it would have worked out for them if they'd changed careers twenty years ago or said something different to a certain girl. What most people don't think about is how things can change if only one atom is different from one universe to the next."

"I imagine it wouldn't change the universe much at all."

"Correct, which is why people don't consider it. Never mind atoms, every possible movement of every possible particle has the capacity to change over time. That's called its quantum potential. Now this stuff is usually just figured out on whiteboards in universities because you can't actually see it happening. If you could see it you'll have already changed it. So I'm not too fussed about seeing or changing separate atoms. Like everyone else I'm only interested in how an alternate reality is treating me, Buster Ames. You know crystal?"

For a moment I thought he was asking about Meth, or someone called Crystal, then I realised he meant the colourful knobby things that grow out of rocks. I hoped to God he wasn't getting all mystical on me.

"Yes, I've seen a couple of them. Quartz and Amethyst and suchlike?"

"Exactly. OK, if you can imagine here and now being the centre of a crystal, all the events that can happen and will happen and could happen and have happened and could have happened branch out from that one central point, a bit like the layers of a crystal. It's a crystal with many dimensions, so there's a lot of room for different things to happen. So far, so good. Now I know you're a practical type, you think of everything in terms of what good it will do us in the real world and how we can make a bit of money out of it."

I opened my mouth to correct him but realised he was correct already, so I closed my mouth again. I can't deny that the word 'Money' got my interest going. I really hoped he was going somewhere with all this.

"Here's my thinking. If we want to actually access other realities, all we need to do is create something that will allow us to see them, and then having seen the way, to enter them, probably going through another dimension or two on the way."

He stopped and smiled, waiting for me to say something. I pondered what he had just said and tried to see where he was leading me. I looked over at the four dimensional mirrored headache-machine. It couldn't be...

Buster saw my eyes move.

"Tell me something, Philip, have I ever won the Grand National?"

"The horse race? You mean riding a horse or being ridden? Because technically isn't it the horse that wins the race?"

"Don't be ridiculous, Of course I mean riding a horse."

"You're the one being ridiculous. Of course you've never won the Grand National. You're six feet tall and I don't even think you know which end of a horse the shit comes out of. What's this got to do with anything?"

"Let me show you something."

Buster walked over to the cube and pressed a button on his remote control. The lights came on, flickering as before. He turned a knob and the flickering grew fast enough to be unnoticeable. Then holding the remote he clambered awkwardly onto the table on which the four dimensional cube sat and crawled in up to his shoulders. I heard him grunt to himself as he twiddled more switches and the outside of the cube moved. It was as if each face, edge and corner was loose and could pivot, but in doing so moved the sides around it in a complex knock-on pattern. The whole thing took on a sort of wavy motion and after a few seconds it stopped in mid-wave, going rock-solid. It was still a cube but a bit skewed.

Buster then crawled right into the cube. His feet vanished

and one of the faces of the cube swung open. Buster crawled out, sat on the edge of the table and pressed a big red button on the remote. The cube righted itself to its normal shape and the lights went off.

I was slightly disappointed. I was expecting at a cool magic trick or a bunch of electric sparks arcing off the thing but all it had given me was a brief moment of dizziness. Buster himself looked completely unchanged.

"You OK?" I asked.

"Yeah, fine," he replied.

"OK. So what was all that about?"

"Tell me Philip," said Buster with a sly smile. "Have I ever won the Grand National?"

"I don't know why you're bringing that up now," I said. "Of course you've won the Grand National. You won it in 1993."

"And do you remember the circumstances behind my winning?"

"Well, I didn't know you at the time but I remember it on the news. There was a false start and all the other horses got recalled or something and when they re-started the race your horse was the only one not exhausted because it hadn't been able to get out of the gate the first time round. You won it by a mile. I think we spoke about it when I first met you."

"Didn't you say before I went through the cube that I didn't win the race, and that I didn't even know which end of a horse shits?"

"Hmm. I must have forgotten about you winning."

"Strange thing to have forgotten, wouldn't you say?"

"I suppose so."

"You know why?" said Buster gleefully "Because it never happened before I went through the cube!"

"What? do you mean to say you've crossed over into an alternate reality?"

"Exactly, a world exactly the same except for my winning the Grand National in 1993."

"Well, what about me? Have I crossed over with you?"

"No, you've always been here. I left the old you behind in the other reality."

Well let me tell you, that gave me pause for thought. In all those alternate reality stories the action always follows the person who is going from one reality to another. They never mention the people living in those alternate realities already.

"So if I crawl through that box and go back to where you came from, I'll be back in the reality where you didn't win the race?"

"Yes, and no. Yes, in that it would take you there if you knew how to steer it in that direction, and no because you'd never be able to find the way."

"Well how did you learn how to find the way?"

"I didn't, I was fooling around with the cube last night and chanced on the horse-race reality, so I made a note of the settings to show you. If you went through it blind you'd probably end up in one of those Nazis-won-the-war realities."

"But this is preposterous! How can a metal box, a few mirrors and some lights possibly transport you across spacetime and dimensions and stuff? It takes a Hadron collider and a trillion volts just to send a neutrino back in time one nanosecond!"

"You could say the wheel was even more simple technology than my box and yet it allowed the ancients to move mountains."

"Fair enough."

"So do you still want to have a go?"

It was tempting, I'll admit. I could go to a reality where I was mega-rich and my girlfriend was the hottest babe in the world but I've learned one thing about Buster's projects over the years and that is it's better to let Buster work them.

"Not really, but thanks anyway. Hey, I've just had an idea."

Buster raised an eyebrow

"Go on."

"Is it possible to pull things from other dimensions and times and realities into our world?"

"Such as?"

"Anything. Gold bars, tomorrow's newspaper, stuff like that."

"I have to say, I never thought of that. I suppose it's possible. You'd have to..." Buster lapsed into silence as he pondered this through.

"Hmmm." he finished. I waited for him to continue but he didn't. He went over to the cube and regarded it for a while, motionless. I was worried he had gone into one of those fugue states he'd been on about. I'd seen him do this before. You'd be talking to him and suddenly his brain would shut all the doors to the outside world and that would be it. I could wait for him or I could go, and I think it was time to go.

"Buster!" I said. "I have to be off. You have a think about what I said, OK? About pulling things back from other dimensions. I hope you're thinking about that now because I think that's where the money might be. I reckon sending people off into alternate realities will only come to grief. At least that's what always happens in the movies."

"Mmmn." said Buster, looking at the remote control again. I think he was only half-listening to me. I let myself out and walked back to my car, hoping that in this reality it hadn't turned into a horse or something.

Chapter five

The car was still a car, albeit with a ticket on it. However I spent the next week checking entries on Wikipedia a little too often, trying to see if Buster had been fiddling around with his and our reality again. Nothing seemed to change much. The picture of England raising the World Cup in 1966 briefly turned into a picture of a man's testicles and for one horrifying minute I had a vision of Buster making a wrong turn in his cube and changing the course of sporting history but it turned out to be a hacker attack on the website which was quickly corrected.

I next caught up with Buster about ten days later, or rather that's when he caught up with me. Going against his normal habit he came to visit me at my place, a fairly decent house in another part of London which I won off my ex-wife in our divorce.

"Well if it isn't Doctor Who himself," I said cheerfully when I opened the door. "How's the ninth dimension been treating you?"

"Piss awful, as it happens."

I looked down and saw in his hand a long thin cloth bag, like the kind you'd transport a tripod in.

"What's in there?"

It turned out to be the results of Buster's latest experiments with the cube. He plonked the bag down on my kitchen table and unzipped it.

"I'm going to show you, in chronological order, what happened when I followed your suggestion that I try and pull things over from other realities."

"Oh, you should have told me you would be doing that. A spot of time-fishing sounds like great fun."

"Believe me, it wasn't. Every time I messed about with another reality I got an electric shock and this godawful smell would fill the place. Anyway, first I tried poking about in the cube with this:"

Buster drew from the bag a small child's fishing net, or rather the remains of one. The net was all burned away and the stick badly charred.

"That's what happened to the first implement, so I went with something sturdier." He held up a metal pole with a crank handle at one end and a hook at the other. It looked like a thing for opening high windows. The end with the hook was all twisted and buckled.

"What did you think you were going to catch with that?" I said. "A window lock?"

"I don't know. I had a whole bunch of them. Found them at the University."

Buster regularly steals stuff from University College London. He'd spent an unhappy year there and still harbours some kind of grudge against the place. As a result he has no qualms about walking in there and just taking stuff. The next window opener Buster held up was cleanly lopped off half way down its length.

"Somewhere in another universe there's the end of this," said Buster, regarding the chopped off rod. "Now check this one out:"

The crank he brought out next had a normal handle but from half way along it was all stained and pitted with rust. It looked like a roman spear dug up from an archeological site.

"I waved it about in there for about twenty seconds and now look at it. It's aged about a thousand years."

I touched the hook. Flakes of rust came away in my

fingers, then the whole end snapped off and crumbled in my hand. I shivered.

"Any more?"

Buster looked into his bag.

"Oh, yes, look at this."

It started, like all the others, with a crank handle and a shaft rising up to a hook, but before it reached the top it split in two, then two again, then again and again until it resembled an elegant tree in winter, every branch and twig ending in a tiny hook.

"That's so cool." I said, turning the thing over in my hands. "Can you do more of these? I might be able to flog this on the art market."

"That's the thing," answered Buster. "I'm not sure I can. Every time I stick something in that cube it comes out different."

"So you can't find the same reality twice, and you can't bring anything back?"

"Oh, I brought something back all right. I had to pay a visit to the UCL Geology department and get a probe they use for sticking in volcanoes, but I did get something back."

"Excellent! Let's see it."

Buster dug into his pocket and threw what looked like a burned rag over to me. I unfolded it and held it up. It was about the size of a piece of A4 paper pitted with holes and scorch marks and it was clearly only a fragment of a much larger piece of fabric but the red, white and black pattern was unmistakable.

"Bloody Nazis again," I said. "They're all over these dimensions."

"Oh, you haven't seen anything. Look at this!"

Buster dug down in the bottom of his bag and withdrew a green cylinder about the size of a rolling pin. It had a pointed top and what looked like fins half way down the sides.

"Jesus Christ!" I yelped, jumping backwards. "That's a bomb!"

"I know," said Buster, completely unruffled. "And the funny thing is I didn't get it out with a stick or anything, It just fell out of the cube while I was moving it. Luckily it landed in a bowl of porridge that was on the floor. Do you want to check it out? I've cleaned it."

"No! Get it out of my house! Sell it to a collector."

"I already tried but he said it looked recently made and was obviously just a reproduction, so it wasn't worth anything."

"Throw it in the bloody Thames then. Hang on, wasn't the building where you live bombed during the war?"

"Yeah, pretty badly. You saw the old photos didn't you?"

"Well couldn't this be one of the bombs that fell on your building, but instead of falling on your building it fell right through your time tunnel or whatever you call that contraption?"

"I'm sure it is."

I was suddenly in the position of having an insight that hadn't occurred to Buster. I spoke slowly so my brain had time to pass the words to my mouth,

"It may be a bomb, but it's the only thing that made it through that cube of yours unscathed. At least until it blows up. Everything you stuck in that thing got messed up in there or messed up on the way out, but the bomb didn't. Also, the bomb is the only thing that you weren't actually fishing for. So obviously you're going about this the wrong way. Things have to be moving in the universe that they're in, and you have to be holding the cube

Buster's Cube

in just the right place so that they'll fly through and we can catch them. It doesn't work if you just stick something in from over here. Instead of spear fishing you should be trawling, using the cube as a net."

I was particularly proud of the fishing jargon. I've never been one for constructing my own metaphors, in fact I can't do it for toffee but now and then I surprise myself. I certainly surprised Buster. He leaped up, nearly dropping the bomb as he did so.

"That's brilliant, Philip!" he spluttered. "Let's get back to mine and go time fishing!"

Chapter six

The phrase 'easier said than done' doesn't apply to everything. There are a great number of simple tasks which would be easier to do than for me to describe to Buster. However Buster's suggestion that we 'go time fishing' implies a fun and easy task that manhandling the 4D cube turned out not to be. Unlike the little fishing net that Buster had started off with, the cube was not built for whisking around. It was also heavy. Not so heavy that we couldn't lift it but almost too heavy for us to wave it about in search of a moving object we couldn't see in a universe we knew nothing about.

Making things even more difficult was the need to keep the cube plugged in for the lights and mirror-motors to work. Even with an extension it was hard to keep the power cable from getting in the way. Indeed one time a loop of it fell into the cube and came out with different colour insulation. At least it didn't have swastikas all over it.

We tried holding it this way and that, upside down and right way up, not that there was a right way up for this contraption. At one point some kind of flying insect came out of it and I got all freaked out because it might have wandered through from the Palaeozoic era or something. Buster was all for capturing it and studying it but I just wanted it dead. Who knows what kind of diseases it may have been carrying? The work was suspended for half an hour whilst we hunted it down and swatted it with a rolled up tank-modelling magazine (don't ask). It looked like a perfectly normal house fly, by the way.

The work went on for another hour after we killed the fly. Buster adjusted the interior angles of the mirrors, which cube faces to open and the frequency of the lights but nothing came out of the cube except for the fly and an occasional nasty smell. We had a brief argument over whether objects from the future are more valuable than those from the past. Eventually Buster put his end of the cube down on the floor and slumped heavily into an armchair.

"This is no good," he said dejectedly. "We're working blind here. If I can't get into the cube with the glasses on while we're shifting it about then we have no idea where or when we're trying to grab things from. There doesn't seem to be much going on at this point in spacetime. At least nothing moving through the air."

"Except for that fly." I offered.

"Great. A fly that may or may not be from another dimension and is now squashed. Worth a fortune if we could get anyone to believe us, which isn't going to happen. Even I don't believe what we're doing half the time."

"So let's think this through," I said. "If we can't tell what time we're trying to scoop stuff up from, we're going to have to maximise our chances of getting something good by going to an eventful place. Obviously this location is a bit of a blank spot in history except briefly during World War Two, but what if we went somewhere like the Tower of London or Stonehenge? There must have been all sorts of people and things that've been moving about there for thousands of years. The only problem is getting power to the cube somehow."

"That's not the problem," countered Buster. "I can rig this thing up to batteries easy. The problem is walking into one of those places carrying this thing with all its wires and stuff. They'll think it was a bomb."

"Or else it'll let another German bomb through. This is your neighbourhood, Buster. Where around here have valuable objects been moving around or carried around for a good long time and we could get to without being apprehended?"

"Well the insides of banks are off the list. The cube is too dodgy looking for that. Art galleries ditto unless we pretend it's art but I've been banned from pretty much all of them by now. There's Richardson's, the old auction house round the corner, but again it would be hard to get the cube in there, and even then if something came through, how would we get it out of there? Maybe if we took it to a park we could catch some future Frisbees, or old…"

"Wait!" I interrupted. "That auction house you mentioned. Does it have a service entrance, for deliveries?"

"Yes, as it happens, there's a side door in the alley across the main road. Hey! If we were to stand out there…"

"We could dip into the history of everything that's ever gone in or out of that doorway!"

The more we thought about it the more it made sense. Every week they had some auction or another in that place, from diamond encrusted Faberge eggs to Ringo's drum kit. I'd seen them delivering to that alley, often bringing stuff in an armoured van with security guys all around. Of course when the place was closed the alley would be deserted and no one would pay attention to two guys lugging a metal box down there at night, at least I hoped not. I looked at my watch. It was 10.30pm.

"Buster, how long would it take to make this thing mobile?"

"You mean put wheels on it?"

"No, just to make it battery powered."

"Oh, about ten minutes."

Which meant an hour and forty minutes at least. You have to square Buster's time estimates to get a figure closer to reality. I settled down on a cracked leather armchair, the only near-comfortable item in Buster's lab. Buster rarely sat in it. He seemed to spend all his time in the lab wandering around and did his sitting upstairs.

"Philip! Wake up."

With a start I opened my eyes and briefly wondered where I was. Buster stood in front of me with the remote control in his hand.

"It's ready."

Chapter seven

I looked at my watch. It was half past midnight. I went to the end of Buster's alley to check out the area. It was empty until a single car shot past from left to right. The auction house stood across the road, looking centuries old. The service entrance on the right side of the building opened onto an alley not much wider than Buster's.

Buster was finishing taping down the new wires and batteries to the outside of the cube when I got back. With all the extra equipment the cube was even heavier but the excitement of what we were about to do gave us the power to lift it. As we manoeuvred the cube down Buster's alley I had a sudden attack of morals.

"Buster, isn't this stealing?"

"It may look like stealing, but the way I see it is this: we're not stealing from our own reality so in reality we're not stealing."

I pondered this. The argument seemed shaky and dependant more on wordplay than on actual logic but it was good enough for now. I figured we'd see what came through the cube and take it from there. We emerged from the alley and looked around. The street was deserted.

"Now we don't want to spend any more time lurking around that doorway than we have to," I said. "So you'd better activate the cube before we go over there. What year are we fishing for?"

"It doesn't matter," answered Buster as he switched on the lights and angled the interior mirrors. "I'm still getting to grips with how this thing works so I really have no idea what year it's focused on. We're bound to grab something."

I looked up and down the road. It was clear in both directions.

"OK, let's go."

Buster took the front of the cube and we shuffled across the first half of the road. The metal edges of the cube pressed into my skin and I made a mental note to wear my leather gloves next time. However it was an irrelevant note to make because we were halfway across the other side of the road when the cube exploded.

One second I was shuffling behind Buster, the cube as heavy as ever, the next second it was ripped out of my hands in a cataclysm of shattered mirrors and flying cable. An intense blue flash threw me to the ground. I may have been knocked out for a couple of seconds or maybe it was one last fugue state but when I came to I was sitting against a bollard with gravel and fragments of mirror stuck to the side of my face.

I checked for Buster. He was standing in the middle of the road, his back to me, swaying slightly. He turned round and looked back in horror at what had become of his machine. There was debris all over the road, splaying out in a fan shape from the place where we had been standing when it had disintegrated. Luckily most of the force of the explosion seemed to be directed to the right and not towards us. Buster looked over from the twisted metal and glass to me.

"Are you OK?" he asked.

"No. What the hell happened?"

Buster dropped a strip of metal onto the pavement. It was the last part of the cube he had been holding before the explosion had torn the rest of it out of his hands.

"I don't know, but I don't think there's going to be any treasure hunting tonight." he said.

"Yeah," I sighed, getting up and joining him on the side of the road. "We were so close. Damn."

We pondered the bits and pieces of the cube. It looked like

a recycling truck had gone over a bump and shed random bits of metal all over the place.

"We'd better get out of here, come on." I said, heading back to Buster's alley.

"Got to clean up this mess." he replied, crouching down and scooping up some bits of mirror.

"What?"

"I drive on this road and all this broken glass might give me a flat tyre. Besides this is my neighbourhood and I don't want to shit in my own Jacuzzi. Give me a hand."

Tired as I was, I went back to Buster's storeroom and found a broom to sweep up the shattered remains of the cube, leaving the debris in a box in the corner of Buster's lab.

I called Buster the next day from work. He sounded pretty despondent. I tried giving him a pep talk about a 'temporary setback' and told him I'd help him build another cube. He said 'sure' but I could tell his heart wasn't in it any more.

It's not like I didn't ever see him again. I went round to his place every now and then but each time I'd see the box of bits from the cube gathering dust in the corner. Once or twice I asked him when we were going to make another 4D cube but the subject seemed to upset him. I think it was because he'd gone through the cube once and knew that he wasn't really from this reality. Even if he did build another one, chances that he'd be able to find his way back to the world where he hadn't won the 1993 Grand National were slim. Sometimes I'd see him deep in thought, his hand resting on the little sculpture of a horse on his shelf, his award for winning the race.

Chapter eight

A year went by. I was busy with a new scheme. I'd had a great idea while suffering the worst Christmas of my life. My ex-wife had got it into her fool head to invite me over for turkey and even more fool I accepted. She'd re-married and her new partner was a talentless ugly snob. He had a little girl by a previous relationship and it was her turn to spend Christmas with him, along with me and my Ex.

In order to curry favour with Mr. Ugly-Snob she had bought the four-year-old kid a very expensive synthesizer. I knew it was expensive because I Googled the model number on my phone in the toilet. It was bad enough that she couldn't play it but when she discovered the demo button everything went to musical hell. I was surprised that such a high-end synthesizer had two hundred and fifty five tacky tunes programmed into it but it did and little Jocasta played them all, and not just once. She had a particular fondness for 'Jingle Bells' and sat there pressing the Demo button again and again with an imbecilic look on her face. I think I prevented myself murdering everyone in the house by drinking copious amounts of wine.

The next day, my head feeling like burned plasticene, I pondered how difficult it was to learn how to play piano properly and wondered whether the kid would ever stay the course. I wished I'd learned how to play. Whoever programmed that damn synthesizer knew how to play and now his legacy was hard wired into my brain forever. I recalled my own childhood synth, a crappy Bontempi with four demo tunes: Greensleeves, Charlie Is My Darling, Blow The Man Down and some unidentified Russian folk song. The closest I ever got to playing it properly was the odd impromptu gig in the kitchen, miming 'Blow The Man Down' on the keyboard to the pretend delight of my mother.

That little memory triggered something on the way up, a

little train of thought that quickly became a speeding locomotive. What if you were to programme the synthesizer so that each time you pressed a key on the keyboard it played the next note of the song? It didn't matter which key, middle C or high F, the programmed tune would advance as fast as the keyboard player hit the keys in any sequence. The effect, I reasoned, would be that you could fake being able to play the correct notes with no musical ability at all. Only someone who could play a keyboard properly would be able to tell, and then only if they watched which keys you were hitting.

The result of this little piece of reasoning was my Karaoke Piano Bar, developed by Benson UltraTainment. My previous company Benson Enterprises Ltd was history by this point, its two shares 'not worth the paper they are printed on' my accountant had told me bluntly. The premise of the Karaoke Piano Bar, in case you haven't worked it out yet, was this: One at a time, the patrons of a chic little cocktail bar with a nice looking fake piano in it would take turns tickling the ivories and if they liked, sing along.

You'd have the option of about five hundred songs, real piano classics like 'One for my baby' and 'Blue Moon' along with some contemporary stuff and a bunch of Elton John. If you wanted to sing you could even have the option of autotune on your voice for the complete talent-proof package. The success of the new twist on the karaoke format was down to the feeling it gave the players that they really were playing the song properly on the piano. I even had some really talented actual piano players become regulars, real maestros.

That said, most 'proper' pianists despised my invention, figuring it would put them out of business. Some of them even organised a picket line outside the bar which got me in the papers and increased business 500%. At the height of the controversy I held a raucous party in the bar during which I taunted the picketers outside, playing Rachmaninov's third just to piss them off.

In the end though it was Westminster council and the musicians' union that did for the Karaoke Piano Bar. Apparently you need a public entertainment license to do what I was doing, along with payment of royalties to the composers of the songs. I tried to argue that no one was really playing the piano and that Rachmaninov had been dead for over sixty years but it wouldn't wash. Also I had picked up a stalker. A ratty little Steinway-pounder had gleaned my home address from Companies House and had taken to lurking around my neighbourhood, putting polite little notes through my letterbox signed 'Sparky'.

It was around this time that I got a call out of the blue from Buster. He sounded excited and much like his old self.

"You were right," he said. "I'm an idiot."

"I never called you an idiot, Buster."

"No, I'm calling me an idiot. How soon can you get round here?"

I looked at my pile of letters. Two bills, some junk from an estate agent and a new note from Sparky.

"I'll be right over."

The first thing I noticed at Buster's was the box of pieces from the exploded cube had gone. I soon saw what had become of it: It was all laid out across two tables, looking like a collision between a robot and a disco ball.

"Don't tell me you're going to try and put this lot back together."

"Oh no," he replied "This is what was left after I'd combed through the wreckage. It can all go." To make his point he swept a bunch of tangled wiring into a big bin.

"So what's the big fuss? Have you finally built another cube?"

"No. Not yet. But I'm going to."

"That's the spirit. What was it that finally spurred you on?"

Buster went to another table and came back with a shoe box which he held with great reverence, as if it was the holy grail itself.

"I was an idiot for not properly examining the pieces of the box after the accident. If I had I would have found it earlier."

I didn't bother asking him what he had found as I assumed it was in the shoe box. He lifted the top of it and took out an object swathed in bubble wrap.

"At first I thought it might have been something we'd picked up off the road by mistake but after a few experiments I realised what it was -and what it *meant*."

By this time my curiosity was well and truly engaged. I leaned forward as Buster carefully unwound the bubble wrap. Inside was an triangular shaped white lump about the size of a large mango. One side of it was translucent and the opposite side was completely smooth and polished.

"What the hell's that?"

"Before I tell you, have a feel of it."

"It's not radioactive is it?"

"Probably not. At least I don't think so."

"You haven't tested it?"

"Do I look like the kind of person who has a Geiger counter knocking about?"

"Absolutely you do."

"Just feel it, will you?"

"OK" I sighed.

Buster put the lump in my hand. It was light as a bubble. I put my other hand on it, expecting something that felt so insubstantial to float away or crumble in my grip. It didn't. In fact it felt surprisingly hard and durable.

"What is it?"

Without answering, Buster took the lump and placed it on a dark green square on the table.

"This is an induction pad," he said. "It's for charging mobiles without having to plug them in. You can get them at Maplin's. Now watch this."

He switched on the induction pad and immediately the translucent side of the lump glowed incredibly brightly. I had to put my hand to my eyes to keep from being dazzled.

"Got it yet?"

"It's a light?"

"And more. You'll get it in a second. Let me tweak the voltage frequency."

Buster turned a knob on the side of the induction pad. It looked like his own modification; the sellotape holding the knob on was a bit of a giveaway. The side of the white lump stopped glowing and started flashing yellow.

"It looks like a hazard light." I said.

"Bingo!" cried Buster. "Now do you get it?"

I wished Buster would just tell me what was going on. Hazard lights, induction pads, a strange white material which was almost weightless…

"OK," Buster said, "What do you think happened to the cube?"

"It exploded."

"Not quite."

"Yes it bloody did! I've still got metal shards embedded in my skin."

"Where were we when it happened?"

"We were carrying it across the road."

"And was it switched on at the time?"

"Of course it was."

"Don't you see what happened? *It was hit by a car!*"

"No it wasn't, the road was…"

I stopped in mid-sentence, finally cottoning on. It might have been a year ago but it wasn't the kind of event that you forget in a hurry. The road was clear when we were carrying the cube across but many cars had been in that location in the past and it was reasonable to assume that many more cars would be going down that road in the future. If the corner of one of those cars-to-come had hit the precise location of the cube…

"Good Lord," I said. "Is that thing a car headlight?"

"Not only is it a car headlight," said Buster triumphantly. "It's a car headlight from the future!"

"And that's what caused the cube to explode?"

"The cube never exploded. It was smashed into by a car that won't be driving down that road for years, maybe hundreds of years."

"So where's the rest of the car?"

"Still in the future, but minus one of its headlights. Whoever was driving it is going to be pretty mystified as to what happened."

"You mean, what will happen."

"Whatever. Now we know why the pieces of the cube all flew in one direction, because the momentum of the car threw them that way. Only the front corner of the car came through because the cube wasn't big enough for the whole car to come through and as soon as the cube broke up it cut off the gateway. That's why this edge of the piece is so smooth. It's been sheared off at a molecular level."

I was silent for a while, trying to piece together the sequence of events that led to this inter-temporal car wreck.

"Let's hope he had insurance." I said.

"Will have insurance." Buster corrected me.

"Either way. I'd like to see the claim form."

I picked up the corner of the car again. As it left the induction pad the flashing yellow light went off.

"What's this made of?" I asked Buster.

"No idea. It's light, and strong as hell. I tried chipping it with a hammer but couldn't even scratch it."

Buster went off to the corner of the lab and put the kettle on. As the sound of boiling water filled the room an idea built in my brain.

"Buster, did you say you're going to build another cube?"

"Well, yes. Now that I know that the first one didn't explode due to some inherent fault. I'll be a lot more careful when and where to switch it on, though."

"And where and when are you going to switch it on?"

"Well I think I'll start with our original plan to nab some relics going into the auction house."

"Screw the auction house. Your next cube will have to be about eight foot across."

"Eight feet? Why ever so big?"

"Because we're going to catch *an entire car*!"

Chapter nine

It took some persuading for Buster to come round to my plan. Firstly, the auction house idea was too risky. What if we got something priceless from the year 3000 that wouldn't be worth peanuts today, like an old iPod? What if we accidentally lopped off the arms of the poor sod who was holding the item? What if we got caught? We could still get caught stealing a car argued Buster but my mind was made up.

"Think how things might have turned out if Henry Ford had got hold of a Ferrari in 1910?" I reasoned.

"You just want a new car, don't you?"

"Bloody right I want a new car. Newer than any car will be for years and years. Not only that, I'm going to reverse engineer it and start the most groundbreaking, advanced car company in the world."

"Have you any idea how much work it will be to build a 4D cube big enough for a car to drive through?"

"A fair amount." I conceded.

It turned out to be an unfair amount as Buster had to do most of it, but I helped where I could. Firstly the materials. We needed mirrors, big ones. Glass mirrors were too expensive and fragile but luckily I found a firm that made mirrored Perspex which was a lot lighter and cheaper. Buster handled the installation of the lights and motors. These I obtained through an all but defunct technology company I had originally started to try and manufacture Christmas tree ornaments that moved up the tree and hung themselves automatically (another disaster. They kept confusing trees with small children.)

Eventually the massive new cube started to take shape before a stupid and totally avoidable setback halted work. Buster had just finished bolting the framework together when we both realised at the same time that it was too big to get out of his lab so we had to take it apart again.

In fact finding a location where we would be able to assemble the big cube was a bit of a problem. It would need a large enough door to get the cube out of and be close enough to a road for us to wheel it out there for the car capturing. Moreover it would have to be a significant road that would be in use for a good few years to come but not too busy late at night so we could set it up without a present-day car slamming into it.

Finally I found somewhere. It was an industrial unit in a part of west London called Park Royal. I don't know if there's a real park there but if there was I didn't see it, only massive industrial estates. Many of these had big shuttered loading docks which were as wide as a heavy goods vehicle so it would be easy to manoeuvre the cube out. Better still, the industrial estate was right near the A40.

Of course it wasn't our plan to set the cube up on the A40. That would have been madness. The road we were interested in went parallel to the big A-road and serviced all the industrial estates alongside it. It was fairly busy by day but empty at night and Buster said there was a reasonable chance that it would be there for some time. I was slightly concerned about the quality of car we would capture along this grimy backwater but Buster said that even the rankest white van driven by the most sweaty-arsed builder of the year 4000 would be worth grabbing for the stereo alone.

On a freezing night in mid February Buster finished the cube. The two of us stood watching it go through its paces. I've been referring to it as a cube but purely because I can't keep writing stuff like 'Tesseract Hypercube'. Just bear in mind that it was the same shape as the previous two- that of two normal cubes humping each other. It was impressive, and very big. It was eight feet across and don't forget it was also eight feet high and eight feet deep, and that was only one of the cubes. With all the triangular linking faces the whole shebang was remarkable even before you looked inside. The closest face slowly swung open at Buster's command on his new wheeled control podium that had replaced the old modified Fisher-Price remote. When he hit the interior lights there should have been music playing or something it was so cool.

Buster had made a few improvements to his original design. Instead of just strobing white lights he had made it so the lights could change colour as well, all at once or each separately. he said it was something about light frequencies controlling the direction of the cube's reach into other dimensions but I suspect he just thought it made the cube more badass. When he made the lights change colour it looked like an art installation I saw once called "Infinity Mirror Room Filled with the Brilliance of Life" by some nutty Japanese lady. Google it. It's very groovy and saves me time trying to describe what the inside of Buster's new giant cube looked like.

"It's a pity it'll probably get smashed up." said Buster.

"It had bloody better not," I replied. "After all the time and money we've sunk into this. I'm on my last few quid. It's all gone to entertainment lawyers and multi dimensional hypercubes. What makes you think it'll get smashed up anyway?"

"What if the car is going so fast when it comes through that it hits the sides of the cube? Or what if some heavy goods vehicle runs into it that won't fit? It'll be just like the first time. All we'll have is a radiator grille."

These possibilities hadn't occurred to me. I just figured that if the thing didn't work there were always the festivals.

"All I know," I said "is I'm going to be standing well back from that thing when we activate it."

Before it came to that we had to get the cube out of the unit and over to the road. I didn't want any cock-ups at this point so I'd put a lot of thought into this part of the operation. Firstly I had struck up a friendship with the other clients of the industrial estate, and a funny bunch of people they were. You don't realise this unless you work in one of these places but there's a real community going on there. People have copies of each other's keys, they take in mail for their neighbours, some of them have lunch together, they lend equipment to each other, the whole deal. In the twelve unit estate we were on there was a paint warehouse, a ball bearing manufacturer, a swimwear distribution outlet, a couple of internet shops and a guy who sells samurai swords and guns. I'm not kidding, he's got a warehouse full of guns. Maybe they're fakes, I don't know. Best not to ask. That's another thing, people are friendly but mind their own business which suited me fine.

I'd become friendly with Painter Pete, the paint warehouse guy who'd lent me his forklift. I was a bit apprehensive as to whether the cube would fit on the forklift or even if Buster could drive one (he can't) so I had put in some practice with pallets of emulsion at Painter Pete's and I was OK at it by the time Buster had finished the cube. The cube was a lot bulkier than the paint pallets but didn't weigh as much so I thought it should be fine as long as I went slowly. Along the way I discovered that Painter Pete's first name wasn't actually Pete, it was Gary, but his surname really was Painter. Funny how things go.

Chapter ten

Buster held down the button that raised the steel shutters on our industrial unit and they went up with a slow clatter. Cold air wafted in from outside along with a pulsating roar from the A40 round the corner. Very carefully I engaged the forklift motor and reversed the wobbling cube out of the loading bay. I sighed with relief when we got it out into the estate forecourt. It was 1am and the place was deserted. A light shone out of the gun guy's place but it was always on whether he was in or out.

When I put the forklift in forward gear I realised we had a problem. The cube was too big to see around and I had no idea where I was going. Buster suggested opening up some of the faces of the cube but with all the reflections it was like trying to drive a forklift through an MC Escher painting. Then he had the idea of fixing a camera to the front and putting a TV panel in the forklift so I could see my way via video link but that would have meant putting the experiment off while he set up the camera and panel. I was getting impatient. The lease for the industrial unit expired in a couple of days and we didn't have time for any more setbacks. In the end we just went with a plain and simple solution. Buster would walk in front of the cube and shout directions to me.

We turned the corner out of the estate and slowly made for the road. We had decided to put the cube half way down the road because we had no idea from which direction the future traffic would arrive. Gently I placed the cube down and drew back the forklift. I was too excited to find somewhere to park the forklift so I ran it up onto the pavement.

Buster darted around the cube making checks and adjustments then ran back to get the control module, leaving me alone with the cube. It was a slightly surreal situation, standing there alone on a chilly February night in a filthy industrial access road next to a dual carriageway minding a portal to another dimension. I wondered if this was the kind of situation the Science Museum would be making a tableau of in years to come, like the Wright brothers' first flight at Kitty Hawk. 'Benson and Ames puncture the Space-Time continuum in Park Royal'. Maybe we could look through the cube and see. Come to think of it 'Ames and Benson' had a nicer ring to it, even if it did put Buster first.

My reverie was interrupted by Buster wheeling the control module round the corner. He lifted it up onto the curb a good twenty metres from the cube and I went over to join him. I was getting rather excited at this point. He flicked the master control switch on the panel. Nothing happened.

"Damn, forgot to power up the cube." he said, darted three steps forward then abruptly sat down on the pavement.

"What are you doing?" I said.

"Doing this Russian style."

"What?"

"Russians," explained Buster "Always sit down for a bit before they embark on a journey. It lets them contemplate the road ahead and provides a quiet moment for them to remember anything they've forgotten."

We sat in silence for a minute until I started to shiver.

"Do you feel we've sat down long enough? My arse is getting cold."

"OK," said Buster, hauling himself to his feet. "Let's do it."

He went to the cube and connected up the battery packs around its base. The cube didn't do anything but a light glowed on the control panel. Buster hurried back to where I was standing.

"Now see this?" he said, indicating a black loop that dangled from the side of the panel. "That's the abort handle. If anything happens and we need to shut the thing down, you yank on that and it cuts all the power. Even if everything goes well you'll need to pull it in case anything bad happens next. Got that?"

I nodded. Buster took position in front of the control panel.

"Here's the sequence." he said. "First the doors, then the lights, then the mirrors."

"Have you worked out how far into the future we're going to be reaching? I don't want to end up with a horse and cart."

"How about a Tyrannosaurus?"

"Jesus, we'd make a fortune if it didn't eat us." I said.

"OK. Here goes. Doors."

Buster pressed the first on a line of six buttons along the top of the panel. The nearest face of the cube slowly swung open revealing a dim interior. He pressed the fourth button and the face directly away from us opened as well.

"Lights."

He turned a knob and the interior lights of the cube flickered to life. He turned it further and the flickering sped up.

"Aren't you going to switch on the colours?" I asked.

"Let's see where plain white gets us first."

The flickering got fast enough for it to become a continuous blur. Buster concentrated fiercely on the cube. I needed to pee but kept it to myself. Now wasn't really the time.

"Now the mirrors."

Buster worked a joystick and the mirrors began their rolling motion. Once again the interior of the cube resembled infinity in a washing machine. Here we go, I thought.

"How long do you think before something happens?" I asked.

"Could be a second, could be an hour. It depends on how busy this road will be in the time we're focusing on."

"What time are we focusing on then?"

"I told you, I have no…"

Buster was interrupted by a loud honk behind us. I spun round and to my horror a shabby estate car was making its way down the road towards us. I could just make out the baffled face of its driver staring at the cube.

"Shit!" we both said together.

"Keep your eye on the cube and your hand on the abort handle!" shouted Buster. "I'll get rid of him."

He ran full pelt towards the car waving his arms. The car stopped and I could see Buster leaning in to the driver's side window. A noise behind the cube drew my attention away from the scene but it was only a couple of winos staggering off down the road and round the corner. After a few seconds animated conversation with the driver of the car during which Buster made some complicated hand gestures the car made a clumsy three point turn and trundled off. Buster hurried back to me.

"Poor bastard was lost. Had his whole family in there. They were looking for Heathrow airport."

"Who the hell goes to Heathrow at two o'clock in the…"

I was interrupted by an almighty crash behind me. Buster's jaw dropped and I whipped round to face the cube. It hadn't exploded and for a split second I missed what it was that had made the noise because I'd been looking in the wrong direction.

The good news was it was a car. We had actually captured a car. The bad news was it had come shooting straight out of the top face of the cube and was flying vertically up into the air. In retrospect I suppose it made sense. There was no guarantee that anything driving into the cube would come out in the opposite direction; we're talking about multiple dimensions here. We were just lucky it didn't come out of the bottom face and plough straight into the ground.

Not that lucky though. The car slowed down as it ran out of momentum and slowly turned over as it began to fall. With horror we both realised that it was going to come straight down on top of the cube, probably smashing itself and the cube to pieces. I grabbed the abort handle and yanked it so hard the control panel fell over on the pavement, then stepped back to watch the carnage.

The carnage never happened. What did happen was something the two of us, living in our world of modern vehicles, hadn't expected. The car floated gently to the ground, zigzagging left and right like a piece of paper. It was a profoundly disturbing thing to see a car do, not unlike watching a massive oak tree float off like a dandelion seed. The irregular motion of the car drew it away from the cube and set it down a few metres to its right, bouncing once and coming to rest.

Buster and I ran up to it. To my relief it didn't look like a builder's van, but neither did it look like the Batmobile which is what I had been secretly hoping. It didn't look bad, though, like a big white Jaguar E-type, very sleek, with a large passenger compartment and slightly thicker chassis. The bodywork was scored with lines in the appropriate places for the doors but there were no handles on the thing. The bonnet was one solid curved piece, punctuated only by two translucent panels which I recognised as headlights slightly differently shaped to the one that had come out of the first cube.

Buster peered into the window trying to make out the car's interior. It was dark inside and the street lights were reflecting off the glass. He cupped his hands around his eyes and leaned his head against the car. The small pressure he put on it almost flipped the whole thing onto its side.

"Watch out!" I cried, righting the vehicle.

"It's so light," said Buster. "It's like it's made of polystyrene or something."

"Same stuff as that headlight, do you reckon?"

"Yeah… Shit!" exclaimed Buster suddenly. "We did it!" He held out his hand. I grabbed it and in a completely spontaneous show of emotion pulled him towards me and hugged him. We disengaged and regarded the car again.

"I wonder where the driver is?" I said.

"I must confess I was wondering if we'd get a driver as well. Maybe in the future cars drive themselves. Maybe it was on its way to pick someone up. I'm kind of glad we didn't pull someone across though. Imagine all the explaining we'd have to do. Also he wouldn't have wanted to give us the car. It's ours now."

I looked at my watch. It would be dawn in a few hours and these industrial estate types were early risers.

"We'd better get the cube back to the lockup," I said. "How badly did it get damaged?"

Buster studied the cube for the first time since the car came through.

"The top face is all smashed up, and the lights and motors may have taken a few knocks but it's not too bad. I think we should get the car squared away first though."

"How are we going to drive it?"

"We'll work that out later. Just take the front end and we'll carry it."

The car turned out to be absurdly easy to lift. I've carried IKEA boxes that weighed more. Buster and I carried it round the corner and back to the industrial estate where we encountered a problem I should have foreseen.

"Uh-oh, there's not enough space in the unit for the car and the cube." I said.

"Put it upright." said Buster. We raised the car up vertically against the back wall, resting it on its front bumper, though it didn't have a bumper or even a radiator grille, just a smooth curved front end. The rest of the night we spent collecting the cube with the forklift and getting it back into the unit, then clearing up the evidence of what we'd done.

Chapter eleven

The first thing I did when I got back home after washing the oil stains off my hands was to call a hire company and book a car transporter. We had to get the car out of the industrial estate and over to Buster's ASAP. I know I could have had a tow company take it but the appearance and lightness of the car would have provoked questions. To my chagrin my credit card was turned down. A quick login on my bank's website confirmed my fears: I was broke.

The silly thing was, in this car we had a major asset on our hands. Eventually when we'd unlock its secrets we would score some big-time dough. As soon as we found out how to get into it and drive it we could even make a couple of quid minicabbing but for now, infuriatingly, we were in a hole. First priority was to get it safely inside Buster's lab so we could tinker with it. There was also the problem of the cube. It needed to get out of the industrial unit before the lease was up in forty eight hours. They don't mess around on these industrial estates. Either you came up with the rent or out you went. God knows what the bailiffs would make of the cube, or even the car. They'd probably chuck the whole lot in a skip. I did what I usually do when confronted with a Buster-related problem. I called on Buster.

When I rapped on his door there was no answer. I put my ear to it and heard muffled clanging noises so I was sure he was in. I tried calling his phone but got voicemail. With my ear to the door I tried to listen out for when the clanging noises stopped so I could knock on the door and possibly get his attention but as my knocking was merely making more clanging noises I didn't think he'd notice I was out there. I pulled my head away from the door to give it a good kick but was surprised to find my clothes were stuck to it.

Well, sort of stuck. It wasn't as if the door was sticky, there

Buster's Cube

was something in my pockets that held my trousers and jacket to the steel door. It was my keys and a metal pen. They were stuck to the door through the fabric of my clothes. I'm no scientist but I could see what was going on. Magnetism. Incredibly strong magnetism. What the hell was he up to now?

"Buster!" I shouted as loudly as I could, and finally I heard the clanging stop and footsteps come down the stairs.

"Who is it?"

"Me, Philip! Who did you expect?"

"Oh! Sorry Philip." I heard the locks being opened. "Were you waiting long?"

"Look, before you open up, I should tell you…"

The door opened, dragging me in a tight quarter circle as I went with it.

"…That I'm stuck to your door."

"Oops, sorry," said Buster "I'll sort you out, hang on."

He reached behind the door and flicked a switch. A low hum that I hadn't been aware of died down and my clothes released themselves.

"I turned the door into an electro magnet." he said. "Er… if you have any credit cards they probably don't work now."

"That's OK, they've all been cancelled anyway."

We went up to Buster's lab and he made some tea. The lab was in its usual state of disarray but I've become able to recognise the new disarray amongst the permanent background disarray. It seemed as if Buster had been playing around with a big metal sheet and several hunks of darker metal which were stuck to it.

"So. Magnets, is it?"

"Magnets."

"Buster, we should be concentrating on the car and the cube instead of playing around with this stuff."

"God, Philip," said Buster, exasperated. "Do you only ever think in straight lines?"

He went to his work bench, grabbed the white corner of a car we had first captured and brought it over to me. In his other hand he held a classic U shaped magnet.

"Watch this."

Buster slowly moved the magnet toward the white lump. A dimple appeared on it which stretched out into a C-shaped groove. The groove multiplied into several, deepening and bunching together the closer the magnet came.

"Cool." I said.

"Very cool," He confirmed. "I'm thinking that a big magnet will be enough to pop one of the doors open."

"Sounds like a plan." I said. "All we have to do is go get the car and the cube from the unit. And there's a little problem on that score. I can't hire a transporter because I'm out of cash."

"Why do you need a transporter? Surely the car's light enough for us to lift into a big van?"

"What about the cube?"

"I'll have to disassemble it."

"There's still the problem of getting hold of a big van. The hire companies need a credit card."

"We don't need a hire company. I'll borrow my mate Davo's Luton."

I have to admit Buster's favours-instead-of-money system does sometimes work.

Chapter twelve

Buster's system may sometimes work but it would be charitable to say the same for Davo's Luton, or indeed Davo himself. The most I could say for the wreck on wheels that the van turned out to be was that it sometimes didn't break down. It had bald tyres, no tax, a body that rain leaked into and an engine that oil leaked out of. Still, beggars can't be choosers and we really were down to the begging level at this point. We moved the car and the cube the next evening, Buster having spent most of the day taking the cube apart so it would fit.

Getting the car into the van was easy apart from one dicey moment when we were lifting it down from the back wall of the industrial unit and it slipped and fell right on top of me. I'll admit it was pretty terrifying to see the car coming down but it merely plopped onto me with no more impact than a tea tray. We laid it along one side of the Luton's boxy interior avoiding the gaping hole in the floor and fetched the panels of the cube. For once I had come prepared and wore gloves for the handling of the mirrors which had some evil edges to them. Buster handled the panels without gloves. His hands are tough as rhinoceros hide but oddly he is extremely sensitive to hot objects.

Finally we said goodbye to Park Royal, Painter Pete and the gun guy and trundled off down the very road we had grabbed the car from. We didn't actually say goodbye to anyone, it wasn't that kind of place but I had a sense of closure as I saw it recede in the van's one working side mirror. How we got through the security cordon around the City I'll never know. The so-called 'ring of steel' was set up specifically to stop the kind of dodgy van that we were driving but as usual the checkpoint was unmanned and the only police we saw the whole journey were hassling some Sikh guy.

We were both exhausted by the time we got to Buster's but

the work still wasn't finished. His alley was too narrow for the Luton so it was a long night of shuttling pieces of the cube from the van to his store room, followed at last by the car, which we got in by turning it sideways through the door. We couldn't even relax once we'd got everything in because one of us had to return the Luton to Davo. I volunteered to do it on condition that Buster wouldn't mess with the car until I got back.

Naturally he couldn't keep his promise and when I returned I saw he'd been playing about with his magnets again. He hadn't appeared to have slept.

"How's tricks?" I asked.

"Yeah... made a bit of progress, you know."

"Have you managed to open the doors?"

"Not yet, but I might have come up with a workaround," he said, wolfing down the almond croissant I had kindly brought him, "The way I see it is this: In the future, well in any time, cars need to be secured against anyone but the keyholder getting into them, and we know that the only thing that has the slightest effect on this white material is a magnet, so I'm assuming that there's some kind of magnetic key to open it."

"Fair enough. So did you try running a magnet over the door frame?"

"Yeah, that's the first thing I tried. It dimpled a bit but otherwise no luck. So I tried two magnets together, then a magnetic key I had from an old padlock, then a whole combination of magnets of different polarities... nothing."

"So what did you do then?"

"Well I got a bit pissed off so I kicked it."

"Any use?"

"No, but it made me feel better. The thing is, it's entirely possible that coming through the cube messed up the mechanism, so even with the right key it wouldn't work."

"So what the hell are we supposed to do now?"

"Kick it again."

I was disappointed in Buster. He doesn't usually resort to brute force until all his other options are exhausted.

"Look," I said "Just whacking the door with your foot might work with Davo's Luton but this is new technology we're dealing with. You can't expect…"

"I'm not going to kick it with my foot," he interrupted. "I'm going to give it a magnetic kick."

He went to his tool bench and brought back an evil looking club-shaped object about three feet long, wrapped all around with copper wire and sporting a thick cable coming off the handle.

"The hell is that?"

"A magnetic kicker," said Buster proudly. "It'll direct a powerful electromagnetic pulse for a fraction of a second. The good bit is it can pulse a thousand times a second. I made it myself."

Buster pointed it towards the car's right hand back door.

"Hang on," I said "Shouldn't you be aiming for the driver's side door?"

"No, I don't want to risk frying the controls. Best stand back."

He held the kicker in both hands and switched it on. I heard a dangerous sounding hum and felt the air crackle as the hairs on my arm shivered and stood to attention. Buster gripped the kicker tightly and pointed it at the passenger door. He pressed a button on the handle and it made a single 'tick' noise that was a bit of an anticlimax. In the millisecond of the tick I thought I saw a round hole appear in the door, about the size of a ship's porthole. The ticking grew more rapid until it turned into a continuous buzz and the hole became a stable-looking entrance in the side of the car's door, just below the window. Buster turned to me and grinned.

"Open sesame!" he said above the sound of the ticking. "Want to get in?"

"Is it safe?" I asked.

"As long as the kicker stays on and focused. If you're half way through and the power goes off the door will slice you in half."

I looked back at the hole. It was moving slowly around the door in tandem with Buster's grip on the kicker.

"Turn it off."

He slowed the ticking and powered it down. I told him there was no way in hell either of us were going to entrust our lives to that 'thing'. Buster was crestfallen.

"It's one in the afternoon," I said. "We've been up since nine AM yesterday. You're coming home with me and sleeping in my spare room."

"What? Why?"

"Because I don't trust you. If I go off now you'll be up tinkering for twenty four hours. What's your record for staying awake? Nine days?"

It was true. During a short-lived office job Buster had once spent so much time playing an online fantasy game that he'd had to take a sick day just to catch up on his sleep, then he'd spent that whole sick day playing the online fantasy game.

"Come on." I said.

Ben Slotover

We both fell asleep on the tube.

Chapter thirteen

When we got back to mine I discovered my electricity had been cut off. Fine by me. I'd had my fill of sparks, crackling air and electromagnetic pulses and just wanted to have an analogue night in.

Six hours later I woke up shivering. Throwing my duvet around my shoulders I shuffled into the living room. Buster was gone, and he wasn't in the spare room either. I checked the kitchen and found a note from him saying 'Had an idea.'. I quickly checked the window, fully expecting to see a mushroom cloud in the direction of his place. When had he gone? Had he got any sleep at all? To be fair, we'd both had quite a good sleep on the tube yesterday. We'd woken up two stops from my house and then one stop later I realised the train was moving away from my house, not towards it. That could only have meant we'd been asleep right to the end of the line, then back in the other direction. We might have even gone back and forth another time or two. I called Buster's mobile.

"Hi Philip!" It didn't sound like he was home, the sound dynamics were all wrong. It sounded like he was outdoors. I could hear roaring and crashing in the background.

"Buster, where are you?"

"I'm at the dump."

That figures. Buster is a big fan of recycling insofar as it provides him with a steady stream of spare parts for his work. It's a one way street though. I've never seen him separate his paper and glass and stuff and leave it out for the council. It must be something to do with his living off-grid. When he has a bag of rubbish he goes round the corner from his place where there's a loading bay and a few giant commercial bins and just chucks it in one of those. Most times he comes back with something from those bins that has caught his eye. Often he comes back with more than he threw out.

"Which dump?"

"Yours."

"I have a dump?"

It turned out to be called a 'Recycling and Re-use centre'. To Buster it was Disneyland. Eight massive steel containers were arranged in two rows, each container big enough to contain four skips. One was full of garden waste, one was for metal, one paper- you get the idea. I found Buster by the junked household appliances, wrestling with a washing machine.

"Oh, hi." he said, looking up. "Help me get this off, will you?". He was struggling to tear the door from its hinges.

"Don't you have a toolkit on you at all times?"

"Take more than a screwdriver to get the door off a Miele. They're built like brick shithouses. Try the re-use shed."

He pointed to a container that had been laid on its side and was full of miscellaneous objects: old picture frames, books that pre-dated the internet, computers that pre-dated the books. There were no tools of any kind but there was a metal chair that was falling to pieces and I took one of its legs back to Buster.

"This is all I could find," I said. Buster used the chair leg to lever the door off the washing machine. It came free with a loud crack.

"What are you doing with that anyway?" I asked him.

"I need a metal ring, and the Miele machines all have them around their doors."

"I hope this has something to do with getting into that car."

"Oh, it has everything to do with getting into the car."

We headed for the exit, Buster looking about nervously for the Recycle centre staff. It was a cold day and they were all in their portakabin drinking tea. He explained that technically you weren't allowed to take anything that wasn't in the re-use shed but they didn't know him at this place; he'd been banned from his local recycle centre. Buster told me it would take him a day or so to set up the metal ring and that he'd call me when it was ready.

Chapter fourteen

Buster never called me nor did he answer his phone for two days, so on the evening of the second day I decided to visit him. He didn't answer his door when I knocked but unlike before I could hear no clanging or any other noises coming from upstairs. Where was he? I tried his phone three more times and although he didn't pick up I thought I could hear his ringtone coming faintly from inside, a nasty piercing sound that Buster claimed was easy to hear whatever other noise was going on.

"Buster!" I shouted, banging on the door. "It's me!"

The door shifted a little in response to my thumps. Looking up, I saw the reason why: The frame had been damaged getting the car in and the door didn't sit properly in it any more. I kicked the door and it burst open, taking some of the frame with it. Oops. I hoped Buster hadn't just gone out for milk.

"Buster?" I called from the doorway. Still no reply. The car was there, right side up and jammed against the staircase. I grasped the car by its corner to get it out of the way but couldn't move it. The car had suddenly got heavier. Not as heavy as a normal car, because I could still shove it if I pushed hard, but about as heavy as a person...

"Buster!" I shouted, peering into the car. There he was, unconscious on the back seat. I rocked the car from side to side and to my relief he finally stirred, sitting up and rubbing his eyes. He saw me and his mouth moved but I couldn't hear a thing. I assumed he couldn't hear me either as he went into a complicated series of hand gestures, miming a circle and pointing at the floor.

That's when I saw the metal ring from the washing machine. It was wedged half under the car below Buster's door, wrapped all around in copper wire with a thick black cable running off to the wall.

I looked over at Buster. He was miming a pen writing on paper. I understood what he wanted but even if I had pen and paper it wouldn't be much use. How was I to get it to him? Then I had an idea. I took out my phone, launched a notepad app and held it against the window. Buster gave me a thumbs up and started to tap on his side of the glass. It worked. When he was done I withdrew the phone and saw what he had typed: HOLE RING UP TOO DOOR AND SWITCHON.

I picked up the ring and placed it against the car door just below the window. Finding what looked like a toaster dial taped to where the cable was attached I turned it on. It hummed in my fingers and I saw the car door in the centre of the ring part like a set of curtains.

"Thank God it still works," said Buster, leaning down to speak through the hole. "Now whatever you do don't move the ring or switch it off. I'm coming out."

I kept the ring clamped in place to the door and stood out of Buster's way as he crawled out through the hole and flopped ungracefully onto the concrete. As soon as he was out of the car I switched the ring off and gingerly laid it on the floor.

"I see you managed to get into the car." I said drily.

"Yeah, getting in was OK. Getting out was… a problem."

"How long were you in there?"

"I'm not sure. What time is it now?"

"It's ten past eleven at night."

"OK, so I was only in there for fifteen minutes. Hang on," he checked his phone. "OK, I was in there for twenty four hours and fifteen minutes."

"What was it like in there?"

"Very quiet. I think the compartment's completely sealed

off. Airtight."

"Lucky you didn't suffocate."

"Must have some kind of air purification system, I don't know."

"Must have been scary."

"Actually it was OK," said Buster. "I figured you'd turn up sooner or later so I caught up on some sleep. I think I slept the whole clock round."

"Oh yeah, talking of me turning up, I broke your door getting in."

"Maybe I should give you a key one of these days."

Buster went off to the toilet while I tried to find his latest kettle to make some tea. He's always cannibalising his kettle in pursuit of a knob or switch or heating coil, then having to get a new kettle.

"So how'd you get stuck in the car?" I asked him when he came back from the loo.

"Silly really," he said. "I made the magnetic ring on the assumption that it would create a gap in the bodywork big enough to crawl through, and it did. So I attached the ring to the car door, climbed through and as soon as I was in the car the ring fell off and I was trapped in there."

"How did you attach the ring to the door?"

"Blu Tack."

I didn't know what to say. Buster should have been killed fifty times over pulling stunts like this. He's so used to dicing with death he doesn't even seem to notice when he's doing it any more.

"Well, at least it's safer than that magnetic kicker thing." is all I could say.

"Does that mean you want to give it a try?"

"I don't know. Is that ring the only way in and out?"

"I'm sure there's a mechanism somewhere inside for opening the doors. I couldn't find it but then you know more about cars."

"Ehhh…"

"Go on, try it. I'll stay out here with the ring in case you get stuck."

The problem was not so much getting stuck inside the car as getting stuck in the ring while half way in. Buster held the ring tight against the door but I was all too aware of what would happen if he lost his grip: instant slicing in half by magnetic forces. As it was I managed to scrape through at the cost of a couple of buttons from my clothes and fell exhausted onto the rear seats of the car.

Sitting up, I surveyed the interior. The first thing that struck me was how quiet it was. Buster had removed the ring and the only noise in there was the sound of my own breathing. I could see him out there, waving and speaking but couldn't hear a single thing. There was also no smell. All cars smell of something. The residue of oil, petrol, stale dropped crisps and old farts seem to figure prominently in most. Even spotlessly clean cars smell clean. New cars smell of new plastic and seat cushions, and if you've ever been in a smoker's or a dog owner's car, forget about it. This car smelled of nothing, even though Buster had just been in it for twenty four hours. I leaned over and sniffed the front seat headrests. Zero. It was also scrupulously clean, as if no human had ever sat in it before. I had an image in my head of car's original owner, dressed in his shiny metallic spandex jumpsuit that they all wear in the future, ordering his robot to hoover the car again.

I climbed through to the front and fell into the driver's seat which was on the right hand side. For all its fancy white sleekness from the outside the car was remarkably minimal within. The dashboard was featureless. No gearstick, no dials, not even a glove compartment, just two buttons. The colour of the dashboard was the same as the seats- a uniform charcoal grey. I felt under the driver's seat and was pleased to find the bar to move the seat forward and backward. Simple technology that never changed. I gave myself a few more inches of legroom and pondered the controls. Seeing as the car was parked up against the back wall of Buster's storeroom I didn't think it wise to try and start it up yet so I concentrated on getting the doors open properly. If possible I wanted to avoid another trip through Buster's ring of death.

Buster was holding up my phone to the window. On its screen he had typed 'DO YOU WANT TO GET OUT?' I tapped on the phone through the glass: 'GOING TO TRY DOORS'. The door was even more featureless than the dashboard. No handle, no seat pocket, no window control, just a dark grey wall. There was a strip just below the window that was shinier than the rest of it and I concentrated on that. Think, I told myself. If this door doesn't open with a handle then maybe it's touch sensitive. But if it is then there would have to be a system to stop you opening the doors by accident with your elbow. It would have to respond only to a deliberate movement. My phone has a system like that. You have to run your finger in a straight line across the screen to unlock it. Gingerly I stroked the door along the length of the shiny strip below the window.

The door opened. It didn't swing outward like a normal car door, nor did it do a fancy gullwing or even fancier recess into the floor. It simply disappeared in a line from left to right as if it had been wiped out of existence. My ears popped as it opened and I could suddenly hear the sounds outside the car again.

"Hey now!" said Buster. "You got it open!"

"Not especially hard," I said, getting out. "Only took a bit of common sense."

Buster's face fell as I spoke and I wondered what the problem was now. He was looking over my shoulder and I turned round to see the door I had just got out of closed up tight. I touched it, sliding my hand across it like I had done on the inside but to no avail. The car was sealed again.

"Bugger," I said. "The damn thing must have an auto-lock. What we need is some way of keeping the door open when we're not inside it."

"We wouldn't be able to leave it anywhere with the door wedged open. What we need is a key."

"Hmm."

We both thought about the problem for a while.

"Well," said Buster finally, "We've got a way into it and we've got a way out of it. That's a start. What I'd like to do is drive it."

"Damn right, except for one thing. I'm not crawling through that ring of yours again."

"That's OK, I'll go through the ring and open the door for you from the inside."

"Nope. You're going to devise something safer than that ring and then we'll think about a test drive."

"But the ring is safe! We've both been through it."

"Listen Buster, there's a difference between being safe and escaping with your life. Sooner or later that thing's going to slip off while one of us is half way through and you know what that will entail." I looked at my watch. "It's midnight now. Let's reconvene tomorrow afternoon at 2pm and then we'll carry it outside and see if we can get it started. In the meantime you work on the door problem."

I got home to find another note from Sparky. They were

starting to get a bit less polite, these notes. This one said *'Did you really think that no one would find out what you were doing? Did you really think that you would get away with it?'*

Chapter fifteen

I was back at Buster's the next day at two pm as arranged. He opened the door smiling. He looked proud. I hoped this was because of some kind of real progress with the car.

So I was shocked to find the car gone and in its place a horrible wreck of a vehicle. Every panel was dented and looked like it was about to fall off. Large parts of it were held together with bungee cord.

"What's this?" I demanded. "What have you done with the car?"

Buster's grin got wider.

"I disguised it," he said. "I got hold of some panels from the car yard and made it look like an old wreck."

"But if the police see that…thing… on the road they're going to pull it over in ten seconds! They'd be after an MOT, emissions test, the whole nine yards. Anyway, I thought you were going to work on the key problem."

"Oh, I sorted that out in half an hour. Look."

Buster unclipped a dented panel from the car's front passenger door, revealing the shiny white car beneath. There was a metal cube stuck to the bottom left of the window. I could dimly see something else on the inside of the glass. Buster grasped the cube and slid it across the window from left to right. The door silently slid open in its disappearing trick fashion, leaving an inch of door and window remaining on the right. Buster reached in and pulled something off the inside of the window. It looked like part of a Cyborg. It was a curved metal rod about six inches long with a cube at one end and what looked like a real human finger at the other end. On closer inspection it was a rubber finger.

"Got that at a joke shop ten years ago. Always wondered when I'd use it. The two magnets go on either side of the glass and hold the rubber finger against the unlocking pad. If you're outside the car you slide the magnet across the glass which moves the finger along the pad and open she goes."

It was an elegant solution. Instead of wracking his brains trying to fabricate a magnetic key he had done the future-car equivalent of shoving a coat hanger through a crack in the window.

"Nice one, Buster. We'll be driving this thing yet. That is as soon as we get rid of this nonsense."

I waved my hand over the battered shell which Buster had plated the car with. He moaned about it of course, telling me he was up most of the night installing it but I pointed out that in order to get the car out of his store room we'd have to carry it on its side through his door and we wouldn't be able to do this with the extra bulk. He couldn't argue about that so I helped him take the dented panels off and leaned them against a wall, sincerely hoping that they wouldn't become a permanent fixture there but suspecting they would.

Finally we had the car placed in the alley in front of Buster's old car, the one with the hinged side. I had a go with the rubber finger and the door opened like silk. I would try driving the car first. In a rare moment of self-awareness Buster agreed that he couldn't be trusted in an untested machine like this until I had worked out the basics of how it ran.

We sat side by side in the front. I fixed the driver's seat and pondered the controls, what few there were of them.

"Can we assume that the steering wheel turns it left and right and the pedals are an accelerator and brake?" I asked Buster.

"I think that's safe to say. There's no gear stick though. How are we going to get it in reverse?"

"No idea. Maybe it doesn't have a reverse."

"Well what kind of future is it that decides to do away with the reverse gear on a car?"

"Not just reverse, they've done away with indicators, wipers, handbrake, light controls, speedometer. In fact there's no display at all. There isn't even a key for the ignition."

"Maybe it doesn't even need a person driving," said Buster. "Maybe it's so automatic you just need to tell it where to go."

"Hmm. Car, go to London Bridge."

Nothing happened.

"Why London Bridge?" asked Buster.

"I reckon there will always be a London Bridge, even in the future. Didn't seem to get the car going though."

"What about those two knobs on the dashboard?"

"I'll try those next. Jesus, it's like if two cavemen discovered a photocopier."

I studied the two buttons. On close examination they were slightly different. The left one pushed in and the right one turned. I tried the right one first and it clicked as it started going round, like a power/volume knob on an old amplifier. Nothing happened, so I turned it back. It clicked again as I turned it off. I tapped the left button. Still nothing.

"Well, some road trip this is turning out to be," said Buster. "I'm beginning to wonder if we've just got a display model of a car. Maybe that's why it's so light."

"This is why I'm driving and you're not. I'm methodical. Now, if there's a safety feature built in to the starting mechanism it might not start up unless I'm, say, holding the brake down. So let's try that next."

I pressed the left pedal firmly down, that being the brake on an automatic. At the same time I pressed the left button. Finally something happened. Without a sound the car jumped backward and collided with Buster's car behind us. There was no sound but we felt a jolt as the two cars connected. I pulled my foot off the pedal.

"Well, I think I've found reverse." I said.

Buster got out and inspected the cars. The future car didn't have a scratch on it and surprisingly Buster's car hadn't been too badly damaged either. There was a new dent in the front and the license plate had come off.

"Sorry." I offered.

"Don't worry about it. Actually that's given me an idea,"

Buster went round the back of his old car and returned with the rear license plate. Taking the front one that had fallen off, he attached them to the future car and got back in.

"It won't hold up to a license check but it'll make us less likely to be pulled over."

"While you're at it why don't you stick the Tax disc in here as well?"

"Good idea."

Buster got out again, retrieved the tax disc from his old car and taped it to the inside of the windscreen.

"Totally illegal," he said. "But at this point we might as well. Let's try that again."

I pressed the left pedal down more gently and touched the left button. A soft vibration thrilled through the car. Easing off the left pedal, I touched my foot onto the right pedal. Slowly and silently the car crept forward.

"We're moving!" I said.

I reached the end of the alley and waited for a gap in the traffic. My hand automatically reached up to where the indicator is in my own car. Naturally it met nothing. Spotting a gap I pulled out onto the main road and turned right.

"Woah!" we both said simultaneously. There was something very strange about the way the car felt going round the turn. When you're in a normal car and it turns there's a pull, a slight force drawing you left or right. It's so slight and we're so used to it that it's become all but unnoticeable. That is, until you take it away. How can I describe this? There was no force acting on us. It was as if London was rotating and we were sitting still.

"Did you feel that?" Buster asked me.

"I felt nothing." I replied. "Weird, isn't it?"

"Try accelerating."

"Hang on, we're in traffic."

I eased the car through the scrum of vehicles that was a permanent fixture around Tower Hill and headed east. There was a long stretch of road through Wapping where I could get a bit of speed up. Luckily it was mid afternoon and the real rush hour hadn't kicked in yet. Eighty metres or so of road opened up in front of me and I pressed harder on the accelerator. The car leaped forward and hit ninety miles an hour almost immediately. As with the turn we felt no G-force whatsoever which made it feel like it wasn't happening. However as the car ate up the distance the back of a plumber's van shot toward us at high speed. I hit the brake and the car stopped as quickly as it started. In a regular car we would have headbutted the windscreen or at least suffered severe whiplash but in this car the view outside simply stopped.

"That was scary." I gasped as soon as either of us could

speak. Buster looked grave.

"How was that possible?" said Buster. "By all the laws of physics we should have been thrown back and forth like rag dolls by that kind of acceleration."

"Listen, by all the laws of physics we shouldn't have got hold of this car in the first place." I answered. "Let's just take it easy and learn how this thing operates. We've established pretty conclusively that the two pedals are stop and go, plus if you press the stop pedal when the car isn't moving then it reverses. That button on the left is the ignition, and the one on the right we don't know. It didn't do anything when I turned it earlier."

"Maybe because the engine was off when you turned it. Maybe it'll do something now we're moving."

"OK, give it a go." I said.

We really should have pulled in before trying anything new with the car but I was getting used to the weird way it handled and I was also getting cocky. Buster turned the knob just enough to make it click and nothing happened, so he turned it all the way.

I don't know if you've ever seen that film 'Tron', the original one. When Buster turned the button the windscreen became a crazy mishmash of coloured lines and shapes, numbers and letters, readouts and info-graphics. I nearly ran into the back of the plumbers van again.

"Shit! Turn it off!" I yelled.

Buster grabbed at the knob and whirled it back round until it clicked off. The windscreen returned to normal transparency. I pulled off the main road and into a side street somewhere in Limehouse.

"What the hell was that?"

"It looked like a HUD." said Buster.

"A Hood?"

"H-U-D. Head Up Display. They have them in jet fighters and attack helicopters. Projections on the screen giving readouts from the aircraft's computer."

"What's it doing in a car?"

"Nowadays it's cutting edge technology and very expensive. I think some of the top end cars might have it. Nothing like as fancy as this though. Is the car on? I want to see it again."

I slowly switched on the HUD and by degrees turned up the knob. As I turned it more and more information came onscreen. Firstly it was just a few things around the edges: a couple of gauges, a speedometer and some text that was too small to read.

"Well, that's the gauges and meters accounted for." I said.

I turned the knob further. More graphics started encroaching on the screen. The funny thing was they seemed to fit around what we could see through the windscreen already. The entrance to the Limehouse link tunnel was up ahead and a label suddenly hovered above it reading 'Limehouse Link' alongside little graphics showing the locations of futuristic speed cameras which wouldn't be in operation for years. At the bottom of the screen in large white letters was written 'NO ROUTE' and below that 'UACIN OFFLINE'

"What's UACIN, do you think?"

"Probably the system they have in the future like GPS," said Buster. "Is the knob turned up all the way?"

"No." I replied, and turned it up as far as it went.

Here's where it would have been useful if you'd seen 'Tron'. The entire view out of the windscreen became computer generated. The gritty East London street ahead of us faded into a blocky, three dimensional, exactly corresponding simulated overlay. Gone were the dog turds and bits of broken glass in the gutter. Everything was smooth, straight and glowing. It wasn't a still image either. Every car that crossed our view was represented by a CGI car that looked a bit like ours. People became robotic stick figures and the shops by the side of the road looked like little websites.

"Look- the road has its name written on it." I pointed out.

"Augmented Reality." said Buster.

"What?"

"They'll have a different name for it in the future but this kind of thing is currently called Augmented Reality. It's a real time view but enhanced with information from the car's computer and info from the network. iPhones can do it but this is way ahead of the curve. This is so augmented there's no reality left. Try driving with it on."

I pulled out from the kerb. The projection changed along with the view out of the windscreen. A computer generated car passed us on the other side of the road and I saw the real vehicle shoot past my side window, looking very different. Then a party of school children crossed ahead and were represented as a crowd of little robots. I pulled in.

"This is doing my head in," I said. "The silence and no G-force is off-putting enough but I can't drive through this living sat-nav. I need to see what's in front of me."

I turned the knob down and reality returned.

"I don't blame you," said Buster. "We're not accustomed to this level of technology. What if you gave Henry the Eighth a pinball machine? He'd freak out."

"I don't know, Buster. I'm wondering what kind of future built a car like this. It's totally cut off from the outside air, you don't feel it moving, you don't even have to see what's actually in front of you. I'm sure the bloody thing would drive itself if we could work out how. How bad must the outside be if this is how people travel?"

"Maybe in the future people are just really crappy drivers."

"People have always been crappy drivers. Do you know what happened to the first guy to invent a car? He ran it straight into a wall."

"You should try and run this car into a wall, see if there's a safety system."

"You can do that yourself when it's your turn to drive. I'm heading back."

We drove back to Buster's in silence. At one traffic light a guy in a Ford Escort wound down his window and asked us what kind of car it was. Buster told him it was a Nakamichi Dragon and that seemed to shut him up.

Chapter sixteen

The next day it was Buster's turn to drive. He grumbled about the steering wheel being uncomfortably low and fiddled with the HUD controls until he found a level he was happy with. Like me he preferred the view uncluttered by labels and robots, going with the gauges and little else. He got the hang of the controls pretty quickly but then a monkey could probably have driven this car. We headed out of town towards the nearest motorway and I braced myself for a terrifying run down the M2.

"The indicators are automatic," exclaimed Buster. "How the hell does this car know when I'm going to turn? Don't tell me it's telepathic."

"Maybe it can track your eyes," I offered "Or it's learned your driving style and can predict your intentions by the way you move the steering wheel. Pretty impressive."

"I pity the car that gets inside my head. Let's see it predict this."

Buster swerved across three lanes of traffic and floored the accelerator. The car, silently as ever, shot forward at a speed I don't think has ever been reached outside Germany. The view ahead almost blurred but that could have been my eyes dilating with sheer terror.

"Slow the hell down!" I shouted, but Buster had already done so by the time the words had left my mouth, narrowly missing a coach.

"God, Buster. What are you trying to do, trigger the airbags?"

"Sorry."

"Turn it around and let's go home."

I don't know if they still have traffic in the future but they certainly did that afternoon on the M2. It was two hours of nose to tail all the way back from the Ashford bypass. I tried to get some congestion updates on the HUD but it still said 'offline'. It was getting dark by the time we got to the alley and I had a headache. Things weren't helped by Buster getting the car stuck while trying to reverse up to his door.

"Why don't we just get out and carry it?" I asked.

"Listen," snapped Buster, turning the wheel all the way and moving forward six inches- part 22 of a 100 point turn. "We can't always rely on being able to lift the car up into a parking space, it's too conspicuous. If there's one place I can practice my tight maneuvering it should be here." He turned the wheel back, pressed down on the brake and reversed another six inches. "Damn it! It would be easier if this bloody steering wheel wasn't set so low."

"Why don't you adjust it?"

"Can steering wheels be adjusted?"

"Of course they can, and I should hope they can in the future. Check for a lever or something. It's usually on the steering column."

Buster felt around under the steering wheel.

"Is this it?" he asked.

"I can't see with your legs in the way. Try pulling it or flipping it or something. You should feel the steering wheel go loose, then when you have the wheel at the right position flip it back and it'll lock."

Buster flipped the lever over and the steering wheel loosened. I watched him raise and lower it until he had it at a height he was comfortable with. There was a very generous range of movement- most steering columns only give you a couple of inches but after Buster released the lock this one could be moved at least a foot in any direction. I wondered if it was some fancy feature to convert the car from right hand to left hand drive and was too busy watching the wheel to notice what it was that made Buster shout "Jesus!".

I looked up. The view out front was the same as before: the brick wall of the alley, but when I looked through the side window I let out an involuntary squeak. The car was hovering four storeys up in the air. Without a word Buster moved the steering column down and the car floated to the ground. He raised the column slowly and the car lifted off again. Before it was six feet up he brought the column down a bit too fast because the car hit the ground with a bump. Neither of us spoke for a few moments, then Buster calmly flipped the lever and locked the steering wheel before turning to me.

"Philip," he said. "I think this car can fly."

Chapter seventeen

We exchanged seats and I had a go, just to double check that it hadn't been a hallucination and that the movement of the steering column really did make the car levitate. More tests in the alley demonstrated that once the steering wheel was freed to move in three dimensions the car did likewise. It was a remarkably intuitive system. The column worked like the stick of an airplane and turning the wheel swiveled the car left and right like the tail rudder. Within a minute I felt as if I could fly the car all over the sky but we agreed that we'd give it a rest for now. This new surprise had given us a lot to think about.

And argue about, as it turned out.

"I can't believe we suffered two hours of bloody traffic on the M2 and we could have flown home in five minutes." said Buster.

"And how would you propose to hide the fact from all the other people on that motorway that your car can fly? Switch on the cloaking device? Pretend it was a Back To The Future publicity stunt?"

"Well, what's the point of having a flying car if we can't fly it?"

"Because we can't risk it being seen by the authorities. At best they'll just take it off us in the name of national security and we'll never see it again. At worst they'll shoot us down!"

"So what do you want to do with it? Sell it to a car company? I bet you're already thinking about how much you can get for it."

I have to admit it had crossed my mind, but I wasn't going to admit it to Buster at that point. I tried to make him see reason. This car was dynamite. I couldn't just let him joyride it all over the city.

"Look," I said. "Let's just think this through. Neither of us want to turn the car over to a big university research lab, NASA or any government department, right?"

"Definitely. Screw those guys." I could see real venom in Buster's eyes. He hates what he calls 'Big Science'.

"Great, so we're on the same page already." I said. "So we've established that we're keeping the car. Now what's better than one car? The capability to reverse-engineer this beauty and make many cars, right?"

"Might I remind you that you can't even pay your electric bill, let alone reverse-engineer a car from the year 3000?"

"I know I can't. I don't even think you can. But if we had enough money we could. We could hire labs, employ a team of engineers, the whole deal." I patted the car for effect. "There might be more new technology locked up in this bad boy than in the bloody Mars capsule."

"I wondered when the phrase 'if we had enough money' was going to come from your lips," said Buster acidly. "And how exactly do you propose we raise this money? Invite some venture capitalists round for a spin in our flying car?"

"Er…" I said. In fact that was exactly what I was going to propose. Ten minutes flight around London would secure as much funding as we'd ever need, I was sure of it. I could also tell from his tone that Buster and I had slipped onto separate pages.

"Can't you see that's just the same as turning it over to the Government?" said Buster, "OK, you might get a payoff but they'll screw you and take the car from you whichever way. Here's how it goes: Small fish is lucky enough to find a load of fish food. He asks Big Fish to help him. Big Fish eats the food and then eats Small Fish as well. The end."

Buster went over to his kettle and flipped it on, angrily.

"You're small fish, Philip. We both are."

We sat in silence while the kettle warmed up. I considered how I could present our options to Buster.

"How do small fish get bigger?" I said. "By eating a big fish? No, by eating other small fish."

Buster pondered the logic of this.

"Go on." he said.

"Now, I respect your opinion about raising big investment from big-money people, and if you respect my opinion about our need to exploit this car for our own profit, then you have to agree that we're going to have to raise the money somehow to get things started."

"I just want to be able to fly it. You know, go places."

"And you will, but we've got to do it within the commercial system so the car won't get taken off us."

"How do you mean? Charge people for rides in it?"

"For starters, yes. We'll compete with the private air charter companies rather than the companies that make the planes. Like I said, we eat up the small fish. It'll be lucrative without attracting attention."

"Apart from the fact that we'll be flying a car instead of a jet."

"Ah, but they won't know it's a car because you're going to disguise it."

"What, by bolting a couple of wings onto it?"

"Exactly. Now you're getting the idea."

"Dumb it down to look like a weird, boxy airplane? It's a ridiculous idea!"

"I think it's an entirely sensible idea, not ridiculous in the least. Do you know what they had to do with the first cars? The Horseless Carriages? They had to mount a wooden horse's head on the front so it wouldn't freak people out. We're just doing the same thing, at least until people come round to the idea of flying cars. Which we will sell them once we've cracked the workings of this one."

Buster thought about this for a while. I could see he was coming round to my point of view.

"It wouldn't be very aerodynamic." he said at last.

"It wouldn't have to be. The wings are just for decoration. As long as the car can lift the weight of them they wouldn't serve any purpose other than to make it look like a light aircraft. You'll probably have to stick a nose on it as well, and a fake propeller or two. Maybe even a speaker to make plane noises."

"And you're sure we can make money in the executive jet market?"

"There's tons of money in it. With this car we can undercut anyone."

"How much are we talking about?"

I whipped out my phone and went online. Within five minutes I found the price of chartering a turboprop to be upwards of £2000 an hour, and a jet even more. Buster couldn't help but be impressed by the moneymaking potential of my plan, plus it was under the radar, so to speak. He would get to fly the car, the government wouldn't be on our cases and we'd make a healthy profit besides. Then when we'd amassed enough dough we'd implement phase two and assemble a team of engineers to plunder the car for the secrets it contained. There was just one thing to do first.

"We have to work out the limits of it." I said.

"Eh?"

"It's no good going into the private jet business when we don't know how fast or how far the car can go. What would we tell people who call us for a quote? We'd sound like rank amateurs."

"That's true," Buster conceded. "So how are we going to do that, other than take it for a test flight?"

"There is no other way. We'll have to test fly it to the full extent of its abilities." Buster's face lit up.

"Cool! Isn't that a bit risky, though? What if we're seen?"

"The sky's a big place, Buster. We'll do it at night, on a new moon, preferably when there's low cloud so we'll not be spotted from the ground."

The plan appealed to Buster because it gave him an excuse to take the car up and shoot across country in it. There was the possibility of our showing up on radar but what the hell, I thought. Might as well take a chance on it. If we're going to be flying it back and forth on the commuter routes we ought to have a dry run anyway. I went online again and found the next new moon to be in eight days. The long range weather forecast was for normal English February weather: wet and cloudy. We penciled in the date for the test flight and shook hands on it.

"What are we going to call our airline?" asked Buster, making the tea.

"How about a combination of our names?"

Our first names wouldn't combine to anything sounding very commercial. BustLip sounded like an injury, and PhiliBuster implied delay and obstruction, also not good concepts for an airline. We tried our surnames, Ames and Benson. Rejecting Ameson and Bensames I suggested BA but there was another airline with a similar name. We settled on 'A to B Airlines' which contained our surname initials and had a nice direct ring to it.

Chapter eighteen

In the eight days before our test flight Buster worked on the disguise our car would wear to make it into something that wouldn't end up in the UFO files. In the meantime I researched what would need to be done to make the whole enterprise a bit more Kosher.

Flying permits, maintenance inspections, certificates of airworthiness, pilot licenses, and that was just for starters. Once you got up in the air you had to watch out for controlled airspace zones, air corridors, military training areas, you name it. The car had no radio and as far as I knew no transponder, which is a box that sends your craft's identity and location to everyone whose business it is to monitor the airways. If you fly around without a transponder, especially in sensitive areas, you run the risk of having the RAF on your tail or even a missile up your arse. It was a depressing day of fact-finding.

One piece of good news was that if you go below a certain height and don't stray into any controlled zones, of which there are many, you can pretty much fly where you want, using something they called Visual Flight Rules. The idea of this is they trust you to spot other air users and avoid them. The bad news was the Visual Flight Rules only applied to daytime flight, so we had to decide whether to fly the car in daylight and run the high risk of being spotted or fly at night and run the low risk of being shot at. Buster still favoured the night flight and after a bit of consideration I agreed- on one condition.

"We can't fly out of your alley here in London," I said. "We'll have to drive out into the country and take off from there."

"Oh, come on!" exploded Buster. "The whole point of a flying car is not to have to hike out to an airport!"

"We're not going to an airport for the very same reason

that we're not taking off from the middle of London. Look."

I unfolded a big map I had bought online showing all the air control zones in the UK. They were represented as big blocky chunks over all the airports and major cities, as well as military bases and other places like nuclear power stations. When you excluded all of them there weren't many places you could fly with much degree of stealth, but a zigzag route up the east coast would take us to Scotland if we were careful.

"The closest place out of the London zone is in bloody Norfolk!" said Buster.

"Norfolk it is, then."

I got to work looking up the most remote, desolate place for our inaugural test flight. It wasn't hard. A quick session on Google Maps revealed that Norfolk was full of them. We settled on a spot about three miles north of a town called Fakenham. It looked like nothing but flat fields for miles around and very little in the way of local interference. You could probably fly an Airbus 380 out of there without anyone noticing. Buster was also amused to find two villages nearby called Great Snoring and Little Snoring. They sounded like made-up names in a story about steam trains, he said.

We set off in the car the next afternoon. Firstly the usual routine of carrying it sideways out of Buster's ground floor doorway. I noted that he had repaired the door frame and stuck a bigger, heavier door on it. Sooner or later, I thought, he'd need to put in a proper garage door so we wouldn't have to keep carrying the car in and out. I drove us to Norfolk. I couldn't entirely trust Buster not to flip the steering wheel lock and shoot up into the air at the first sign of traffic. We didn't use the HUD to navigate. For one thing it put me off and it also wouldn't work properly without being connected to this UACIN network it kept going on about. Instead I stuck a sat-nav to the windscreen and we used that. We passed the time on the way trying to work out what UACIN stood for, or was going to stand for. We settled on "Universal

Automotive Control and Information Network", although there was some bickering over whether it should be 'Automotive' or 'Automatic'. We also discussed whether my sat-nav would work once we were in the air.

For once the weather was on our side. A thick blanket of cloud had hung over the east for the last week and we'd almost forgotten what sunlight looked like. The nights in London had been dark enough even with the cloud lit up orange from street lights but out in the country, with a new moon no less, it was going to be inky.

At eight o'clock we stopped at a Morrisons on the outskirts of Fakenham and stocked up on sandwiches. We stood in the supermarket car park and ate them, facing north towards our planned take-off site.

"Do you think we should get some fuel?" asked Buster.

"You know, that's a very good question. Have you seen anything like a fuel tank or a power socket on this car?"

"No."

"What about the HUD? Did you see a fuel gauge on that?"

"No, but that thing's insane. I'm still trying to get to grips with it."

"We're just not evolved enough," I sighed. "You probably have to grow up with that to work it out."

"Hey, I'm trying my best."

"Maybe the thing's got a fusion engine or something and doesn't need fuel."

"Maybe, but we don't want to find out it's empty at 6000 feet."

"Remember we're not talking about a normal aircraft," I

said. "If we run out of fuel we'll just float to the ground, call the RAC and go home." I said. It's funny, but Buster was being the cautious one now. Me, I was dead excited.

"I'm going for a pee," I said.

We got back in the car and Buster entered the co-ordinates for our lift-off site: 52°54'38.69"N 0°49'26.22"E. There was almost nothing there, just fields and some old farm buildings but Buster had spotted the site from Google Earth and was convinced that the triangular shape of the fields belied an old airfield. He'd dug out one of his World War 2 maps and discovered an old Bomber base, RAF North Creake, which was returned to agriculture in 1947. In his mind it was the ideal spot, remote and forgotten. I had argued with him about this on the way up.

"This is vertical take-off flying car," I had said. "The whole thing about it is we don't need a runway. We can take off from a layby if we wanted to."

"And if someone sees a car rising vertically off a layby, they're going to think something's up. If we take off from an old airfield they won't bat an eyelid."

"Yes they will, that airfield hasn't been used for over sixty five years!"

"Then they'll just think it was a ghost plane, and they won't tell anyone because no one will believe them. They'll take it to their graves."

"I still think there's no reason for it."

"You want a reason?" said Buster. "OK, try this: When this car is all dolled up to look like a cheap Cessna, you or I are going to need to take off from a runway to complete the illusion. Now we can't just drive to a working airfield and ask them if we can test our flying car on their tarmac, so if you want to practice a horizontal takeoff this place is the next best thing. Or would you like to try it on the Tottenham Court Road?"

"Well, now that's a good reason, Buster. Why didn't you tell me that five minutes ago?"

"I wanted to make my point about ghost planes."

The Sat-nav told us we had arrived but it looked like nothing out there, just a dead straight road with hedges on each side as far as the car's headlights could illuminate. To our left a dirt track branched out alongside the border between two fields. Buster consulted his black and white World War Two map.

"Down there." he said, pointing, down the track.

I eased the car along the track and followed it for half a mile. It was hard to imagine this area being a busy wartime airfield with two thousand men and four hundred women working there. Buster had told me about the Halifax and Lancaster bombers that took off from here. Apparently they had once lost seventeen Halifaxes on a single mission. The track turned to the right and I followed it round, then stopped.

What we saw was eerie after all this country driving. We were at the end of a runway. It was pockmarked and cracked and had weeds growing between the cracks but it was undoubtedly a runway.

"Wow." I said.

"You ready?" asked Buster.

"No."

"You want to do the Russian thing?"

"No, I want to do the English thing. I'm going to have a piss behind that hedge."

I stroked open the door and got out. It was cold and blustery. We had certainly picked our time and place. The night was pitch black, the clouds blotting out all the stars. The only lights I could see were from the windows of a distant farmhouse and a slight orange glow from somewhere over the horizon, maybe Norwich. The car lit up the old runway starkly ahead and enough light spilled out for me to find the hedge and relieve myself. I hoped Buster wouldn't need a pee on this trip but he never seemed to go. Not as much as me, anyway.

I got back to the car and Buster let me in. When the door sealed behind me I noticed once again how it totally shut out all outside noise.

"Right," said Buster, fiddling with the Sat-nav. "Using your air traffic control map I've plotted a course on this that takes us through the least busy and least monitored airspace I could find. We go up the east coast, staying fifteen miles inland until we cross the Manchester air corridor. We have to stay low to avoid any planes going from Manchester to the continent, which there shouldn't be at this time of night. We squeeze between the Teeside and Bradford control areas and then it's a straight run up to Scotland as far as the Firth of Forth. The Sat-nav has all the waypoints programmed into it and it'll go a bit mental trying to plot a route because it'll think we're driving on roads, right? But ignore it. Just follow this arrow at the bottom which points a direct route to our next waypoint as the crow flies. As long as you keep the arrow pointing straight ahead we'll stay on course. Have you got all that?"

"Follow the arrow?"

"Follow the arrow."

"All right, let's do it. No wait, Hold on."

I fished my wallet from my pocket and pulled out my driving license.

"What you doing?" asked Buster.

"If anything should happen and this car blows up or crashes or catches fire I want them to be able to identify me, so I'm putting this somewhere safe in case I get burned to a crisp."

There was no glove compartment so I shoved it down between the driver's seat and the central armrest. "OK, I'm ready."

I touched my foot down on the accelerator and the car trundled down the runway. It was a bumpy ride but the lightness of the car made it sail over the worst of the surface. When I guessed we were going as fast as a plane would on takeoff I reached under the steering wheel and unlocked the column. Then I drew back the wheel and the vibrations ceased as the car smoothly lifted off. The thrill of flying the car was diminished, I have to say, by the lack of G force, making it feel like we weren't going up at all. The view was pretty minimal too, not much more than our headlight beams shining out into the darkness. However we were both elated to be finally in the air. The view below spread out and Buster said he could see the lights of several towns out of the side window.

Then everything went completely black as we hit a thick layer of cloud which we didn't come out of for a good couple of minutes. The only way we could determine the angle of our ascent was by a half full bottle of Fanta that Buster held onto the dashboard. In theory, he said, the surface of soft drink in the bottle would act as an artificial horizon. By the time we broke out of the clouds I had no idea how high we were and wished we'd brought an altimeter.

I gently leveled the car off and tilted the steering column until the arrow showed straight ahead. Above us I saw stars, hundreds of them. Below was thick cloud as far as I could see. The Sat-nav arrow pointed steadily ahead but the street view was going bananas, one minute telling me to go up the A16, the next minute re-routing me down a residential street in Skegness. Most of the time it just said 're-calculating route'. Still, the occasional flashes of road on the main display gave me an idea as to which part of the country we were flying over.

"I'm beginning to wish we hadn't chosen a moonless night to fly," said Buster. "Imagine what this would look like with the moon lighting everything up. It's darker than a black cat's arse out there."

"Yeah, but remember the moon would have lit us up as well," I replied. "And anyway black cats have pink arses."

An orange glow to our left lit up the clouds from below.

"Where do you think that is?" I asked.

"I don't know. Lincoln?"

"We should have brought a road map."

"Should have brought a road map, a weather chart, a compass and an inflatable raft."

"Plus a couple of parachutes." I said.

"Hey, the Wright brothers didn't have parachutes."

"Wasn't one of them killed in a crash?"

"Nah, you must be thinking of someone else."

"Yeah, I must be thinking about one of the thousands of other people who died in plane crashes."

"Look out, the waypoint's changed." said Buster, pointing at the Sat-nav.

The arrow had flipped over to the left. I tilted the steering column until the car fell in line with the new heading. The silence and darkness made it feel as if we weren't really going forward at all but I knew we were because the Sat-nav continued to track us up the east coast. Scarborough passed below us, then Hartlepool, then I dropped down and flew just over the top of the clouds to avoid the Manchester air corridor. With the wisps of clouds shooting past I got a sense of how rapidly we were going. It seemed impressively fast and I wasn't even pressing half way down on the accelerator.

"Hey, shall I open her up? See how fast this crate can go?"

"I don't know," said Buster. "We don't want to risk a sonic boom. Besides I want to be the one to do that."

The rest of the way up to Scotland went by fairly uneventfully. The waypoints on the Sat-nav took us between the Bradford and Tyneside air control areas, no RAF jets appeared and ten minutes later the Sat-Nav informed us that we had arrived at our destination. I looked down to see the same featureless bank of cloud below us.

"How long did that take, then?" I asked.

"Er... when did we leave?"

"I don't know, I thought you were checking the time."

"I forgot. It was about an hour, though."

"Christ, we're going to have to get our act together when we start flying passengers."

"Let's time the way back, then. It's one AM right now," said Buster, looking at his watch. "We're somewhere off the east coast of Scotland, at least that's what I can tell by the Sat-nav. This bloody cloud bank must stretch all the way across the North Sea."

"OK, I'll turn it around." I said.

"Hang on, it's my turn to drive."

"What? can't you drive next time?"

"It is next time!" protested Buster. "You drove up to Scotland and I'm driving back."

"Well where am I supposed to land the car? On an oil rig?"

"You don't have to land it, we'll just change seats."

"In mid air?"

"Sure, it's no big hassle," said Buster. "Haven't you ever changed drivers while a car is moving?"

"Of course not! Have you?"

"Yeah, me and Davo used to do it all the time in his van."

"You've got to be kidding."

Buster just fixed me with a stare that convinced me he wasn't kidding. He doesn't usually kid around. His own reality is nutty enough that he doesn't need to.

"OK, let's do it." I conceded.

"Right. There's a way of doing this. Firstly, put this in the footwell and rest it on the accelerator." Buster handed me his bag. I stuck it down by my feet and gently laid it on the pedal.

"OK, it's on there."

"Right, now let me hold the steering wheel while you get out of the seat. This is actually a lot easier in the air than it is on the motorway."

"You did this on a motorway?" I yelped, hitching myself out of the seat and perching astride the central armrest.

"Of course I did it on the motorway. If I was on a minor road I could have just pulled over."

"Of course. How silly of me."

Buster shunted himself across and landed in the driver's seat with a thump. I tried not to look outside at the wavering horizon as I got myself into the passenger seat.

"Here," said Buster, reaching down into the footwell and drawing out his bag. "Stick this somewhere would you?"

I threw it in the back and returned my gaze to the dark

cloudscape outside. The stars shone brightly overhead.

"OK, so which direction is home?" asked Buster.

I reached over to the Sat-nav and set it to take us back the way we'd come. It started by telling us to turn left on somewhere called Castle Terrace. Buster turned the car so that the arrow pointed straight ahead and hit the accelerator.

"Woah, watch the speed."

"Hey, did we come up here to test the car out or not?"

"Test the car, yes but not break any air speed records."

"I wonder what our air speed is? Shall we try the HUD?"

"No!" I said "That thing'll just confuse us. We'll work out how fast we've gone after we land. All we need to know is our distance and how long it's taken us."

"Fine," Replied Buster. "Can you program the Sat-nav?"

"I already did."

"Then why isn't it telling me where to go?"

I checked the Sat-nav. The arrow had disappeared and the street view just said 'Calculating route'.

"Give it a minute to re-locate the satellites." I said. "In the meantime just hold your course."

We waited a minute, then five minutes more. The Sat-nav continued to be non-responsive.

"Damn." I said. "Something's up with it."

"Hey, do you think we've run into a magnetic field?" asked Buster.

"God knows. It didn't act like this on the way up."

I re-started the Sat-nav and set our course again. Nothing. I told it to re-locate the satellites.

"You know, it might have gone out of range of the satellites." Offered Buster.

"This isn't the bloody Blackwall tunnel," I replied. "It ought to locate the satellites easily. There look, it's found ten of them, signal's clear as a bell."

"It must be confused by our being up in the air, or maybe we're going too fast for it to lock on. I have been a bit heavy on the gas."

"OK, slow down and see if that helps."

Buster touched on the brakes. I looked outside but could still see nothing but cloud below us and stars above.

"Shit, I don't know where we are," I said. "We might be in a controlled airspace for all I know."

"Look, why don't I drop below the clouds and we'll navigate by sight?"

"At night?"

"Sure, all we need to do is follow the coast until we get to the mouth of the Thames and then we'll find London."

"Yeah, but we're not aiming for London," I said. "We need to drop this thing somewhere nice and quiet."

"RAF North Creake?"

"If possible. Hopefully the Sat-nav will kick in again when we get closer. I'd like to stay above the cloud as much as possible, though."

"Hey, I've got an idea." said Buster. "Why don't we look for the biggest orange glow in the clouds? That will be London.

When we took off it was southwest of us, so we'll duck under the clouds when the glow is ahead and to our right."

"Nice thinking, Buster. This is like navigating in the old days. Just give me a ship and a city of eleven million people to steer her by."

"Eh?"

"Never mind."

We went on for a few more minutes in the darkness. I kept checking the Sat-nav but it was out to lunch, now claiming to be in touch with twenty satellites but still not showing our location, the piece of garbage. I was concerned but not panicked. The relative comfort of our little capsule in the sky and the absence of any feeling of speed did a lot to keep me calm.

"Look!" cried Buster. "An orange glow!"

I peered through the windscreen. It did indeed look slightly orange ahead, just enough to light the sky up a little. Something wasn't right about the look of it, though. If you've ever been on a plane at night, (and who hasn't?) the light from cities below the clouds is a dull, drab orange. This was a bright, clear, reddish orange, and what's more it was tinged with blue around the outside.

"Hang on, that's not London," I said. "That's the sun coming up."

"Can't be," replied Buster. "It's one thirty in the morning. The sun won't come up for another five hours."

"In England, maybe."

"What?"

"If the sun is coming up in five hours in England, then where in the world is five time zones ahead of England?"

"I don't know. Turkmenistan?"

"Buster, I think we're…"

I was about to finish my sentence when something happened which made both my and Buster's jaws stop working. The sun came up. I had been right all along but I didn't have time to relish the fact, nor could Buster admit I'd been right because both of us were transfixed by the scene. It wasn't just that it was a very nice sunrise, which it was. The fiercely glowing colours of a sunrise seen from the air are always impressive, but as I said, that wasn't what had muted us. It was two things, really. Firstly, it was the horizon. It wasn't straight, it was curved. Very curved. The second thing was that the stars hadn't gone out.

"Buster." I said. "I think we're in Space."

Buster's first reaction was to slam on the brakes as hard as he could. Lucky the car had its G-force damping on or we would have been smeared all over the windscreen. The sun stopped rising and hung over the horizon. Buster pushed further down on the brake, absurdly looking over his shoulder as the car reversed. The sun went down below the horizon and stopped, leaving us hanging there in the shadows. Actually we were going 650 miles an hour backwards. I looked that up later.

"So it's a spaceship." Murmured Buster.

"Looks like."

"Do you think it's a submarine as well?"

"Wouldn't surprise me," I said. "I do know one thing, though."

"What?"

"We can chuck the whole airline plan."

Chapter nineteen

I suppose I'd better tell you how we got home again. After the amazement and the wonder wore off we took stock of our situation. Our main priority was to get the car back on the ground, preferably in the UK because neither of us had brought our passports.

First though, there was the problem of finding the UK under a big blanket of cloud that covered Northern Europe. Luckily Portugal and Italy were all lit up and using these two as the base of a triangle we headed for the top point which we reckoned was the North Sea.

Then there was re-entry to worry about. I was sure that any car able to go into Space shouldn't have any problems coming back to Earth but Buster played it safe and took his time dropping down through the atmosphere. When we broke through the cloud we saw nothing but black below us and guessed it was the sea. At that point thankfully the Sat-nav started to work again. I think the problem had been that it was getting confused by all the satellites it could see up there. We followed the arrow west, skimming along the water until we saw a string of lights ahead: the Norfolk coast.

Aiming for a gap in the lights we flew over a flat beach and a strip of grass and landed on a quiet road on the other side. The second our wheels hit the ground I unzipped my door and ran out for a piss. Buster joined me, keeping an appropriate distance. Over the sea I could see the first grey streaks of dawn rising.

"Just made it." I said, relieved in more ways than one.

"Do you think anyone saw us?"

"Who can tell?"

"What the hell are you doing here?" came a voice behind us. I zipped up and turned round to be confronted by an elderly man with a shabby looking dog. In the rising light I saw a small cottage behind him.

"This is a private road. Would you mind clearing off?"

"Yes, I'm sorry," I said. "We… we got lost."

The man stared at me.

"I'm waiting." he said at last.

I looked over. Buster was still peeing. The old man poked the car with his stick. It rocked alarmingly.

"Now look here, you come here from the city in your fancy sports car…" the man continued, but the rest of his diatribe was drowned out by the sudden roar of a fighter jet as it shot overhead. We scrambled for the car and got the hell out of there. A fine welcome back on Earth for the 537th and 538th people to go into space.

Chapter twenty

"I'm not going to bloody New Mexico," said Buster. "And that's final."

We were sitting across from each other in a roadside cafe somewhere outside a place called Stowmarket. It was 8am and I was on my third cup of coffee. We had been awake now for twenty four hours but I was still buzzing from the trip we had just made. We had been in space. Space! We were official astronauts, downing plates of bacon and eggs in a layby in Suffolk. Buster was moody, though. While we had waited for the food I had done a bit of surfing on my phone and discovered some facts about private space tourism.

"Have you any idea how much they're charging to take people into space?" I asked Buster. "Two hundred K. Two hundred thousand pounds! Per person!" I felt like I had discovered El Dorado.

"Yeah, for a glorified fairground ride. Not even an orbital flight."

"Precisely! Think what we could charge for a few times round the earth. 500K easy. We could clear a million quid on one trip!"

"From New Mexico."

"Well, of course. That's the only civilian spaceport in the world."

"Bugger spaceports. Why should the Americans have a monopoly on space tourism? You can get to space from anywhere. What's the matter with taking off from the UK?"

"Look, Buster. It was risky enough pretending to be a light aircraft and playing hide and seek with the air traffic controllers.

Last night we lit up someone's radar going from Turkmenistan straight to the Norfolk coast the same way a nuclear missile might have done. They've got systems in place to shoot that kind of thing down. We're lucky to be alive. In New Mexico on the other hand there are sixty private aerospace companies and they're all shooting shit up into space all the time. It will be safe, above board and very, very profitable."

"And hot."

"What?"

"It's ninety bloody degrees in New Mexico. I can't stand that kind of heat."

"It's America. They have air conditioning."

This wasn't good enough for Buster. He reeled off every obstacle in our way, tapping the table to punctuate his list.

"Import permits, setting up a company out there, work visas. Flight plans. Vehicle inspections, probably. And what would the US government do when they find out what we're sitting on? We might as well just land it on their embassy roof and have done with it."

"Well what do you want to do? Go back to Plan A? Shuttle executives to Inverness?"

"What about your plan to reverse-engineer the car and make more of them?"

"We're still going to do that Buster, and a lot sooner than before. It'll only take two or three flights to get the ball rolling now and New Mexico is crawling with aerospace engineers."

"Well, I'm not going to New Mexico," said Buster "And that's final."

I closed my eyes and wished we were in a movie right then so we could just cut to our first official space flight from the

Mojave desert with a million pounds' worth of passengers in the back but when I opened my eyes here we were, still in a Suffolk roadside café that someone had described on the internet as being 'The worst I've ever eaten in'.

We paid up and left. I drove us back to London and got caught in a delightful traffic jam. Buster lolled in his seat with his head against the window. I thought he was asleep until he jerked his head upright and craned it round to follow something he'd seen out of the window.

"What is it?" I asked

"Dreams…" he replied, and left it at that.

I fell asleep in his armchair when we got back and woke up that evening. *Damn these night expeditions*, I thought when I woke up with a dry mouth and crick in my neck. *My sleep cycle is all gone to hell.* I fumbled around for my phone but couldn't find it.

"Buster?"

In he walked, carrying my phone and studying the screen in interest.

"Sorry about this morning, Philip," he said. "I was tired and didn't have the patience for the whole New Mexico thing."

"Does that mean you've come around to the idea?" I asked hopefully.

"No, but I've figured out a workaround."

Brace yourself, I thought, here comes one of Buster's workarounds.

"It came to me on the way back."

"Ah, the dream you had."

"No, I was wide awake."

"Oh. It's just that when you said 'Dreams' I thought…"

"No, it wasn't a dream of mine. I'm talking about Dreams the bed place."

"What?"

"Didn't you see it? The Dreams Bed Superstore?"

"No, I was busy fighting traffic. What was your idea, turning the car into a flying bedstead?"

"Of course not, Whoever heard of a flying bedstead? Don't be silly."

Buster telling me not to be silly. That's a good one.

"I'm talking about their balloon." he continued.

"They have a balloon?"

"Yeah, not a big one, but big enough to be seen. It was floating on a wire by the road with 'Dreams' written on it."

"So?"

"You know you said we should disguise the car as a plane to fly it to Scotland?"

"Yeah?"

"We're going to disguise the car as a balloon to fly it into Space."

Chapter twenty one

I sat for some time turning the idea over in my head.

"OK, how would we disguise the car as a balloon?"

"We get a big balloon and fix it to the roof."

"And what are people going to think when they see a car flying around with a balloon on the roof?" I asked.

"They won't be thinking it's a UFO or a missile or a flying car from the future. They'll think 'there goes one of those novelty balloons', that's all."

"But novelty balloons don't go all the way into Space."

"That doesn't matter. The balloon's just to give the car a reason to be up in the sky until we're virtually undetectable. Then we dump the balloon, hit the gas and up we go."

"We'll still be a massive blip on the radar."

"I know, and it still doesn't matter. In fact I'm counting on it."

"Eh?"

"There'll be so much stuff on the radar we'll get lost in the noise."

"What noise?"

"This noise."

Buster gave me my phone back. Onscreen was a picture of one of those hot air balloon festivals, hundreds of big colourful teardrop shaped balloons all in the sky at once. Classic desktop wallpaper stuff. I think I could see what he was getting at and for my benefit he put the whole picture together.

"The Norfolk Balloon Festival, Second week of August," he said. "Two flights a day over three days. Hundreds of balloons, Hundreds of authorised blips on every RAF and Air Traffic radar. We go up, disguised as a balloon, we slip away into space behind all the radar noise, do our thing, and come back down along with all the other balloons wherever they land. We'll have six windows going up and six coming down and the best of it is we won't have to go to bloody New Mexico."

"No, we'll be going to bloody Norfolk again. It's impressive Buster, and could nearly work, but for one thing."

"What's that?"

"When we come down we won't have our balloon attached any more. How are we going to explain that?"

"That? You think that's the problem? My god, Philip. That's a piece of cake! All we need to do is devise an automatic balloon inflator on the roof and have it blow up a new balloon for the way down. We might not even need a new balloon. We could have one single balloon that we deflate and inflate however we see fit. It wouldn't even need Helium in it seeing as it's a big fake anyway."

That was typical of Buster, claiming that making some bizarre car-mounted automated inflatable-deflatable phony balloon was the easy part of the plan. Still, if anyone was brilliant and crazy enough to try and make one it was the man standing in front of me. He held his chin in the palm of his hand and looked all serious for a moment.

"There is one big problem, though," he said. "One that you'll have to take care of, I'm afraid."

"What?"

"When we get to the balloon festival you'll have to keep all those other balloon bastards away from our car."

Chapter twenty two

We parted on good terms that night and I went home for a proper rest and to think about Buster's plan. When was the best time to disguise a strange object in the sky? When there are a hundred other strange objects in the sky, and some of them really did take the biscuit: balloons shaped like crocodiles, condoms, beer barrels, tortoises, cows, Darth Vader, even cars. Our little craft wouldn't even merit a second glance. A quick search brought up seven balloon festivals in the UK that August. If we weren't ready for one, another would be along soon. Until then we both had our tasks: Buster had to make the car-mounted balloon and I had to find some passengers for our first commercial space flight.

How do you find passengers for a space flight? On the face of it it sounded easy. So far, not counting the Russians there was only one operator on the planet who were selling rides into space and they had been besieged by people wanting to sign up. They were the ones offering the miserable sub-orbital hop for 200K. A go-nowhere thrill ride with a bit more freefall than a vomit comet. However we were offering a far superior package. We could orbit the earth, pop in for tea at the International Space Station, even drop them in another country for an extra charge. Norfolk, England to Norfolk, Virginia in ten minutes. £150,000 extra. It was a license to print money.

Then I realised I was getting way ahead of myself. The competition may be offering an inferior service but then they were one of the New Mexico brigade. They were all above board, licensed and backed by millions of dollars. I had about four hundred quid left in my overdraft. We needed startup money badly, but with Buster being all difficult about investors we'd have to start off financing ourselves with passenger fares. I looked at the other operator's website. The actual flight was the least of it. They were selling the whole Astronaut Experience: training in boutique spas on tropical islands, personalised spacesuit fittings, rides in a centrifuge in Florida, meet-and-greet parties with the other astronauts, you could even book a whole spaceship for a party. They were clearly going after Snob Money. 'We went to the Caymans for our holiday.' 'Oh, really? We went to Space.'

To be fair to them, who's got two hundred grand lying around to splash out on a space flight anyway? Rich people. I have nothing against them. In fact I've been a paid-up rich person a couple of times in my life. It's just that when you're trying to attract big money clients the nonsense you have to throw in is just ridiculous. There has to be Champagne everywhere. When you start the service, mid-way through, at the end. It's as if these people need it like Oxygen. Then every letter you send them has to be on extra-thick paper. Watermarked if possible; costs you 1p extra. Crap like that. Plus they treat you like dirt. Buster and I may be about to offer the most incredible service in the history of commerce but to these people we'd just be service industry scum.

I looked down at the piece of paper. All it had written on it was £500,000. I scrunched it up and threw it away. Without all the spas and training retreats and champagne and heavy bloody paper there was no way we could charge that kind of money. Not yet, anyway. When we were all set up and above board we could really start gouging people. What we needed right now was a loss-leader. A cheap deal for people with less money who weren't as fussy about things like safety certificates and insurance. We'd do a couple of trips at a vastly reduced price but make enough to open a front office. Then hire someone to answer the phone, lay in stores of paper and champagne and get an aviation lawyer to start work on the permitting.

At last I felt like I was on familiar territory. Setting up companies is something I've done so often I could make money doing it for other people. I knew how much it cost to prepare yearly accounts, the whole lot. Benson UltraTainment still had an office above the now-defunct Karaoke piano bar and the lease still had a couple of months to go so we could run it out of there. We needed a name for the company and without consulting Buster I just changed A to B Airlines to A to B Spacelines.

I like this part of a new commercial venture, the early quirks and hardships. Bill Gates working out of a motel room in the middle of nowhere. Those Apple geezers building stuff in their garage. I was confident that if handled properly, after a couple of cheap flights for the right people the word-of-mouth would spread, demand would rise, our prices would go up, we'd build a fleet of Space Cars and next thing you know we'd have an empire on our hands.

When I had made a tally of our startup costs as well as a few debts I needed to settle and divided that number by the number of seats we could sell for our first two trips I came to a price of £2000 per head. It was a bargain. Some lucky punters would go into space for less money than anyone had ever spent, or probably ever will. Except for me and Buster, of course.

If someone had told me that our projected cashflow had been reduced 99% I would have hit the roof but Buster just shrugged it off.

"Hey, you're the businessman," he said. "How's the search for passengers?"

"I think we should announce the offer quietly," I replied. "We can't afford a big glossy campaign. We'd have a mad rush on our hands and then the authorities would be more likely to get wind of it."

"Why don't you put a classified ad in Private Eye?"

"Private Eye? Do people still read that? I was thinking of Craigslist."

"If you advertise rides around the Solar System on Craigslist it'll look like you're insane or you're preying on the insane. Either way it's not a good tag."

I was still doubtful.

"What about an ad in an aviation or astronomy magazine?" I asked, "Wouldn't that be more appropriate?"

"No way. That kind of person would be asking questions non-stop. Same goes for scientists of any stripe. Let them pay extra when we're established and our prices go up."

"OK, give me a minute," I said, reaching for my notebook. "I'll try drafting something."

"I'm going to have a go as well. Can you give me a page of your notebook?"

We scribbled on our papers for a few minutes.

"OK, how's this?" I said at last. "'Journey into space. Go on the trip of a lifetime, ten orbits of the earth from our UK spaceport. Very exciting, lovely views. From £1999 per person.' Then I'd put my number. I made it a pound under two grand because…"

"Yeah, yeah I understand. Ten orbits? Is that the package we're offering?"

"We have to start somewhere. Why, what did you put?"

"'Interplanetary adventure awaits! Explore the Solar System and beyond the infinite! Make contact with alien races and save the Earth! No refunds.' I added that last bit in case we don't find aliens."

"Explore the whole solar system? What are you, Buck Rogers? We don't even know if this car will make it to the moon."

"Well yours sounds like a canal trip on the Norfolk Broads. Lovely views?"

In the end we settled on something between my pedestrian tourist brochure description and Buster's wild hyperbole: *'Behold the infinite! Be an astronaut for under two grand. Fly into space and orbit the earth on the journey of a lifetime. Return trips from*

London to launchpad included.'

I went online and placed the ad, giving my mobile number as the contact. For a while we considered knocking up a website but the thing about websites is they're a double edged sword. If you have a really slick one that's great but if you don't get it perfect or leave out just one or two details they can actually drive people away from your business. Better to have people call me and then I'd set up a meeting in my office. I'd be able to get a feel for them and answer their questions face to face. That would weed out the time wasters and nutcases.

Buster said he'd had a couple of ideas about the balloon but would need a week or two to set something up so we agreed to meet in two weeks at a patch of waste ground in Docklands for the first test. We needed space but there was no point going all the way out of town seeing as we wouldn't be flying the car.

First though, I had to sort out my finances. I owed the Electricity, Gas, Water, Credit Card, Council Tax and Inland Revenue £5,455.73 all together. A very irritating sum of money. I could sell a bunch of my stuff but I knew I'd get a pittance compared to what I'd paid for it and that went against everything I stood for.

Finally I made a list of money raising options in descending order of preference: rent out a room, sell my stuff, get a job at Chicken Hut, sell stuff scavenged from the re-use shed, become a male prostitute, go to my ex-wife for a loan. I looked at the list and crossed out the option of going to my ex-wife, then after a minute's thought crossed out the prostitute option as well.

Flipping through my address book looking for inspiration I found contact details for all my ex-business partners. It made depressing reading. Many had had ripped me off or I had ripped them off or they had simply disappeared. One or two I was still on good terms with but they were even more broke than I was. A couple had gone on to immense wealth but I knew they wouldn't return my calls, the bastards.

The only thing I could comfort myself with was that soon we'd be raking in the dough from our space tourism operation. Until then here I was in the gutter, scrabbling for coins. With a sigh I found an old promotional postcard for the Piano Bar and wrote on its back: 'Room for rent. Quiet residential street. Share of utilities, no dogs. £200 p/w'

Chapter twenty three

For the next week I laid low, working on cashflow projections and a business plan for A to B Spacelines. My work entailed prodigious amounts of research and I was hampered by having to do it all on my phone as my cable and internet had been cut off. I lived on beans on toast and turned off the heating. The only electricity I used was for the toaster, microwave and phone charger. By the end of the week my eyes hurt and I was farting almost continuously. I did however discover a few things about space travel.

Staying in all day I had become attuned to the local sounds, especially the regular ones. At 8.30 every morning someone wearing high heels click-clacked past my front garden. Five minutes later came the skateboarder. The postman was the big event of the morning, turning up at about 10.30am followed by the junk mail at irregular times throughout the afternoon. About once a day someone would ring my bell and make a random demand of my time or money. They came from survey companies, fishmongers and Jesus Christ Himself and I would rebuff them with as few words as possible. One time a middle aged guy with a hangdog face and respectable tones asked me if I could return a certain catalogue that had come through the letterbox last week. My God, I thought, things have come to a pretty pass when it is now financially viable to employ people to go door to door retrieving junk mail.

Once a day I would venture out to the shops if it was morning or just for a walk if it was the afternoon and I hadn't gone out that day. I've always needed to get out at least once a day, even if it's just a walk around the block. Going for an entire day on inside air makes me crazy. I was returning from one of these outings when I spotted a small man darting up to my door with something in his hand. By the time I reached the end of my front garden he had put it through the letter box. When he turned round and saw me he jumped. I noticed he didn't have a sack of junk mail over his shoulder. Whatever he had put through my letter box was for me only.

"Sparky?" I said.

He looked down and mumbled something, then made a beeline diagonally across my front garden, heading for the low wall at the end. I headed him off and stood in front of him. He stopped moving and stood before me, a mousy little man with thick glasses and an overcoat too large for him. His face had a few miles on it and I could see he hadn't shaved for days. I'd put him at about 50. Normally I'd have told him to stop with the letters and piss off but it had been a while since I'd spoken to anybody apart from some imbecile from the Cable company and I was in the mood for a chat. I wanted to put this whole stalker thing behind me, anyway.

"Listen Sparky, why don't you come in and we'll talk person to person. No more of this silly running around, OK?"

He continued to look down but mumbled something that sounded like an assent and followed me into the house.

"What have we here, then?" I said, picking up his letter from the door mat. "Let's read Sparky's thought for the day." He stood in my hall and squirmed as I opened the envelope. "I must compliment you on the heavyweight stationary, Sparky. Lovely quality." I removed the card and read it aloud. "*'You are the agent of my downfall, but I have arisen tenfold in strength and your crime against me will be avenged tenfold also.'* You're very keen on all this tenfold business lately. Would you like a cup of tea? Or ten?"

He didn't say much until I got a cup of tea down him. I offered him beans on toast but he wasn't hungry.

"So what's all this about, Sparky? What is it I'm supposed to have done to you? This can't possibly be about the Piano Bar.

That's all done with, all the pianists are back at work. You won. In fact I'm the one that should be harassing you. I don't have a pot to piss in."

"You took my wife." Said Sparky.

"What?" I was rather taken aback. It had been a while since I had taken any woman, let alone this guy's wife. If I took his wife, why wasn't she here? That was a good one.

"If I took your wife, why isn't she here?" I asked.

"She's at *his* house." replied Sparky bitterly.

"Whose house?"

"The man she left me for. Bloody Martin Haggers."

"Well, may I suggest you go round to bloody Martin Haggers' house and harass him?"

"I can't," he replied. "Court order."

"So why me? In what way does this sorry situation concern me?"

"Because she left me after meeting him at your sodding piano bar!" Sparky exploded.

It took a while for the whole pathetic story to come out. He wasn't a gifted speaker so I'll summarise it here. Sparky, or whatever his real name was, met his wife in the early 1980s when he was a brilliant young pianist and his tinkling of the ivories stole her heart. Things went steadily downhill until she paid a visit to my piano bar with a couple of her friends one night and saw a certain Mr. Martin Haggers miming his way through 'It had to be you'. She was instantly smitten. He was a senior estate agent with no piano playing abilities whatsoever but she told Sparky that he had more artistry on the fake keyboard than he would ever have on the real one. Six weeks later they were divorced.

"Look, mate. No one leaves a proper pianist for a phony unless there was something wrong in the first place," I said. "Your marriage was probably all messed up already and that night at my piano bar was just the tipping point." I know I was being a bit insensitive but this looked like the kind of guy who needed a few truths hammered into his head.

"If it hadn't been for your... your temple of fakery..." he began, but I cut him off.

"If it hadn't been for my temple of fakery she would have run off with the butcher. What would you have done then? Taken it out on the cattle farmers? Face it Sparky, you blame everyone except the one who should be blamed."

"Myself?" he said quietly.

"No, your idiot of a wife! What kind of person leaves a concert pianist for an estate agent? Sod her. And sod Martin Haggers too." I hoped that the pep talk would send him straight round to confront his wife and her new man, and then hopefully to jail and out of my life. Sparky looked up, his face set with a new resolve.

"OK, I'll stop stalking you," he said. "But I'd like you to do me one favour."

"Sure, whatever," I said, picking his mug off the table and taking it to the sink. I hope he doesn't want money, I thought.

"I want a ride in your spaceship."

I dropped the mug on the floor.

I tried to bluster it out but the dropped mug was a bit of a giveaway that I had something to hide.

"What makes you think...OK, how did you know?" I stammered.

"You obviously don't know the ins and outs of stalking,"

said Sparky. "I created a Google alert for your mobile number, and yesterday your ad in Private Eye popped up. They put them online as well as in the paper."

"How did you get my mobile number?"

"It was listed in Companies House. I assume Benson UltraTainment is you?"

Damn it, I thought. You can't do anything in this country without leaving a trail.

"You realise, of course, that that advert was a joke?" I said, trying desperately to lie with a straight face. "The idea is to develop a spaceflight simulator. We couldn't possibly launch a real space vehicle."

Sparky gave me a sly look.

"Enjoy your little *simulated* trip to Scotland the other week? The one that took you over the North sea at Mach 5?"

"Er…"

"You had your phone switched on. I tracked you. At least until you vanished off the face of the Earth, and I mean that literally."

"Look…" I started, but now Sparky cut me off.

"Just one ride and I'll leave you alone. No one need know about your shenanigans in Outer Space."

"But why? How come you're so keen on going into space?"

"I'm performing 'The Planets' in a couple of months. Doing the Celeste part. Before you ask, a Celeste is a piano that rings little bells instead of hitting strings."

"What, and you'd like to go into Space to get you in the

mood?"

"People think piano playing is just hitting your fingers on the keyboard but there's so much more. You have to feel the music, understand it, inhabit it."

"You just want to impress your wife, don't you?" I challenged Sparky. "After all, who stays with an estate agent when they can be with an Astronaut, eh? What if I refuse?"

"Then I'll continue with the notes, but I won't just write them to you, I'll pop a few into the hands of some people who would be very interested in what you've got stashed at your friend Buster's place. Oh, yes, I know all about your trips into the City."

"All right," I said, throwing my hands up. "All right, you got me. One ride, that's all. And not to any planets. Just a few orbits, OK?"

"Fine. my concert's at the end of May. That gives you six weeks to make good or I start looking up the address of the Ministry of Defence."

As soon as Sparky left I called Buster.

"I have to see you," I said. "ASAP."

"Er... can we handle it on the phone?"

"If we have to, I suppose. What's going on over there?" I could hear some kind of engine running in the background.

"It's the compressor. Hang on, I'll turn it off."

I heard clanking noises on the other side, followed by a loud bang and some swearing from Buster.

"What the hell was that?"

"Nothing. Just another balloon burst."

"Listen, we have to move up the launch date. We have to do it in six weeks at the latest."

"Does that mean you've found a passenger?"

"Yes, and he's demanding a flight sooner rather than later. And there's one other catch..." I couldn't continue for a moment.

"Yes?" prompted Buster.

"He, er, won't be paying. He's a freebie."

"Oh."

"Look, I'm really sorry but I have to do this guy a favour. I got into a situation and I owe him and he's threatening to spill the beans if we don't get him into space before six weeks. I've looked it up, there's a balloon festival outside Bath, end of April. That's a month away. Do you think you can get the balloon fixed up by then?"

"I can try, but I might have to take a couple of short cuts."

"Whatever you can do, Buster, and I'm really sorry about this."

"That's OK. I was going to tell you, but I invited Davo as well. As a guest."

"What? We've got two freeloaders on this trip?"

"Hey, if you're allowed one then I should be allowed one. Anyway, we owe him for the lend of his Luton."

"We're giving Davo a trip into orbit in the most sophisticated car in the world in return for an afternoon in that piece of shit Luton?"

"Like I said, we owe him."

"All right, fine! But we can squeeze one more person in

and they're paying full whack. We're making a grand apiece on this trip or it's not worth the hassle."

"Minus the cost of the balloon."

"Which is how much?"

"Eight thousand."

"WHAT?" I shouted as my whole business plan went down the toilet.

"Yeah. I haven't spent the money yet, but for it to work that's what we're looking at."

"Do you have the money?"

"No. Do you?"

"Don't spend the money, Buster! Find some way of doing it for less. Much less. Like five hundred."

"Hmm. OK."

"Are we still on for the test inflate next week?"

Another massive bang shredded the air on Buster's side.

"Yeah," he said. "See you there. Everything's cool."

Chapter twenty four

The USA has Cape Canaveral, we have Barking Creek. It's a dirty trickle of water that, I'm told, connects the river Roding to the Thames. I'm sure the river and the creek and the whole area has some rich Victorian fishing heritage but the only bit of it I saw was a smelly brown turd of a waterway dominated at its end by something that looked like an industrial guillotine for giant robots that needed to be executed. It was a massive steel sheet held 38 metres up in the air by two concrete towers. They say it's some kind of flood barrier but to me it looked constantly poised to come crashing down. The flood barrier of Damocles.

On both sides of the creek were industrial estates, recycling plants and scrap yards. There was just one patch of greenery surrounding the flood barrier and it was this green patch that Buster had designated the test site of A to B Spacelines. I wasn't even sure we were allowed to drive onto the waste ground but nonetheless we drove through an open gate and soon found ourselves in front of the Barking Barrier.

I eased the sleek white vehicle to a stop in the middle of the grass behind Buster, who had led the way in his hinge-car packed with the balloon that took up all the back seats and a worrying amount of Buster's vision. Still, he didn't seem to take the loss of rear view too badly. It's something he doesn't really do much of anyway.

He got out of his car as I drew to a halt and started to pull endless swathes of coloured nylon out of the car like some kind of giant magician's trick. All creased and folded like this I couldn't tell what it was or how it would look inflated. Then Buster got to work attaching something to the roof of the car. I watched in interest as he planted what looked like metal hooks into the roof of the car and wandered over to have a look.

"What are you doing?" I asked him.

"Watch this."

Buster showed me a metal hook about three inches long. It had a screw thread at the base and looked like the kind of thing you'd screw into the wall or ceiling to hang something from. He held the hook by its curved end and touched it to the roof of the car. The material of the roof went soft and let the end of the hook glide in, whereupon Buster let go and the surface hardened, leaving the hook firmly embedded in the car, I tried to remove the hook but it was stuck fast. There didn't even look like a join between the hook and the car.

"Cool, right?" he said.

"How did you do that? That's some Excalibur shit you've got there."

Buster held up a very normal u-shaped magnet in the palm of his hand. With the same hand he withdrew the hook which came out of the car's roof like butter.

"Magnets again?"

"Our old friends the magnets," replied Buster. "Remember that electro-magnetic ring I made from the washing machine door? I had to run it at full power to keep a hole open for us to climb through, but I found that if you lightly magnetise a hook or any other metal object you can get it embedded. All you need is another magnet to get it out."

"Cool."

"Yeah, cool, and very important. Remember we need to attach a fake balloon to our roof and somehow keep it attached throughout a space flight. A couple of bungee cords aren't going to do it."

"So what are you using?"

"Hooks, steel cable, Metal welded framework, stuff like

that. I'm not too concerned about it warming up on re-entry because we can take it slowly. I just want the thing to stay on." took one end of a cable and ducked under the nylon sheet.

"Yeah, well I hope it does stay on or we're going to have a lot of explaining to do to those hot air balloon guys," I said. "Like why we landed without a balloon and we're not dead or anything."

"Rather explain that than *be* dead." said Buster. I suppose he had a point. It was quite a relief to know that our lives wouldn't be depending on this... thing. And it did look like a 'thing' all spread out around the car. The car itself was just a lump in the middle of a large colourful nylon pancake. I still couldn't see what it was.

"Right," said Buster, crawling out from the edge of the pancake, "Ready?" Without waiting for a reply he took the end of the cable that came from the space-car's roof over to his own car's engine. The cable had red and black alligator clips which he clipped to his car's battery. Immediately I heard the drone of an air compressor from somewhere within the lump in the pancake and the thing started to inflate. Within the space of three minutes it went from pancake to quivering jellyfish to wobbly triangle until with a triumphant pop its full glory was revealed. It was a giant slide, the kind kids climb up and slide down in fairgrounds. It perched on top of the car, swaying in the breeze.

"Er... Buster," I said. "I thought you were going to have a bunch of self-inflating balloons? Or one big balloon? That... is a bouncy castle."

"That," replied Buster. "Is what you get for five hundred quid."

"And you don't think there's going to be something odd about an inflatable slide sitting on top of a car?"

"Have you seen the some of those balloons? Lot of odd stuff."

"But the whole point is to make something that will look like it would fly. That thing is clearly not flyable. It's full of air. When the car lifts it into the sky they're going to know something's up!"

"Then we'll tell them we're filling it with Helium."

There was no use arguing the point. I had cut the budget and this was now the only way. I just hoped we'd be able to get the thing up without incident. Buster gave me a whole spiel about how the air-filled inflatable was the best option anyway as not being airtight it would automatically deflate as soon as we got out of the atmosphere and the slide would just shrivel up. He would have gone on longer but my mobile went and I had to walk away from the noise of the compressor to hear anything. It was an unfamiliar number.

"Hello?"

"Hello, I'm calling about the spaceflight you do?" said a reedy voice on the other end.

"Yes! Yes! This is, err, A to B Spacelines. How can I help?"

"Do you give actual rides into space?"

"Well, look, Mr…"

"Nigel."

"Nigel, I'd prefer not to discuss this over the phone. The first step in taking one of our trips is a face-to-face meeting. You can ask us all the questions you like, and we'll asses your, er, suitability for one of our packages. How does that sound?"

There was a pause, then:

"Shall I bring the two thousand pounds with me?"

Good Lord, someone's still that innocent these days, I

thought. I'm going to have to warn this person before they fall victim to a predator.

"Yes bring the money, that would be fine." I said, and gave him the address of the office above the piano bar.

Chapter twenty five

"How old are you, Nigel?"

"Seventeen."

I wondered if there was any law against taking a seventeen year old into space. Sod it, I decided. If there is a law it would have to wait in line behind all the other ones I'd be breaking.

"And why is it you'd like to go into space?"

Nigel shrugged.

"Just like to. Looks cool. Better than hanging around here."

"You do understand Nigel, that this is a return trip? We're not leaving you up there."

"S'OK. So how do you do it? You buy space on the Russian rocket?"

"Oh God, no. We have our own craft."

"You go from New Mexico?"

"No," I sighed. "Not yet anyway. We go from the UK."

"Oh."

The conversation abruptly stopped. Nigel didn't seem to have any more questions for me so I asked him some, starting with the most important.

"Do you have the money?"

Nigel reached into the inside pocket of his anorak and withdrew a battered envelope that bulged rather excitingly. He put it down in front of him. From where I was sitting I could see inside the flap and it looked like it was full of fifties. On the envelope, upside down from where I was sitting, were written the words 'Love, Dad.'

"If you don't mind me asking, Nigel," I said "Where did you get this money?"

"My Dad gave it to me."

"Two thousand pounds? Cash?"

Nigel looked peeved.

"Yeah. He does it every time he goes away for a while."

"Goes away? You don't mean prison?"

"Dubai."

"Oh. What does he do in Dubai?"

He just shrugged.

"Look, I'm sorry about these questions Nigel but I don't like the idea of someone your age blowing their parent's money on something like this."

"Yeah, well it's not like it's my life savings, it's his guilt money. He comes back from Dubai with a suitcase full of cash and doles it out."

"Wow, I wish I had a Dad like yours."

"No you don't. He's ashamed of how I turned out and wants me to get a girlfriend. Like I can just go out and buy one. I think he's been in Dubai too long."

I wanted to shake him, tell him clean himself up and use that cash to buy some nice clothes and start hitting the bars. Luckily the desire to do that quickly passed. Nigel picked up the envelope and handed it across the desk.

"Here. Obviously you're not going to fly me up into space but I don't care. I'd rather give it to a bunch of conmen than piss it away. You look like you could use it, anyway."

"Well, that's very commendable Nigel, but we're not conmen. This is a genuine orbital spaceflight you're purchasing."

"Come off it. At best you'll take me to the Planetarium in a limo. At worst you'll give me some guff about how the flight won't happen until a million people sign up."

"No, it'll happen in a month, as it happens. On April twenty eighth."

"Where?"

"I'm not at liberty to tell you that. We'll pick you up from a London location of your choosing and have you back the next day, on the twenty ninth. Don't bother bringing a change of clothes."

Nigel regarded me silently for a few seconds.

"OK," he said, rising from his chair. "You have my number, just promise me one thing."

"Mmm?"

"Promise me this isn't some kind of stupid hidden camera TV stunt."

"I'll promise you that if you promise me something as well. Don't speak a word of this trip to anyone, not even your parents. Keep it to yourself."

"Don't worry. You think I want it to get around that I gave two grand to some rip-off merchants to take me up into space?"

"I told you, Nigel, I'm not a rip-off merchant."

"Tell me when we're in orbit."

Chapter twenty six

We had our passengers, we had a launch date and now I had to plan for the trip itself. I sat down and made a list. At the top went 'Balloon Festival' followed by 'Provisions for trip', 'Passenger pickup locations', 'Maps and GPS', 'Camera equipment' and finally 'Inflight entertainment'. These headings were all I could think of at the time though I was certain there'd be numerous sub-headings to come.

I was correct on that score: under the 'Balloon Festival' section alone I ran into several potential problems. In order to lift off with all the other balloons you had to register and put down a £150 deposit which was returnable at the end 'subject to the good conduct of your team'. Worryingly, they also required a minimum 35 hours flying time for the balloon's pilot. I had never been up in a balloon in my life let alone piloted one and I was pretty sure the same could be said of Buster and our passengers.

In the end I did something really bad. I did a Google image search of a balloon pilot's license and found a picture of some bloke proudly holding one up, probably just qualified. I downloaded the image, Photoshopped his thumb out of it and printed it. It wouldn't stand up to scrutiny but might survive a once-over.

Then there were provisions and in-flight entertainment. The first item wouldn't be a problem, I'd just get some sandwiches and bottles of soft drink. I toyed with the idea of champagne but decided it would be wasted on this crowd. Maybe for a later trip. You're probably wondering 'What's the point of in-flight entertainment on a trip into space?' and you'd have a point but it was mainly for my own use. The way I see it, what's the point of going into space if you can't enhance it with a few tunes on the stereo? Just ask the scientists on the Space Station. They have music playing all the time, I'm told.

I spent, or rather wasted, an enjoyable hour running up a playlist on my iPod, spending fully five minutes trying to decide whether to include 'Rocket Man'. Then I remembered that the car didn't have a stereo, or at least one that we knew about. Maybe within the byzantine workings of the HUD there was some incredible library of every piece of music ever recorded but for the moment we'd have to use a battery operated speaker that I could plug the iPod into.

So, three off my list already. I was feeling good. Then I hit problems with 'Maps and GPS'. How the hell do you navigate in space? It's all very well to look down on the Earth and try to identify coastlines but if there was cloud over the UK we'd have a sod of a time trying to find the balloons over the west country without being spotted by early-warning systems or UFO watchers. Added to this was the problem of the GPS not working once we'd got above a certain altitude.

I got sidetracked on the internet looking for how space probes knew where they were and discovered some interesting facts about Pulsars but generally it seemed like you needed massive computers and ground-based radar stations to properly find your way round. That was OK for NASA but a bit out of our price range.

Then I found an interesting alternative. It seems you can buy tracking devices to attach to your children in case they get lost or abducted. You don't literally attach them to the child, just clip it to their clothing. They had a range of one hundred Kilometres which also happened to be the official boundary between Earth and Space. All we'd have to do is covertly fix it to one of the hot air balloons and we could track the whole flotilla once we got near enough. I went to the company's website and ordered a child tracker, trying three credit cards until I found one that worked.

Then the problem of how to find our way around while we were in space. We'd be OK if we stayed near the Earth, but what if Buster hit the accelerator too hard and we ended up drifting through the Milky Way? It was a nasty thought but I had to consider it nonetheless. I couldn't really come up with a solution so I just wrote 'ASK BUSTER' under that bit on my list.

That just left 'Passenger Pickup locations' and 'Camera Equipment'. For the latter item I would just bring my old Lomo film camera. The thing was almost obsolete like everything else that uses film but I wasn't sure if the electronics of a digital camera would survive Solar radiation. As for the former, I would need to call Sparky and Nigel and find out where they'd like to be picked up and ask Buster about Davo. Davo lived in some kind of craphole squat in northeast London and I hoped he'd just come along with Buster. I was OK with going into Space but if I had to trek out to Leytonstone I'd be seriously pissed off.

Chapter twenty seven

A week before the flight I was at Buster's, watching him fiddle with my Sat-nav. He had hooked it up to a computer and was poking around its workings via some kind of diagnostic application. There was little I could do but watch. I'm a straight shooter when it comes to using technology. I use things for the purpose they were designed. I register my software, apply updates when they tell me to and never use pirated material unless forced to by financial circumstances. Buster is the complete opposite. Once he gets hold of some technology, be it hardware, software or firmware, he considers it his slave for life. What he was doing now with my Sat-nav was the equivalent to what he had done to his hinge car.

I stared at the baffling numbers and graphics on the computer screen. The last time I had seen anything like this was when a guy came round to fix my cable box. He had accessed a whole level of menus and configurations that were not for the likes of me, the customer. Buster had found a similar set of pages on the Sat-nav and hummed to himself as he perused them. Every now and then he made a noise that could have been disappointment, exasperation or thoughtfulness. He had a notebook beside him and consulted it periodically. I had a peek at it but it was even more cryptic than the computer screen.

"Ah!" he said eventually.

"Yes?"

"See these?" he explained, pointing out a long list of numbers on the screen. "These are the frequencies of all the GPS satellites. This is what your Sat-nav is looking for when it's trying to find your position."

"OK." I was with him so far.

"Now, as we know the thing went haywire when we went into space because it was picking up too many signals. Then again, if it can't pick up enough signals it won't work either. You need at least three, preferably four signals to find out exactly where you are."

"I see, so you're going to tell it to only listen out for three or four satellites?"

"No, I'm going to tell it to ignore the GPS satellites completely."

"Then how…?"

"The GPS satellites are in Medium Earth Orbit, or MEO," said Buster. "That means they're always moving relative to the planet. If we narrow down the number of satellites then we'll lose track when they go round the other side of the Earth. Anyway, they'll be no good when we go further out into space."

"So you're going to… OK, what are you going to do?"

"I'm going to reconfigure it to listen for other radio signals."

"Ah! You mean Pulsars."

"How did you know about Pulsars?"

"Internet."

Pulsars I should explain, are pulsating stars that give off distinctive radio waves that scientists think might be used for beacons in deep space travel. A bit like GPS but on a much bigger scale.

"We're not using Pulsars for two reasons," said Buster "One, you need a radio telescope to hear them and two we're not going far enough out for the signals to be useful. Luckily there are plenty of radio emitting beacons right here in the solar system."

"Such as?"

"The Sun, for one."

"Really?"

"Oh yes, the Sun gives off tons of radio waves."

"What else?"

"Jupiter."

"Jesus."

"You mean, 'By Jove.'"

"What?"

"Never mind."

I tried to put this all together in my head without triggering the buzzing in the bridge of my nose.

"So, you're going to get my Sat-nav to listen out for the Sun and Jupiter?" I said.

"Yes, and the Earth too, of course."

"The Earth emits radio waves?"

"Yeah, but not naturally. Luckily there's no end of man made radio coming off the Earth."

"What are you going to use, the BBC World Service?" I asked.

"No, the Buzzer."

"The Buzzer?"

"It's a transmission that comes from somewhere in Russia," said Buster. "It's been on since Soviet times."

"What is it, balalaika music?"

"No, it's this."

Buster switched on a shortwave radio next to the computer and keyed in a frequency. A series of low beeps came through the speaker, about one every second.

"That's the buzzer?" I asked. "Should have been called the beeper."

"Yeah, well the interesting thing is it's not a direct beep over the radio waves, it's a transmission from a microphone pointing at something that's going beep. We know this because once in a long while the microphone picks up people talking in the background in Russian."

"Creepy."

"Yeah," Said Buster. "They think it's something to do with the Dead Hand system."

"Do I want to know what the Dead Hand system is?"

"Everyone ought to know. It's what the Soviets set up to launch all their nuclear missiles automatically if the chain of command was taken out by a first strike. As long as the buzzer is on, we're safe."

I was actually feeling a good deal less safe on hearing this.

"Why do you need to tune into the Buzzer? Why can't you choose a lighthouse or Radio Norwich?"

"Because the Buzzer is a reliable and powerful signal and can be heard whichever way the Earth turns. Unlike Radio Norwich."

"So with Jupiter, the Sun and the Buzzer the Sat-nav can work out where we are in space?"

"Pretty much."

"There's one problem, though," I said, pointing at the Sat-nav. "We haven't got a map of Space in this thing. It only covers the UK."

"Not a problem. I've reconfigured the scale of this map so London covers whole solar system."

"What?"

"Look," said Buster, pulling up a map of greater London on his computer. "Here's London. Now if I overlay a map of the Solar system on it, choosing somewhere nice and central such as Bank tube station as the Sun, you get this."

He shifted a transparent map of the Solar system over the top of the one of London.

"This is a map showing the exact locations of the planets as of yesterday morning, I got it from an Astrology website. If the Sun is at Bank, then Mercury is at the end of Fleet street, Venus is in Trafalgar square, Earth is in Shoreditch and so on."

I examined the map. It was interesting to see the relative distances of all the planets. Mars was on the South Bank, while Jupiter had taken up residence in Brixton.

"Where's Pluto?"

"Watford."

"Bloody hell. So if we wanted to go to Pluto we'd just key in Watford high street and follow the Sat-nav?"

"That's the idea."

I was impressed.

"Buster, I think this is the cleverest thing you've ever done. You should work for NASA."

"NASA can piss off, those bastards."

Chapter twenty eight

The registration for the Balloon festival came through just two days before we were due to set off. I got a whole package from them along with a welcoming letter, directions and several pages of rules and guidelines which I promptly ignored, figuring that they wouldn't apply to us anyway.

The Child Tracker had also arrived and turned out to be a great deal smaller than I had expected- just a rectangular unit with rounded off corners about the size of my thumb. I suppose there was no point in making a big bulky box with an antenna on it if it was to be carried around by a child. They must have made advances in transmission technology that had nearly caught up with the Bond films. To be safe I gave it a dry run, leaving it at home while I went for a walk with my mobile and watched the map on my screen for a red dot. To my surprise it worked perfectly, showing up loud and clear even when I took the tube two stops away and re-located it. With that and the Sat-nav sorted all we had to do was pick up our passengers and some sandwiches and we'd be good to go.

That night after running through my checklist I called Sparky and Nigel and arranged to pick them up at their homes, both conveniently located in the west London suburbs. As for Davo, thankfully he was being brought by Buster in the hinge-car, the back all crammed with the giant bouncy slide and the framework to hold it in place. I picked up the Space car from Buster's the night before and made a plan to rendezvous at Heston Services on the M4 where we would get the sandwiches and drive out west in convoy towards Bath and then on to the balloon festival and Space.

Nigel and Sparky were suitably impressed by the car but I don't think either of them realised that it was the spaceship and I wasn't about to tell them. I think they just thought I was some flash git with a limited edition Jaguar. We all met up in the car park of the service station and I introduced my passengers to Buster and Davo. Davo looked like he hadn't slept in two days or shaved in a week which made him fresher and better groomed than I'd ever seen him before.

Nigel was indifferent to the others but I could tell Sparky, being the most refined of all of us, was revolted by his fellow astronaut Davo's appearance. I gave everyone twenty minutes to use the toilet and stretch their legs while Buster got the sandwiches in, enough for one meal before we took off and another for the trip.

A middle-aged man with grey hair and handlebar moustache met us at the 'Flyers entrance' to the festival. He was wearing a yellow t-shirt with 'Avon Balloon Festival Security' printed on it. I was in front in the space-car with Buster behind. The security guy knocked on the window but seeing as I didn't know how to open the window I unzipped the door and got out. He seemed momentarily startled at the car's disappearing door mechanism. To be honest I'd become used to many of the special features that had so impressed me in the beginning.

"You flying today?" he asked.

"Yes."

"Can I see your accreditation please?"

As nonchalantly as possible I handed him the sheaf of papers I had been sent along with the dodgy pilot's license. To my relief he didn't look at any of them except for the gate pass and told us to follow signs to pitch V17. The festival was being held in a big, flat field which had just been used for a music festival. I could tell because there was a pile of old banners by the side of the road with stuff like 'Earthlight stage', 'Starlight stage' and 'Healing tent' written on them. The organisers of the balloon festival had sectioned off squares of the field twenty metres on each side using low poles and ribbon. Each of these had a signpost with a code on it to show where the balloon was to be set up.

I reached V17 which was surrounded by the other participants' pitches. Some of them had already arrived and were busy unpacking their balloons from very professional looking trailers. Buster and I parked and we all got out of our cars. Nigel looked around, clearly unimpressed.

"So you're taking us on a balloon ride?" he said.

"No," I replied. "Space flight, like I said."

"This is obviously a balloon ride. Balloons don't go into space."

"It's a two-stage process," I gabbled hastily. "The first stage is a balloon and then we make the rest of the ascent under our own power."

"Well, I don't see anything looking like a rocket in your kit. You're either lying or going to do something dangerous." Nigel turned to Sparky and Davo for support.

"I think these guys are on the level," said Sparky. "They might not be telling us the whole story but they definitely have some kind of transport. I know that for sure."

Davo just shrugged and lit a roll-up. I was rescued from further interrogation by a perky young lady wearing a balloon festival yellow t-shirt and carrying a clipboard.

"Hello!" she said, "Are you Team Franklin?"

I hesitated for a second, then remembered that I'd entered the festival under that name, it being the surname on the pilot's license I had purloined from the internet.

"Er... yes. That's us."

"Great!" she ticked something off on her clipboard. "You have a takeoff slot of twelve noon. That OK?"

"Fine."

"Fantastic. When's your balloon arriving?"

"It's already here," I said, pointing to Buster's hinge-car. He was busy grabbing armfuls of nylon out of it, assisted by Davo who still had the burning cigarette in his mouth. Her smile faltered when she saw them.

"Er… oh," She said. "Are you hot air or helium?"

I paused, wondering which answer would get us into less trouble.

"Helium." I said at last. It seemed to be the right answer because she ticked something else off on her paper.

"Would you like a later slot? I know you helium guys take a while to inflate."

"No, twelve o'clock will be fine. It's not a big balloon."

"OK, can I see your paperwork?"

This was the crunch time, the moment when we would be finally cleared for takeoff or exposed for the frauds that we were. I handed over the sheaf of papers, info about our craft and its passengers which was composed of half-truths and outright lies. She flicked through it, pausing for one heart-stopping moment on the pilot's license. Luckily she was distracted by a loud curse from Davo as he skidded on the slippery deflated slide and fell over. She put the papers into their plastic folder and handed it back to me with a smile.

"There you go, Mr. Franklin," She said. "Have a great flight. Weather's tip top, I'm told. Dead calm up to twenty thousand feet."

How about the other three hundred thousand feet? I wondered, though of course I didn't ask that out loud. I gathered the others round.

"Right lads," I said, looking at my watch. "Take off is at twelve, and I'll need you all on board at quarter to, which gives you just over an hour to stretch your legs. For God's sake go to the toilet before we set off. You won't get a chance later and I don't want to have to initiate a piss bottle. Buster and I are going to set up the…er… balloon."

Sparky and Nigel wandered off in the direction of the refreshment tent while Davo lay down in the back of the hinge car and appeared to pass out. Buster and I started getting the car ready for the flight. Firstly Buster embedded the metal hooks into the roof, then we lashed a metal framework to the hooks using steel cable. It was a complicated looking thing composed of metal rods and poles that had been taken apart to fit it in the car. When it was done it was about the size of four ping pong tables sticking out on each side of the car roof. I hoped it would support the bouncy slide in a convincing enough manner that would make it look like the inflatable was lifting the car as opposed to the other way round.

When the framework was assembled Buster fixed the air pump to the roof and attached a thick air hose to the intake of the slide. We then hauled the voluminous folds of the slide on top of everything and secured the base of it to the metal frame so it would be in the right position when it inflated. We were both sweating and exhausted when we'd finished and hadn't been watching the activities of the other balloon teams. I cracked open a bottle of water from the food and drink store and looked around me.

In every direction people were unfurling great expanses of balloon fabric and unloading gas cylinders from trailers. Some had already started to blow air into their balloons and one or two had even got their balloons upright already. The air was full of excited chatter punctuated by the occasional roar of a gas jet topping up the hot air inside a balloon. Many of the participants seemed to know each other and a party atmosphere prevailed. It occurred to me that there was probably a balloon festival circuit which they all went round every summer.

"What yew got there then?" said a voice behind me. I turned round to face the person who had spoken, a man I'd guess in his 50's with thinning grey hair and a considerable gut. He was wearing a yellow T shirt like the organisers but it wasn't an official one, bearing only a big number 76 in blue. I looked over his shoulder and saw what the deal was. A big yellow balloon, also bearing the number 76 was billowing up behind him.

"Um… it's a little novelty balloon." I answered hazily.

"How many cubic feet is she?"

Oh God, I thought. I really don't want to get into a technical conversation with this guy.

"Er… a million?"

"What?" he barked, his smile gone.

"Sorry, ten million."

By the look on his face I could tell I'd gone the wrong way. I looked it up later and I found out the Hindenburg was only seven million. Fortunately a shout from his own team called him back to his balloon. Buster ran up beside me, holding the end of a cable out of which poked black and red alligator clips.

"Who was that?"

"Some fat-arsed balloonist," I answered. "I think he reckons we're lightweights."

"We're ready to inflate." said Buster.

"Good. Where is everyone?"

"Davo's asleep in the back of my car and Nigel and Sparky went for a wander."

"OK," I said, looking at my watch. "Our slot is in twenty five minutes, so you get the slide inflated and the car ready to go and I'll round up the others. They've probably just gone to the bog or something."

I found Nigel mooching around near the tea stall, eating a biscuit and reading a festival guide.

"I see a lot of people here are offering rides in their balloons," he said. "The going rate is about five hundred quid. Bit of a bargain compared with two thousand, wouldn't you say?"

"I keep telling you, Nigel. We are taking you up into space."

"Well they must have lowered the definition of space to two thousand feet because that's how high these balloons normally go. Says here."

Nigel pointed out a page in his guide.

"That's great, Nigel. We're taking off in a minute so you need to come back with me. Where's Sparky?"

"I don't know. He went off."

"To the toilet?"

Nigel just shrugged. I felt the first tingle of panic. Not actual panic but a signpost to it. Looking around, I scanned the area for Sparky's hunched-over form and saw only jolly teams of balloonists. Many of the balloons were now fully inflated and the whooshing of gas filled the air. I couldn't see more than ten metres in any direction.

"Come with me," I ordered Nigel and walked him back to the car. When I reached it I saw some sort of altercation going on between Buster and Mr.76. The slide was fully inflated and looked pretty ridiculous perched on top of the car but with so much else going on the argument hadn't attracted a crowd, thank goodness. As I approached I heard the words 'children's play area' from a belligerent Mr.76. Buster isn't a natural diplomat and in an argument he likes to tie people up mentally and then run away. The man abandoned Buster and strode toward me, puffing, an angry upside down miniature of his own balloon.

This is going to take all my powers of tact, I thought. Thanks a lot, Buster. If this guy causes enough trouble for our papers to come under scrutiny then we're done for. We'd have no option but to leg it in the cars. Nigel peeled off and went to stand with Buster as the man approached. This wasn't his problem and he'd be no use anyway.

"That," Said Mr.76 pointing at the slide, "Shouldn't be in the balloon launching zone, it should be in the children's play area."

"That's our craft and we will be launching it here." I said, trying my best to appear competent and in charge, mindful of my previous mistake with the capacity of the balloon. This failed to placate him and I realised I was arguing with a veteran of more balloon flights than both Montgolfiers combined.

"You can't launch that, it's unflyable," he said. "It's a perforated inflatable filled with air. It's not going anywhere unless a tornado runs through here. And why you've got it stuck to a car I cannot imagine."

"What's the matter, have you never seen a novelty shaped balloon before?"

"I've seen plenty, and they were filled with hot air or helium."

"But ours is helium."

"No it's not, where are the gas tanks? I can hear the air compressor anyway, I know what an air compressor sounds like."

Of course he did. This guy probably has CDs of different air compressor noises. And a scrapbook of gas burners. How could I argue anyway? He was absolutely right. The slide wasn't going to lift us anywhere. I was going to have to hit him with pure bullshit.

"It's Hot Helium." I blurted out as soon as I thought of it.

"What?"

"It's a new kind of hot air plus helium hybrid bi-mix. It's called Hot Helium."

His face softened slightly with doubt.

"Never heard of it."

"Of course you haven't," I went on, warming to my theme. "We're researchers. University of Carlisle." Don't ask me why I said Carlisle. It was the first place I could think of.

"Oh." Said Mr.76. I could tell he still had plenty of doubts about us but for the moment I had him confused enough not to make trouble for us. I was just about to congratulate myself for winning this little challenge when Davo suddenly stepped in and won it his own way.

"Sod off back to your piss coloured balloon, you fat old shit. Mind your own business." he said savagely. Mr.76 puffed himself up in affront.

"What did you call me?"

"I have not *begun* to call you anything, brother." said Davo, getting right in the man's face. Where had he sprung from? He was messing up everything. He leaned in closer to Mr76 and said something too quiet for me to hear but the words made the fat man turn tail and walk away from us at maximum speed.

"I'm fetching the organisers!" he yelled back at us.

"Oh, great," I groaned. "Thanks Davo."

"You're welcome, mate." replied Davo cheerfully, lighting

up a new rollie. I looked at my watch. It was five minutes to the mass takeoff.

"Buster! Nigel! Everyone in the car!" I yelled.

"Where's Sparky?" asked Buster.

"I don't know! Let's get ready to go and hope he gets back here in time. When he sees all the balloons starting to take off he ought to know he should be back here."

"Unless he's lost." said Buster helpfully.

We all got in the car. I was in the driving seat, Buster in the front passenger seat, Davo behind Buster and Nigel behind me. I switched on the car and unlatched the steering column, waiting to take my foot off the brake and float the car up into the sky. I looked out of the side window and saw Mr.76 coming back with the lady who signed us in. I groaned and was just about to relay the bad news to the guys when I saw Sparky walking up behind them. I unzipped the car door and shouted over.

"Sparky! Get in the car, we're leaving!"

The little man broke into a run, passing the fat instigator and the balloon woman and managing to get to the car just as I opened the back door with one of Buster's magnetic fingers. Nigel squeezed up as he got in and I quickly zipped up my own door, shutting out the approaching couple. Let them shout and rage but they are not stopping us from going up today, I resolved.

Chapter twenty nine

Luckily the issue resolved itself as we were saved by the bell. Mr.76 was grabbed by two people from his team and rushed to his Balloon's gondola. An air horn sounded and balloons started to ascend like an upside down film of rain dripping off a gutter. The festival organiser dashed to and fro for a few seconds but eventually stopped and watched as the balloons all took to the sky.

"OK, everybody ready?" I said. "T minus one and all that. Here we go."

I let go of the brake and pulled the steering wheel back. The car wobbled, rose a few feet into the air and lurched over to the right, directly towards Mr.76's balloon.

"Christ! It's a pig to fly this, now." I said. I was used to the car's smooth handling in the air.

"Yeah, you wanna watch out for that," said Buster beside me. "This thing's really top-heavy and unstable with the slide on it. Plus aerodynamically speaking we're buggered. A cross wind could knock us right over. You'll get the hang of it."

"I hope so," I said. I righted the car and narrowly avoided lurching it over in the opposite direction. I hit the gas and the car rose higher. I did get a feel for how to handle it, a bit like holding a tall, teetering stack of cardboard boxes. No sudden movements, compensate for wobbles, and just keep moving at a slow ascent.

If there's anything more spectacular than seeing a mass hot air balloon lift-off, it's seeing one from the air, though in our case it was a bit unnerving to watch it all through the windscreen of a car. I was reminded of a digital picture-frame I had once bought which had a default screen like this. I kept the photo in rotation as let's face it, sky-full-of-hot-air-balloons is one of the all time great default images, along with basket of kittens and two kids washing a dog.

Once I had the car handling OK, I sneaked a look in the rear view mirror that Buster had blu-tacked to the windscreen. Our passengers looked a bit shaken by the takeoff.

"Relax everyone. Enjoy the view," I said.

"I wish I could enjoy the view," whined Nigel. "I'm bunched up here in the middle without a window to look out of. No one ever told me I'd have the crap seat."

We all ignored him, then Sparky piped up at last.

"Look, it's our neighbours from the take-off field."

I turned in horror to my right to see the big yellow '76' balloon rising up past us. As it rose its gondola drew level. Sure enough, Mr.76 was there staring right at us, along with two other people also wearing yellow t-shirts. They all had looks of amazement on their faces and I made a mental note not to land anywhere near them if I could help it. I hit the gas and we slowly rose higher than the top balloon and hovered just above it.

"OK," I announced. "We are about to begin the next phase of the ascent. Buster, do you know what to do?"

Buster held up a remote control. I noticed it was a re-build of his old cube remote.

"All set." he said.

"OK, initiate deflation." I had been rehearsing that line and was very proud of myself for having thought it up. Buster hit a button on his remote and a vibration that had been present all the time without my noticing it seemingly reversed itself. I craned my head toward the top of the windscreen and could just see our big slide go all creased and floppy, then convoluted and hard, like something shrink wrapped. The car bobbed up and down as the aerodynamics changed. I settled back in my seat and concentrated on keeping the car steady as it rose.

"The slide's all deflated now. I'm switching off the air pump." said Buster, working his remote.

"Hang on," said Nigel "What's holding us up?"

"Sky hooks." I replied, recalling the term from a book I had read as a child, probably Biggles. It was a piss-off answer, designed to shut him up for the time being. Luckily it did the trick. I actually had no idea what held the car up. Maybe it repelled itself from the Earth's magnetic field or something. Sparky looked out of his window at the tops of all the balloons below us.

"Aren't the other pilots going to wander what we're doing up here with a deflated balloon?"

"They might if they could see us," answered Buster. "Think about it, what's the only direction you can't see in when you're in a hot air balloon? Up, because your own balloon is in the way. We'll be too high for them to see us anyway soon, right Philip?"

"Hmmn." I replied. The handling of the car had become much easier now the slide had deflated and I resisted the urge to floor the accelerator and shoot for orbit. Instead I tilted the nose of the car upward and increased our speed fractionally until the balloons were just a cluster of colourful dots behind us.

The car fell silent as we watched the landscape go from what you'd see out the window of a 747 to what you'd see from one of those old supersonic passenger jets. The sky grew a darker shade of blue and the horizon started to show a slight curve. Without an altimeter the colour of the sky and curve of the horizon were my only guides as to how high we were getting. By rule of thumb I reckoned we'd be in Space as soon as we could see the stars in daylight and the horizon became as curved as a rainbow.

After fifteen minutes of steady ascent I checked the rear view mirror. Sparky was staring out of his side mesmerised and

Nigel was craning his head to see round Davo who had, to my annoyance, fallen asleep against the window.

"Look, stars." said Buster.

I looked ahead and up. Sure enough I saw a star, then another one, then like discovering a skin rash I suddenly saw so many of them they all seemed to appear at once. I pressed down slightly on the accelerator and the Earth below us became a vast blue and white ball that slowly began to rotate.

"Wow," murmured Nigel. "I was wrong about you guys. This is definitely worth two grand."

"It's worth a lot more than that," I replied. "Be thankful you got the bargain price. Buster, can you start up the iPod? There's a playlist called 'Space Music.'"

Buster hauled my bag out of the footwell and connected my iPod to the battery powered speaker. It crackled as he switched it on and the silence that followed was punctuated by faint clicking noises as he navigated through the music player's menus.

I'd spent a while selecting the first track, a lot longer than I'd spent working out what our trajectory and positioning would be once we were up in Space. Things like that I could work out once we were aloft, literally winging it. The music though had to be carefully planned. I didn't want to spend the whole flight fiddling with iPod menus.

I was just easing off the accelerator and bringing the car into what I guessed was a low Earth orbit when the music drifted in at a slow fade. It was a piece by Vangelis called 'Heaven and Hell', taken from the old TV series 'Cosmos'. I know to some people this is going to make me sound incredibly unhip but I don't care: when it comes to music for space trips, Vangelis is The Gov'nor. The music swelled with ethereal spaceyness, a mixture of '80s synthesisers and full orchestra. It would have been impressive even down a coal mine, but with the Earth rotating at full tilt below us and the Sun setting behind our backs it all came together beautifully. I made a mental note to raise our prices when we got back to Earth.

"The Cosmos…" Intoned Carl Sagan at the end of the track, "…is all that is… or was… or ever will be…". Davo snapped awake at the words.

"What is this bullshit?" he demanded, breaking the spell.

"It's music." I replied tersely.

"No it bloody isn't. It's wank," He dug into his pocket and withdrew a battered phone. "Here, put this on" he said, handing the phone to Buster.

I have to admit I was a bit put out by this turn of events. I had another forty minutes of Vangelis on my playlist including four unreleased tracks from the 1985 Cosmos TV special. I've always believed in the 'Driver chooses the music' rule but it seems in Space all bets were off. Buster shrugged and plugged Davo's phone into the speaker. I hoped that whatever Davo had chosen it would fit in with the general mood of the trip.

It didn't. It was banging nightmare techno that wouldn't even have fit in at a German funfair. It was, as Ozzy Osbourne once called it, 'music to get your head kicked in to'. I sneaked a look at Davo's phone to see if this horror had a name. It did. It was called 'BRUTAL NAPALM HARDCORE GABBER OLDSCHOOL TERROR MIX'. I checked the display to see how much of it we had to endure.

"Jesus, Davo, this track is nine hours long!" I yelped. "You're not supposed to have an mp3 as long as this, this is for a clothes shop!" I looked around the car. Buster was gently bobbing his head to the noise, Nigel looked pained but didn't say anything. Sparky had his fingers in his ears. At least I could count on his support.

"Come on, switch it off." I said, feeling like the Dad on a family trip to the beach. "This is unlistenable."

"Nah, mate, it's hardcore!" protested Davo. "It gets all jazzy in a minute, just listen."

Nigel perked up.

"I like jazz." he said.

"All right, we'll see it through to the jazzy bit, then it's someone else's turn to choose the music."

The noise went on for two more orbits until a piano could be heard tinkling repetitively below the beat.

"There you go, jazz." said Davo proudly.

"Turn it off!" shouted Sparky, his fingers still in his ears. I needed no more encouragement and whipped the cord out of Davo's phone. It continued playing the horrible racket on its own speaker until Davo took it back, plugged in his own headphones and continued listening.

"Jesus, look at us, the British Space Programme," I said to no one in particular. "The first independent craft to go into orbit and we spend half the time arguing over what music to play. OK, Who's next?"

"I didn't know we were supposed to bring music." whined Nigel.

"You weren't." I snapped.

"I've got something," said Sparky, handing Buster his phone. "It's the piece from 'The Planets' I'm going to be playing."

Buster dropped the phone before he was able to plug it into the speaker and felt around in the footwell for it.

"Hang on, why isn't anything floating?" asked Nigel.

"What?"

"We're in space, isn't everything supposed to be weightless?"

"Er... Buster?" I asked, hoping he would have a plausible explanation. I honestly hadn't considered this. When you're inside a car you don't really notice anything odd when things fall down the footwell because that's what they always do. Nigel did have a valid question though.

"Magnets." said Buster. "If you hold a magnet over a nail and it pulls it up off a table it's because the force of the magnet is stronger than the gravitational force of the whole Earth. We're being kept in our seats by magnets."

"But people aren't magnetic." protested Nigel.

"Yes they are," countered Buster "You just need a magnet strong enough."

"Oh." Nigel murmured. He seemed a little disappointed. I could understand how he felt. It would have been interesting to float about like those astronauts do but there wouldn't have been much room in here to do that anyway. Plus I've heard that all that weightlessness can mess you about inside, make you throw up and stuff. Buster plugged Sparky's phone into the speaker and pressed play.

Now I've never been too much into that classical stuff. It makes for a good movie soundtrack but it's not something I could ever just sit down and listen to. This piece of Sparky's was dead on though, as it ought to be with a title like 'The Planets'. It sounded like spacey Bond film music, all lush strings and tinkly bits that I assumed was Sparky's part on the Celeste. I looked behind me and saw Sparky's eyes closed, transported by the music. It was having a similar effect on Nigel and Buster, shutting down everything except their ears. Davo was the exception, still plugged into his Napalm Horror Mix.

By lucky chance, or maybe because our brains are geared

toward tying these things together, the Sun came up over the dark Earth just as the music reached a climax. The glare of the Sun was automatically eclipsed by a dark spot that appeared on the windscreen and followed it, an automatic safety device of the car, I assumed. The continents slid below us and I could clearly make out southeast Asia, then the expanse of the Pacific.

"We'd better think about getting back," said Buster, looking at his watch. "The balloons will be landing in just under an hour."

"OK, Take a last look at space, everyone." I said. "We're heading home."

"Oh, shit, my camera." Said Nigel, and rifled through his pockets, digging out a cheap looking Olympus.

"Oh yeah, pictures," I said. "Buster, could you get out my Lomo and take a few snaps?"

I heard Sparky's phone making some fake camera-click noises and for a couple of minutes everyone except Davo was busy taking pictures.

"Aren't you going to take any photos, Davo?" I asked.

"Why bother? There's millions of pictures of Space already. Probably look better than any I could take." He had a point, though it wasn't really *the* point. I made a mental note not to take any more freebies up unless they showed sufficient enthusiasm. When I spotted the coastline of West Africa I turned left and made for Europe, covered as usual in a blanket of cloud. By the time we were close enough for the cloud to fill our view it was hard to gauge how high we were or even what country we were over but we had to get within range of the child tracker transmitter for it to work. I looked up. The stars were gone and the sky wasn't too dark either.

"OK, inflate the slide, Buster."

He flicked a switch on the remote, then another, then slowly turned up a knob. Above me I could feel the vibration and saw the closest corner of the slide uncrease itself and bulge outward. The car started to shift sideways, first one way then the other as the slide was buffeted by crosswinds. I held it steady until the slide was fully inflated and then tilted the steering wheel down, bringing us into the clouds.

"Ok, start up the child tracker."

Buster reached into my bag and brought out my smartphone with the receiver plugged into it. This was the real test. If we were too far off course we'd have to circle around until we picked up the signal. The phone started beeping frantically.

"What's the problem?"

"No problem," said Buster. "Signal's clear as a bell. We're dead on course. According to this we're right on top of it."

"Excellent!" I said, dropping the car slowly through the clouds. "I'd better be careful coming out of these clouds in case I land on top of a balloon. Which one did you fix the tracker to?"

"What do you mean?"

"Which balloon did you fix…"

"But I thought you did it." said Buster.

"What?"

"When you went off looking for Sparky and Nigel. I assumed you did it then."

"But that's when I thought *you* did it!" I yelped.

"Well no wonder we've got such a clear signal," said Buster, rummaging through the bag and bringing out the transmitter. "It was only coming from six inches away."

"Oh, crap."

"What's the matter?" asked Nigel, leaning forward.

"Nothing. Shut up." I replied. "Buster, try the Sat-nav."

We waited for the Sat-nav to boot up and find some satellites. Eventually the screen showed our position as directly above Shoreditch in east London. Buster groaned.

"It's still set to cosmic scale," he said. "You know, the Buzzer, the Sun and Jupiter. Wherever we land on Earth it's going to say Shoreditch."

At that moment we broke through the bottom of the cloud. It looked like England, the countryside a green patchwork of fields and forests, but other than that we had no idea where we were. There was no sign of the balloons anywhere.

"OK, everyone look out of your windows." I announced. "Look for any kind of landmark. Something we can get our bearings by."

"I can't see anything from up here." said Sparky.

"I don't have a window." complained Nigel.

"Go lower." suggested Buster.

I tilted the steering wheel down and the car sank closer to the earth. Still no one could identify anything other than endless fields and small towns.

"There's a railway line." offered Sparky.

"Well, that narrows it down," I said glumly. "Christ, at this height we're visible for miles."

"Might as well just land the thing," said Buster. "We'll find a road sign and drive the rest of the way."

I sighed and looked for an empty road. This wasn't how I'd planned to get back at all. Next time we'd really have to be on the ball. It was all that fat Mr.76's fault, distracting us. I saw a field up ahead with an open gate leading out to a road and dropped the last couple of hundred feet to the ground. The slide was being knocked about quite a bit by the wind and I hit the ground on the left two wheels of the car. For a horrible second I thought the whole thing would go on its side but with a lurch it righted itself.

"Quick, deflate the slide!" I ordered Buster and he flicked the switches on his remote again.

"Can I get out?" asked Nigel. "I need to pee."

Chapter thirty

It turned out we had landed in Shropshire. Not bad, considering I'd had no guidance at all, but still a couple of hours drive from our starting point. We fixed the deflated slide to the roof frame of the car as best we could with bungee cord and drove the rest of the way back to the balloon festival. Most of the balloons were packed up for the night when we'd arrived including, thankfully, Mr.76 and his crew. Buster and Davo set to work removing the slide and packed it up into Buster's hinge car while I lay down on a nearby slope and fell asleep, my nerves shot by the whole ordeal.

Still, I reflected on the long drive back to London, we had done it. We had taken a carload of passengers up into space and arrived back in one piece. Not only that, but we had made a little profit. Buster and Davo went off in Buster's car, I dropped Sparky and Nigel off at a tube station and took the Space car home, locking it in my garage.

The first thing I did on getting up the next morning was take Nigel's bundle of money to the bank and deposit it into my parched current account. I kept a fifty pound note and stocked up at the supermarket. It felt great to have money in my pocket again, a feeling which instantly evaporated when I saw the headline on the front page of one of the red-top papers announcing "UFO SCARE OVER SHROPSHIRE" and a photo of our slide hanging in the sky.

Unlike the little independent newsagents that they are rapidly running out of business, supermarkets don't care if you stand there riffling through the paper without buying it, even if, as I was, you are surrounded by your dropped shopping bags and have a freaked-out look on your face. I turned to the centre pages for the full story which contained a massive blow-up picture of our inflated slide, taken on some farmer's phone.

Luckily the car stuck to the bottom wasn't very obvious in

the picture and the accompanying article merely noted that the 'UFO' turned out to be an inflatable slide 'still attached to its trailer' which had been carried away by freak winds from a funfair in Cirencester. I had no idea where Cirencester was but there was a statement by the supposed manager of the fair expressing regret that the slide had got away before it had been fixed down and relief that it had been recovered without anyone getting hurt. The whole matter was being treated with some amusement, it seemed.

Myself, I was more confused than amused. I dumped my shopping at home and went straight round to Busters, newspaper in hand. I called him on the way to say I was coming- a good decision because he greeted me with a cup of tea which I badly needed at that point. Naturally Buster is an expert in UFO sightings, a 'connoisseur' as he puts it, and he took this development with surprising level headedness. He read the article while I sat shaking in his chair, sipping tea.

"Well I must say it's nice to be the cause of a UFO sighting at last," he said, putting down the paper. "And not just chasing up other people's wild stories. Helps you see the thing from both sides, as it were."

"There's only one side to this," I replied. "The 'we're buggered' side. We can't use the slide any more, that's for sure."

"Nonsense. No one's going to connect us with this, except maybe our friend in the yellow t-shirt, and he doesn't know our real names anyway."

"What I can't understand is why they've got this funfair bloke from Cirencester taking the rap for the whole thing."

"There's two explanations for that," said Buster. "The simple one and the paranoid one, which you look in no fit state to hear."

"Ok, try the simple one."

"The newspaper made it up. They got hold of a photo and

they're lazy bastards so instead of properly investigating it they print this fictitious story about a funfair that they reckon is close enough to the truth to get away with. I mean what other explanation would there be for a bouncy slide to fly through the air? That it's come from Space? Inflatables fly off in the wind all the time."

I thought about that, and it did seem plausible. I'm always told that the tabloids fabricate stories, and neither the funfair nor the mysterious manager were actually named in the article.

"Ok, so what's the paranoid explanation?"

"That the Government knew exactly where the slide and the car came from and to conceal it they cooked up this story to explain it to all the witnesses."

"That's ridiculous; the Government can't just dictate what they like to people in the national press." I protested. Buster didn't even bother to contradict me with words. He merely raised an eyebrow.

"OK, it's possible," I conceded. "I liked the lazy journalist explanation better."

"Me too."

"We could always check into it, you know, call the paper and ask about this Cirencester funfair guy." I suggested. Buster shook his head.

"Very unwise. That would be sticking our heads above the parapet. If they're covering up the story they wouldn't help us and they'd know who we were as well."

Buster was right, of course. I sipped my tea and wondered what our next course of action would be. Buster must have been wondering the same thing.

"So what's next for A to B Spacelines?" he asked.

"We lie low, we recalibrate and we reorganise." I said. "We need a proper checklist for one, no more forgetting to place the child tracker and definitely no more freebies. We need to be more careful setting up the slide at balloon festivals," I stood up and paced around, warming to my theme. "Maybe it's safer not to go the official route and just lift off in the field next door to a festival when all the others go up. Then we'll get lost in the flotilla and not have to deal with prats like Mr.76."

"And how long do you think we'll need to lie low?" enquired Buster.

"Oh, a few weeks at least. Why?"

"It's just that I got a call from Nigel this morning."

"Nigel? How did he find you?"

"We swapped numbers yesterday when you were asleep after the flight."

"Oh. What does he want?"

"He wants to go up again."

"Ha! Fine, we'll book him in when we've got another car load of passengers."

Buster looked at me as if he had more to say but was judging whether or not I could handle it.

"What?" I asked.

"He's got three friends who want to go with him."

"What?"

"And they want to go to the Moon."

"*What?*"

Chapter thirty one

The four boys sat in my office. I say boys but they were the size of grown men. These were far too fresh faced to be called men though. Nigel introduced them as his friends Justin, Quentin and Klaus. They looked the same age and obviously knew each other from whatever private school had bestowed their strangulated accents. Accents that, unless they went into the army or the wine trade, they would spend a good many years dampening down.

There hadn't been enough chairs to go round so Buster and I had rescued some stools from the piano bar downstairs. It was being gutted to make way for a juice bar and the landlord had graciously allowed me to hang on to the office upstairs until it was re-purposed as an employee break room and wheatgrass storage facility.

"First, I'd like to impress on you the need for absolute secrecy." I said to the boys. They all nodded. "I don't know why you're nodding, Nigel. You obviously didn't keep your mouth shut the first time."

"These guys are OK. They're my friends."

I resisted the urge to tell Nigel he looked as though he didn't have any friends. These were, after all, customers. I stole a look at Buster beside me. He had insisted on being the driver/pilot for this trip and wanted to get a look at who he'd be taking. He looked at the boys impassively. I got to the point.

"Why do you want to go to the Moon?"

Nigel just shrugged. Good job for him A to B Spacelines is here, I thought. The boy is plainly not NASA material. Justin spoke up. He seemed to be the leader of this little gang.

"Nigel told us about your operation and about the listening to music in Space and all that, and it sounded like fun." he said.

"But why the Moon? Why not just do a few orbits like Nigel?"

"We, ehh…" Justin looked at his compatriots. None of them spoke up. "We want to go to the dark side of the Moon and listen to… well, you know."

"Dark side of the Moon? The album?"

They seemed a bit perplexed by the word 'Album' but there were nods all round. Interesting that what began as little more than an afterthought, bringing music along for the trip, had now become a major selling point.

"You do realise that there won't be any walking on the Moon?" I said. "I mean actual walking on the Moon, not the song. Well you can listen to the song but you won't be able to get out of the vehicle. We don't have any space suits."

"But can we land on the Moon?" asked Quentin.

"Hmm." I said. I hadn't actually thought of the ramifications of leaving tyre tracks all over the place. I turned to Buster, who shrugged. We were on new ground here.

"Let's just say you can land at the discretion of the Pilot, Mr. Ames here." I said at last. It was a bit of a fudge, handing over the responsibility to Buster but in the end he'd be the one at the controls.

"How is your craft powered?" piped up Quentin again.

"I'm not at liberty to say." I liked saying that. It beat the hell out of 'I don't know', sounded more professional as well. Justin took over the questioning.

"Where do you launch from?"

"A Balloo-" began Nigel but I cut him off.

"That's classified." I was certain Nigel would spill the

beans about how we got into the air but I wasn't giving them the location yet. I hadn't worked it out myself anyway.

"How much is the trip?" asked Justin.

"For a Moon shot, it's seven and a half grand. Each." Buster and I had given this some thought. Obviously we would charge more than the orbital flight but we'd still have to avoid pricing the trip out of their range. By their nods all round I instantly kicked myself. We probably could have gone higher. Who knew how much money these boys had at their disposal? For all I knew they'd pay seven point five K just for a night out, or even for a bottle of champagne. Justin withdrew a cheque book in a leather case from his pocket.

"Seven and a half is the cash price. If you're paying by cheque, it's eight and a half." I said quickly, trying to extract whatever else I could from this negotiation. Justin put his chequebook away. At least these guys aren't so money-blind that the difference of a grand means nothing to them, I thought. I'd rather do it off the books for cash anyway.

For the rest of the meeting I outlined the practicalities of the trip. I'd pick them all up in one location, none of this school run nonsense. All of them would have the cash on them at pickup. They'd be away for a maximum of twenty four hours and they were to bring their own packed lunches and music players. I took their numbers and arranged to call when the launch date was fixed.

After they had sauntered out Buster and I had a conference.

"What do you reckon?" I asked him.

"That Justin is definitely a pothead. The other two probably as well. Not so much Nigel, though. I get the feeling Nigel's the runt of the group and he's desperately trying to impress his friends."

"Poor Nigel. If I wasn't so skint I'd give him a discount for bringing us the new customers."

"Is that our client base then?" said Buster. "Rich druggies?"

"Hey, it's thirty four grand. Better we get our hands on it than some upscale dope dealer."

"Dark side of the Moon," muttered Buster. "Jesus."

"Do you think you'll have any trouble finding it?"

"The Moon? Piece of cake."

"Piece of cheese."

"Har har. I'd better re-calibrate the Sat-nav anyway. Update the positions of everything. When do you think we can make the trip?"

"Let me see," I said, picking up a printout of upcoming balloon festivals from my desk. "There's one next weekend but that's too soon and it's in Scotland so forget that. Then the one after that is mid-May, the eighteenth. That's in Sussex. Perfect, not too far from London."

"And we're going to do it guerrilla style this time, right? No registration, no red tape, just inflate nearby and take off with all the others?"

"Absolutely, Buster. I think this will be the one where it all comes together."

Chapter thirty two

The funny thing about money is that while it opens doors in the physical world it also shuts them in the mental world. Take travel, for example. If you want to get from A to B on a budget you have to really give the brain a workout- calculating off-peak fares, roundabout routes, fuel surcharges and stop-off expenses. With a bunch of dough in your pocket you can just hail a taxi or pay up the full fare without any thought and away you go. You don't even need the actual money in your hand for it to short-circuit your thinking, just the promise of money will do it.

And so it was that the thought of the thirty four grand currently bulging out of my inside pocket occupied a big shiny throne in my mind, leaving little room for such bothersome concepts as 'Guerrilla Balloon Launches', 'Covert tagging of someone else's craft', 'finding the Moon on a hacked Sat-nav' and 'Placing your confidence in a bunch of upper class stoners'.

It was mid morning and we were driving in convoy to the Lewes Balloon Festival, the first flight of which was due to take place in a little over three hours. Factoring in driving and setup time plus toilet breaks we should have plenty of time to get to our launch site. Buster was in the Space car ahead with the boys and I followed in Buster's hinge-car with the slide, frame and air compressor. The child tracker transmitter nestled securely in my trouser pocket. No way would Buster take off with it this time. He already had the rest of the equipment with him: the Sat-nav, the child tracker receiver, the iPod speaker and a marine radar. The last item was a new addition. I was concerned that our car would collide with one of those satellites that now permanently orbited the Moon or show up on one of its pictures which would create quite a stir at NASA or the university of Yokohama or wherever it is that they monitor these things.

Distracted as I was in thoughts of this nature and my rear

view blocked by the bundled slide I didn't realise anything was behind me until three massive whoops drew my attention to the wing mirror, whereupon I saw a Police car trying to get past, lights flashing. I slowed down and drifted over to the side of the road and suffered that sinking feeling every motorist knows when he discovers that the Police aren't overtaking you but pulling you over.

As I ground to a halt I saw Buster speed off ahead and out of view. Luckily the cops hadn't twigged that we were in convoy but that was about as far as my luck held. I tried to remember if I had been speeding but was pretty sure I hadn't. I'd find out in a minute what I'd done, though. I just hoped that Buster had the presence of mind to wait for me at the Balloon festival.

The policeman was wearing a blue short sleeved shirt with some kind of utility vest over it containing numerous pockets. Keep calm, I told myself. You haven't done anything wrong. Don't think about the pepper spray or handcuffs in those pockets.

"Good morning, sir," The policeman said. "Do you know why I've stopped you?"

"Erm... was I speeding?"

"Is this your vehicle?"

"No, it belongs to my friend."

"Are you aware that this vehicle is not displaying any license plates?"

Oh shit shit shit, I thought. Of all the things to get bloody pulled over for. It seemed like an age ago that Buster had taken the plates off this one and put them on the Space car to give it a temporary look of legitimacy.

"You also don't appear to be displaying a tax disc."

Oh Christ, he took the tax disc as well.

"Do you have any insurance?"

I honestly didn't know if my own insurance allowed me to drive this car, or if Buster's did, or if Buster even had any insurance. Time to half-lie my way out of this.

"What it is, officer, is that this car belongs to a friend of mine, and I'm just delivering this inflatable slide to an event in Lewes. It does have plates and a tax disc but they were stolen."

"Do you know what the license number of the car is?"

"No."

"Do you have the car's documents? Registration?"

"No."

"Do you have your own license with you?"

"No."

"When were the plates and disc stolen?"

"Yesterday."

"Did you or your friend report the theft?"

"Not yet, no. We've got to deliver this slide urgently and I think he stayed in London to make the report."

"What's your friend's name?"

"Buster Ames."

The policeman stood by my window and made notes in a little book. He was standing with his back to the road and it was a good thing he was because he didn't see what I saw. Just beyond the curve in the road ahead was a stand of trees, and from the top of the tree line rose the all too familiar silhouette of our Space car. For a couple of seconds it hovered in mid air then slowly floated upwards. At that precise moment the policeman started to turn around and would have seen the car had I not made a strangled cry.

"Officer!"

He turned back to face me. Over his shoulder I saw the car rocket into the sky, becoming a tiny dot in a second and a half.

"Yes?" he said.

"I'm sorry."

It was the only thing I could think of at that moment, but at least it distracted him and didn't get me into even more trouble. He gave me an odd look and went off to his car. I slumped in my seat. It was all going to hell before we'd even started. I patted the big bundle of money in my pocket and that made me feel better. My phone beeped its text message alert. It was from Buster and contained merely the letters 'RV RAF NC' He must have typed it singlehandedly while flying the car. I worked out what it meant: Rendezvous RAF North Creake. Our old test airstrip back when we thought all the car did was fly in the air. Well, that stuffs the whole balloon plan. Now all he had to do was deal with the real RAF while I dealt with the Police.

Or rather while they dealt with me. I was ordered to follow the Police car back to the station for further processing. The policeman turned out to be based in Crawley which for those of you who don't know the area is a little town south of London which services Gatwick Airport and has a couple of nice curry houses. Because of the airport the Police have dealt with more strange situations than your usual country cop shop and are prepared to deal with a whole load of contingencies from dirty bombs to deep-frozen stowaways falling out of airplane undercarriages (don't laugh, it happens a lot, I'm told).

However when I opened up the side of Buster's hinge-car and pulled metres upon metres of inflatable slide out of it several of the coppers came out to gawp in wonder. Some made jokes about it being the new generation of emergency escape for when the car lands in water. Others made dark comments about Gypsies and fairground travelling folk. I tried to convince them that I had never even knowingly met a Gypsy but the label stuck and in the end I accepted it. Considering the shenanigans that Buster and I were up to, being labeled just another Traveller with a dodgy car was something I ended up accepting like a man.

They impounded the car, of course. Even though they found Buster's details on the DVLC computer and matched the hinge car to him I had the hardest time trying to persuade them that I hadn't stolen the car and removed the plates myself. They tried to get Buster on the phone but the call went straight to voicemail for the reason that he was halfway to the Moon. In the end I paid a whopping great fine for driving without insurance or tax and was told Buster would have to come down to collect the car from the pound after bringing his paperwork and paying another fine. Then they let me go.

By the time I got home it was early evening. I threw a sandwich down my throat and jumped into my own car, an unexceptional Volvo that had so far played no part in this whole escapade. I didn't use it that often because it smelled of petrol and made a whistling noise at high speed that drove me mad but I revved it up and headed for the fossilized runway of North Creake.

Chapter thirty three

With only one stop for provisions at the supermarket in Fakenham I made it there in two hours. I would have been there sooner but as Buster had turned my Sat-nav into a cosmic positioning unit I had to navigate using an out of date AA road atlas with half the pages stuck together and a Google Maps printout balanced on my lap. Turning down the narrow rutted track that led to the old runway I fully expected to find the area taped off by Military Police but in the gloom it was the same as ever- a triangle of fields and a single runway that hadn't seen action since 1947. At least I haven't missed them, I thought, unless they've already missed me.

The first thing I did was switch on the child tracker. Other than a dull red LED light there was no indication that it was transmitting anything. I had serious reservations that it would be able to guide a vehicle down from Space but at least it was more use down here than sitting in the footwell of the very car it was supposed to be guiding. Although now wasn't the time for such thoughts I suddenly had a vision of Buster following the wrong tracker and landing the car in the back garden of some paranoid parent.

I switched on the Volvo's hazard lights and rooted around in the boot for anything else that would help Buster find the landing site. I knew there was a torch in there somewhere and after a minute's grappling with various boot-junk I found it in an emergency kit along with a bonus: a glow stick. The torch was nearly out of juice but it had a flashing yellow light that still worked. Cracking the glow stick, I laid it on the grass with the yellow flashing torch and the car forming a triangle. It was a pretty weedy trio of lights but might help with the final approach. Now all I could do was wait.

An hour went by, then another. Despite the time of year it was chilly and I stopped wandering around looking at the sky and curled up in the back seat instead. It had been a hectic day. First the drama with the Police, then the dash out to Norfolk, then making this improvised space port landing pad. Not for the first time I wished we were running things above board in New Mexico instead of all this furtive creeping around. My anxieties were soothed by the thought of that massive bundle of fifty pound notes waiting for me back at my place.

I dozed for another hour and woke just before dawn, scanning the field and the sky for the car. Nothing. I started to worry that something had gone wrong up in Space. Maybe they had got lost, or the car had exploded, or imploded.

I got out of the car and relieved myself against a hedge. The sky was greying on the horizon and I could just about make out the old runway stretching ahead of me. Then I heard it. In the films when you see craft landing from Space they usually make swooshing and beeping noises. With one obvious exception their approach is not normally heralded by the theme from 'Flash Gordon' but that was what I heard coming from above, getting louder every second. I looked up and made out the shape of the car descending at a steady rate directly above me.

I was momentarily puzzled that I could hear the speaker blaring the Queen song- in my experience the car was totally soundproof. The answer became apparent as the car landed. Both of the front doors were unzipped. Now why would Buster do that? The music stopped as soon as the car touched down and a cheer came from within. Nigel and his friends piled out of the car in high spirits. I went round to the driver's side and found Buster sitting there looking drained. It was good to see him.

"You made it." I said.

"Just about," He replied and handed me a large paper McDonalds cup. "Get rid of that, will you?". It felt weighty but the contents were not sloshing around.

"What is it?"

"A cup of shit."

With an involuntary retching noise I threw the cup into a hedge.

"How did it go?" I said.

"I'll tell you later. Let's just dump this lot first."

Luckily the boys didn't ask to be driven back to London. One of them either owned or had access to or knew someone who lived in a big country pile and Buster dropped them all off at its gatehouse. I then followed him to the horrible roadside café outside Stowmarket that we'd gone to after our first space flight. In the car park I got a proper look at the car in daylight. It was filthy on the outside, covered in a layer of grey-brown dirt.

"What is this, Moon dust?" I said, running my finger over it.

"Er, no," replied Buster. "It's Mars dust."

"You went to bloody *Mars*?"

Chapter thirty four

Someone at the roadside café must have read their reviews on the Internet because the coffee was better than the last time we were there. Either that or I just really needed a cup. Buster told me his story between mouthfuls of bacon and eggs.

"When I realised you weren't behind me any more I stopped round the corner. I thought you'd just needed to catch up but when you didn't follow me I reversed round just enough to see the cop car so I scooted back round the corner. If it had been up to me I'd have waited however long it took for the Police to be done with you but that guy Justin started panicking and demanded that we get out of there pronto. Then the others started panicking as well and it was pretty tense in there for a while."

"Why were they so freaked out?"

"Think about it. Dark side of the Moon? Obviously they had drugs on them. Anyway, I realised that without the inflatable slide there was no point going to the Balloon festival and the road was pretty quiet so I chanced a take-off right there and then."

"Yeah, bit of a risk, that. The policeman nearly saw you."

"Well you should have heard those pricks carry on. Nigel was all right but that Justin guy was bloody insufferable. Ordering me about like I was the family chauffeur."

"You *were* being paid to drive them."

"I suppose. You still got the money?"

"Most of it. I had to pay all sorts of fines for the missing license plate on your hinge car plus the tax disc and all the rest of it."

"Ah, so that's why you got pulled over." said Buster.

"Yeah. Your car's in the Crawley vehicle pound, by the way. Anyway, go on with the story."

"OK, so I was just about to shoot for orbit when I realised we'd need to rendezvous somewhere so I texted you before I got out of range. Glad to see you got the message."

"Yeah, about the only thing that went right on this trip." I muttered.

"Tell me about it. So I floored the gas and we were in Space in about ten seconds. That shut them up for a bit, I can tell you. The majesty of the infinite and all that. We got into a low Earth orbit and I let the car do a couple of loops while I got the Sat-nav and the marine radar organized. We're going to have to find a way of fixing that stuff to the dashboard, by the way. It kept falling off. The good news was the Moon was where it was supposed to be, on Old street. I just followed the Sat-nav from Shoreditch and we were there faster than it would have taken me doing the same trip on the ground. I could probably have done it by sight anyway. The Moon's not hard to miss." Buster put his fork down and took a sip of coffee before continuing.

"By this point the boys had left me alone to fly the car and were busy taking photos and stuff. Then that Quentin guy got something out of his bag which got them all worked up. I couldn't see it because I was driving but I could hear it. It was rattling like a pill bottle which was exactly what it turned out to be. God knows what the pills were but Justin, Klaus and Quentin all took one."

"What about Nigel?"

"He didn't want one. They tried to persuade him but I stepped in and told them to leave him alone. Then Quentin told me to shut up and drive the car and they all started laughing. I tell you, I nearly ditched them in Space. Anyway we got to the Moon and I steered round it to the so-called Dark Side and can you believe it? Justin starts bitching because it's not dark enough. I tried to explain to him that the 'Dark Side' merely refers to the side that faces away from the Earth and it's lit up by the Sun as often as the side we see but he was having none of it."

"So what did you do?" I asked.

"I orbited the Moon until all we saw was the part in shadows. Technically only half of what we were looking at was the side away from the Earth but as long as it was all literally dark they were happy, the nitwits."

"What did it look like, the Moon?"

"Like the pictures."

"Did you land on it?"

"Yeah, but only because I was sick of driving." said Buster. "I remembered what you said about not leaving tyre tracks around the place so I just parked in a crater and let them fire up the old Pink Floyd. It wasn't bad, you know. Nice bit of hippy rock or whatever that genre's called. The boys were all into it but three of them were high as kites. They'd have been happy to listen to Davo's Hardcore Terror Mix at that point. Anyway we sit there for half an hour or so and they're all laughing and singing along and talking absolute nonsense to each other and I'm just glad of the break and trying to shut it out. Then I see something on the radar that gets me worried."

"Another craft?"

"Yeah, probably a satellite. I never saw it for real, just a little blip on the scope. But it's coming right for us, like it's going to pass overhead. You know what you said about not being seen by other orbiters? Well I did a bit of research before I left and I found out there's new stuff going round the Moon that has hi-def cameras. Anything looking like a car that's not the lunar rover is going to come under serious scrutiny."

"So what did you do?" I asked. This was getting exciting.

"I got us the hell out of there. Just took off and went in the other direction. We were half way down Pentonville road before I reckoned it was safe. But that's when the real trouble started. Quentin, that little shit, his parents are QCs or something. Really top-level barristers. Some of it must have rubbed off on him because he started yelling about how I hadn't fulfilled the terms of the agreement, taking off before the music had finished. How he managed to spout all this legal gobbledegook on a head full of drugs I'll never know. Maybe you only need half a brain to practice law. Then Justin and Klaus chip in with how I should return the money they paid us. Well, I knew what you'd think about that so we worked out another deal."

"Let me guess, you took them to Mars for free."

"Oh, no. I wasn't going to do that. No more freebies, we said, right? I told them I'd do it for a grand."

"What? Mars for a lousy grand? What kind of negotiation is that, Buster?"

"Well, Klaus had the cash right there on him and it looked like a lot at the time, plus they had me over a barrel on the music issue."

"No they didn't!" I protested. "They were just a bunch of drugged up schoolboys trying it on! And who goes into Space carrying a thousand pounds in cash? Where were they expecting to spend it? On the Space Station?"

"Well by that point I just wanted to get the trip over with. You don't know what it was like cooped up in a car with those animals."

"Ok, fair enough. The thousand will go toward all the fines and impound fees for your hinge car anyway. But next time we've got to put a serious premium on landing on planets, especially if we're the first ones to do so. How was the trip to Mars?"

"Surprisingly easy, as it happens. I put the co-ordinates

into the Sat-nav for Belvedere road on the South Bank and just followed the arrow there. Got there in three minutes at top speed."

"Three minutes!" I yelped. "God, that car can move."

"Yeah, I worked it out. We were going three quarters the speed of light. Nearly crashed into Phobos when I got there."

"So what did you do on Mars?"

"We did a few orbits, then landed on a flat bit and went for a drive."

"A drive? Jesus, Buster. What did I tell you about tyre tracks?"

"I wasn't too worried about those. Unlike the Moon, Mars has wind storms. I figured the tracks would be covered up by one of those. Plus I had to do something while the rest of Dark Side played out. The problem was, Klaus suddenly needed to go to the toilet and asked me to open the doors so he could go behind a rock. He needed to do a number two. I tried to explain that Mars had a carbon dioxide atmosphere and was about two hundred degrees below zero and we'd all die if I opened the doors, but he couldn't hold it in."

"So he went in a cup."

"Bingo. And let me tell you, I almost wished I had opened the doors. Whatever year this car came from they must have toilets all over the solar system."

I changed the subject.

"I suppose that's when all that dust got onto the car, when you drove it around." I said.

"No, the dust got on the car when we, er, did the donuts."

"Donuts?"

"Yeah, it was Quentin's idea. I jammed the steering wheel all the way to the left and spun the wheels. It made the car go round in circles and leave donut tracks in the dust. They do it in their cars at home, those boys."

"Idiots."

"Yeah, well I didn't think it was such a bad idea," said Buster. "The donuts might be mistaken for natural formations if someone ever spots them. Plus I got to admit it was quite fun. So after the donuts I lifted off and headed back to Shoreditch. Earth, I mean. Went a bit slower this time. I didn't want some radar operator thinking an asteroid was about to hit."

"How did the Child Tracker work?"

"Fine." said Buster, taking a sip of coffee. "As soon as I got close to England the blip showed up nice and clear on the phone. I got down to cloud level, then dropped the car slowly until I saw your lights. Nice idea, that."

"Yeah. I heard you a mile off, playing Flash Gordon."

"Oh, God, when we ran out of Pink Floyd they cranked out every clichéd piece of music you could imagine. Space Oddity, Flash Gordon, Theme from Star Wars, Also Sprach Zarathustra, at least there wasn't any bloody Vangelis."

I was slightly put out by that. I still maintain that Vangelis is the best music for space trips.

"Buster?"

"Yeah?"

"Well done, mate. You did all right. It can't have been easy for you."

"Thanks. It wasn't. All this creeping round under the radar is starting to be a real pain. How long before we can go public?"

201

"When we've made enough money."

"But it's never enough money for you!" he whined.

"You don't understand, Buster. Say we split the thirty four grand three ways, ten for you, ten for me and fourteen for the company. It's still not enough to protect ourselves. When we go public we'll need scientists and lawyers working for us, not to mention security. We only need a couple more big scores like the Mars trip to get the ball rolling. In the meantime you can content yourself with the fact that you are one of the first human beings to land on another planet."

Buster drew a piece of paper from his pocket and consulted it.

"Yeah," he said. "Me and... Nigel Cavendish, Quentin Fforbes-Dyson, that's with two effs, The Right Honourable Justin Pentacost and Baron Klaus Von Reichart. I'm not sure I even want my name on that list. We sound like one of those 'Magnificent men in their flying machines'".

"You'll go down in history."

"Only as a footnote. We didn't even get out of the car. The glory will go to the first person to actually set foot on Mars. Some NASA goon. Who do you think the first man in space was?"

"Yuri Gagarin." I said automatically.

"No he wasn't. There were two or three guys before him but they all died horribly. Not the kind of press the Russians wanted so they hushed it up."

"Nonsense."

"True."

"You're on your conspiracy hobby horse again." I said.

"Yeah, well everybody needs a hobby."

"Come on, we're both tired. Let's get back to London and we'll work out what we need to do after a bit of sleep."

Before we got back in our cars I took an envelope out of my pocket, the one with the hinge car impound documents in it, removed the documents and used my credit card to scrape off as much Mars dust as I could from the car's bodywork. This I collected in the envelope and stashed it in my pocket. I figured it might be worth something even though it had probably been contaminated by dirt from the Stowmarket bypass.

Chapter thirty five

We drove back to my place and stashed the Space car in my garage. Buster removed the number plates and went off to get the hinge car out of the pound while I downed another cup of coffee and did something that I knew would put a spring in my step: I went down to the bank and deposited the rest of the money into my account.

Then I went back home and spent a satisfying hour online paying all my debts: credit cards, utilities, loans, even council tax and insurance. I only had about £4000 left in my personal account at the end but I was firmly in the black and there was no better feeling. I felt light, cool, able to breathe. There's a reason they call it 'keeping your head above water' when you're financially solvent.

Then to business. Not wanting a repeat of the Police disaster I went online and found a white Jaguar E-type for sale and copied down its number plate from the picture. Then I went down to my local automotive shop and had them make up a pair of identical plates which I fixed to the Space car with super glue. It wouldn't stand up to a police vehicle check but might survive a once-over.

Now we had money in the bank I resolved to hire a proper car transporter the next time we moved the Space car. No more using Davo's Luton, that was for sure. Finally, although my head was snapping forward with fatigue, I researched office spaces for rent. Whatever people expected from a company offering trips into Space, it probably wasn't a poky room above a juice bar.

This was confirmed to me the next day when I went back to the office to pack up the rest of my stuff in preparation for the move. The juice bar owner had now covered every horizontal surface with trays of wheatgrass in various stages of germination. It looked like a cross between a second hand office furniture store and Hyde Park.

I unfolded some cardboard archive boxes and started to empty the filing cabinet. There was all the paperwork from A to B Spacelines in there, then further back reams of legal briefs and sheet music from the Piano Bar, then behind that even more evidence of previous ventures and misbegotten moneymaking schemes. It wasn't so much a filing cabinet as an archaeological record of high hopes and business disasters.

I was so immersed in trying to sort out what to save and what to burn that I didn't notice the man standing in the doorway until he gave a gentle knock on the door frame to get my attention. I spun round, dislodging a tray of wheatgrass which thumped to the floor, luckily right side up.

"Oh!" I said. "Hello."

"A to B Spacelines?"

"Yes?"

The man stepped into the office and scanned the room with a critical look on his face.

"I'd like to make some enquiries about your operation if I may."

Every sense I had told me to be careful. I have good instincts about people and this guy, whether it was his dark suit or his piercing eyes, had set several bells ringing in my head. He had close-cropped grey hair but his physique was not that of an old man. He had the bearing of a private security goon and just the way he'd said 'make some enquiries' sounded heavy. He certainly didn't look like someone after a joyride into Space.

"Sure." I said as nonchalantly as I could, "have a seat, Mr...?"

"Dennett." he said, moving a tray of wheatgrass from the

chair and sitting down. He fixed me with that scrutinising stare.

"So you take people up into Space, do you?"

I decided to play dumb and give as little away as I could while getting as much info from him at the same time. It's a standard tactic in business negotiation, 'The Art of War' Chapter one.

"Are you interested in going up into space?" I countered.

"I'm interested in what your company does exactly."

"We provide a service. How exactly did you come by us?"

"'Behold the infinite. Be an astronaut for under two grand. Fly into space and orbit the earth on the journey of a lifetime.'"

He was quoting our advert. An advert that had come and gone at least six weeks ago and which hadn't contained my office address.

"Oh yes." I said dismissively "Well, that was just a bit of silly fun. We dress up as astronauts and go up in a hot air balloon."

"And that's it?"

"That's it."

"That's not it, Philip Benson."

I felt a prickle in my throat. How did he know my name?

"Who are you?" I said.

"Dennett."

"And where are you from?"

He fixed me again with those eyes.

"Norfolk." he replied.

Well that put the wind up me, I can tell you. If he'd have said he was from MI5 or the Russian Space Agency it would have rattled me less, but Norfolk? It was a straight answer but it implied he knew all about us. *Get rid of this guy*, my instincts screamed.

"OK, Mr. Dennett from Norfolk, I hope I've been of some assistance. Let me know if you're interested in one of our simulated space rides and I'll book you in."

I hoped he would get the message and get lost. He rose from his seat but he didn't get lost. Instead he went to the window and addressed me while observing the people in the street below.

"You're a nice man, Mr. Benson. You have a nice house, a nice car, a nice friend, but this," he waved his hand across the room. "Is not a nice business. Things that happen to people in this business… are not nice."

"It's not nice to threaten people." I said indignantly.

"The threat is there," he replied, walking to the door. "But it's not coming from me. Thanks for your time. Maybe I'll see you again."

He left without another word. I whipped open the bottom drawer of the filing cabinet in case I had stashed a bottle of something there. I hadn't, so I had to content myself with chewing a clod of wheatgrass which tasted as foul as could be expected.

Chapter thirty six

I drove the whole way to Buster's with one eye on the rear view mirror, nearly hitting a cyclist on Charing Cross road. When I turned down Buster's alley I noticed the hinge car wasn't there, so obviously he wasn't back from the Crawley car pound yet. I knocked on his door but there was no reply so I settled down to wait, periodically jumping up and checking both ends of the alley. Finally I heard footsteps coming my way which did little to calm my fears. I was expecting the hinge car, not someone on foot. Could it be Mr. Dennett? Take it easy, I told myself. It's probably Buster, coming back empty handed due to some legal problem with getting the car out of the pound.

The footsteps got closer until a figure came round the corner. It wasn't Buster, it was Davo. I never thought I'd be relieved to see his shambling form but here he was, the ever-present roll-up wedged between the first and second fingers of his fist.

"All right, mate?" he said. "Buster in?"

"No, he's gone to Crawley. He's got car trouble."

"Not that rocket car o'yours?"

"No, his regular car."

"Oh. I came to tell him about someone who wants a trip in the rocket. Two people, actually. Man and a woman."

"Where do they want to go?"

"I don't know. Up there." he said, flicking his head to the sky.

"Do you have a number for them?"

"Hang on, I've got a card."

Davo handed me a bent business card and turned around to go.

"Tell Buster I was here, OK?"

"Oh, Davo?"

"Yeah?"

"Does the name Dennett mean anything to you?"

"That's your name isn't it?"

"No, it's Benson."

"Then who's this Dennett geezer?"

"Someone who's been asking after me."

"Sounds like a wanker." Said Davo as he shambled off down the alley.

I chuckled in spite of all my worries and looked at the card. It said 'BLESSED COMMUNITY OF THE INFINITE PANTHEON' and under that 'Modal Divinator: Star Baba' and a phone number. I sighed. The card screamed 'Crackpot' but the kind of person to get this card printed would be exactly the sort to want to go into Space.

I heard a honk behind me and turned to see the hinge car trundling up the alley, its original license plates held on with string. Buster got out and stretched.

"Hiya," he said. "Didn't expect to see you here. I thought you were doing business stuff today."

"We need to talk."

Over the usual cup of tea I told Buster about my visit from Mr. Dennett.

"OKaaaayy," said Buster thoughtfully. "Assuming this mysterious Mr. Dennett knows we've been going up into space, let's try and figure how he found out."

"If he's connected to the Government then they could have tagged us on the radar." I began.

"He might also have been in contact with Sparky, Nigel or one of Nigel's friends." Continued Buster. "Or maybe he saw the Private Eye ad and did a bit of checking into it. Sparky found out about us via your phone number and he's not with any agency."

"Or maybe he was tipped off by one of the Balloon festival people?" I suggested. "Mr.76 for example?"

"Yes, or else the car got picked up on a Moon or Mars satellite? Or by the space station?"

"Oh, I just thought of something," I added. "Maybe there's a better resolution picture of the car and slide when it got into the papers and you can see the license plate? They could have traced it back to you."

"How about when we first got the car out of the cube?" answered Buster "Maybe there was some CCTV we never knew about?"

I slumped back in Buster's armchair and sighed.

"Let's face it, Buster. We haven't exactly run an airtight operation. Now the net's closing in. I can feel it."

"Oh come on Philip, what are they going to do? Put us in prison? The worst they can do is take the car away from us and tell us to keep quiet about the whole thing."

"You didn't see this Dennett guy. He said that not nice things were going to happen to us."

"Oh, screw him! Where's the evidence? Some high-as-a-kite aristos who say they've been to Mars? Let's just dump the car."

I was suddenly furious. Why the hell should our only option be to get rid of the car? We'd worked bloody hard to get hold of this car and it was the only one of its kind. It also had the potential to be an amazing money-spinner.

"We're not dumping the car!" I shouted, rising to my feet. "We earned thirty four thousand quid in a single day with that car and no one's going to take it away from us! Oh and by the way, Davo was round here looking for you. He said he'd found some new passengers, not that it's going to do us much good. They sound like lunatics." I threw the business card in Buster's lap. He looked at it idly, then jumped up.

"Where did you get this?" he demanded.

"I told you, Davo gave it to me."

"This is from the CIP! The Community of the Infinite Pantheon! they're one of the richest cults in the world!"

I sat up. Something about the words 'Richest in the world' got my attention sharpish.

"Go on." I said.

Buster filled me in, and don't ask me how he knew all this. The CIP is a religious order that was founded in the 1920s by a group of bored industrialists who had been thrown out of the Freemasons. They believed in some kind of God-is-everything claptrap and sold all their stocks and pooled their wealth for when the 'End Times' came. Because of this, when the stock market crashed in 1929 they were the only ones who didn't lose anything. Their leader, a smart, charismatic fellow with the improbable name of Arch Nemesis, bought up every property, business and patent he could get his hands on, which after the market crash was plenty.

The cult went underground for a few years after that,

quietly building a spectacular fortune with holdings all over the world. With the death of Nemesis in 1970 a new leader emerged called Star Baba who ran the cult to this day. Either that or Star Baba was just the title of the current leader, I didn't quite catch that bit.

The interesting thing is they are one of the few cults that don't actively recruit people. They have so much money that they are constantly inundated with applicants and have a twenty year waiting list for membership. Their headquarters were a vast stately home in the midlands outside Derby.

How Davo got to know them is a mystery. Buster says they have a discreet but sumptuous house in London and Davo may have crashed one of their parties- a particular talent of his, apparently. It all made for a compelling story and certainly took my mind off my current woes. It also showed me a way out of the Mr. Dennett situation.

"Hello, CIP?"

The woman's voice sounded crisp and businesslike. Not like a Cult at all.

"Hello, this is Philip Benson for Star Baba."

A pause.

"May I ask the reason for your call?"

"Yes, I'm the CEO of A to B Spacelines. I believe Mr. Baba is interested in our services."

"Please hold."

Some flutey music came on, the type you hear piped through in Spa resorts.

"They've put me on hold." I told Buster.

A different woman's voice came on the line.

"Hello, Mr. Benson?"

"Speaking."

"Hello, My name's Aurora. I was wondering if you could come down to our London headquarters for a chat?"

"Sure, do you mind if I ask…"

"We're not big fans of the telephone. Mr. Baba never uses one, in fact." said Aurora, interrupting me. She gave me an address in a very nice part of town and asked me to be there at nine the next morning.

"Well?" asked Buster when I'd hung up.

"We're in."

Chapter thirty seven

The address proved to be so exclusive that we drove the Space car past it twice without realising it was there. On the third pass I spotted a driveway that I had thought was a hole-in-the-wall garage but which turned out to be a passage through to a courtyard very much like Buster's arrangement but much, much fancier with ornate stonework surrounding the many windows that looked down on us. The courtyard was paved with stone that looked hundreds of years old and had enough room for three cars to park and turn around. Two cars were already parked there, a Bentley and a twelve seater minivan. I parked the Space car beside them and we got out.

"Mr. Benson?"

A young lady in a smart black suit stood outside the doorway that led into one side of the courtyard. She had a neat blonde ponytail and looked every inch the corporate PA,

"Good morning." I said, extending my hand. "Philip Benson. And this is my associate Professor Ames."

We shook hands formally. I was wearing what I called my 'good first impression' suit. Smart enough to mean business but not too smart to look like I'm going to a wedding. When you're dealing with the very rich I've found it literally doesn't pay to dress better than them. It makes them less inclined to give you their money. Buster's outfit had presented more of a problem. His only suit was a nasty moth-eaten pinstripe which looked like it had been pilfered from a clothes recycling bin. We briefly considered putting him in a lab coat but settled on a look I call 'Tech-wizard casual'.

"I'm Juliana." The young lady said. There was nothing remotely culty about her. In fact the whole setup seemed more like an exclusive club than a religious order. The impression continued when she led us inside. You know I said how I could see streams of money? This looked like the place all the streams led into, a deep volcanic lake of riches. It was in the wooden paneled walls, the pale marbled floors, the carpets, the echoes, the silence.

"Did you see that door we came in through?" Buster murmured as we were led upstairs. "It had massive steel bolts going through it."

"Yeah, either to keep the money in or the people out."

We were shown into an ornate upper-storey room that ran the whole length of the building with high windows on each side. One set of windows looked out over the courtyard in which we had parked, the other presented an incredible view of central London. It wasn't just the view that was impressive, I've seen London from a height before, it was the quietness of it all. There's something very relaxing about watching a thousand hectic scenes below you in silence while you stand above it like God.

"It seems our space captains have arrived." Came a voice behind us. We turned round to find a dapper little man standing before us. He wore a grey tunic that buttoned up to his neck and little round glasses. He was bald but had flecks of grey in his eyebrows. I would put his age at about sixty. He looked like a cross between Blofeld and Ghandi.

"Forgive me," he said. "I am Star Baba. I'm not used to making my own introductions. Aurora usually does that for me. She'll be along in a minute."

"Philip Benson." I said

"Buster Ames." said Buster.

Neither of us extended our hands. I had briefed Buster about this already. I have never seen one of these mystical types shake hands with anyone, either on TV or in the movies. They tend to affect a little bow or a weird hand gesture. In this Star Baba was no exception. He went with the little bow.

"Shall we sit?" he said, gesturing to a suite of antique chairs clustered around a low table.

"Nice place you've got here." said Buster once we'd sat down.

"Thank you, though it's not mine," replied Star Baba. "It belongs to the Community. I'm really just the caretaker. It serves our purposes."

Pull the other one, I thought. I expect the Bentley outside belongs to the Community as well, as does your mansion in the Midlands. Nice lifestyle for a caretaker.

"This would be the Community of the Infinite Pantheon?" I said. "I have to confess, I'd not heard of your… operation before."

"We keep a low profile, at least the religious side of the operation, as you call it. You've probably heard of some of our business holdings." He then reeled off the names of some absolutely massive blue-chip companies. The kind of conglomerates that if they went bust would bring down the economy of, well, the whole world. Not that there was any danger of them going bust. We're talking highly successful businesses. I was pretty jealous.

"The Community is split, you see," went on Baba. "The religious side owns the business side and the business side funds the religious side. None of the companies we own are required to subscribe to our beliefs and I am not on the boards of any of the companies, nor is anyone else on the religious side."

"How many of you are there on the religious side?" asked Buster.

"A few hundred. We admit only those who embody the ideals of the Pantheon. We take care of them financially and we expect them to fulfill their duties in return."

"And what are their duties?" I asked. Star Baba made an

odd, high pitched hum at the question, then looked over my shoulder at the door.

"Ah. Aurora." he said.

I swiveled round in my seat to see a middle aged woman with long, black, flowing hair in a long, white flowing dress gliding toward us. I rose to my feet, followed by Buster.

"Mr. Benson," she said. "We spoke on the phone." At least she shakes hands, I thought as she extended her arm. I introduced her to Buster and we all sat down again.

"Mr. Benson was just asking what the duties of our Community members are." Said Star Baba.

"Yes, I heard. Please forgive us, Mr. Benson, if we're not forthcoming enough for you. There are some aspects of our religion that are not for the uninitiated to know."

"Why not?" asked Buster.

Shut up, Buster, I thought to myself. Let these guys have their little secrets. We're just here to ferry them into Space. Luckily Aurora didn't take offence at the question. She didn't answer it either.

"I believe you have a means to travel to other planets." She said, turning to me. I quickly surmised that she was the brains of the operation. Star Baba was all very impressive in his cuddly cult leader way but she was the one to do business with. I'd seen this before with power couples. One is the philosophical one, the other a hard-headed realist. Bit like Buster and myself, really.

"I know it sounds a bit far-fetched," I answered. "But it's absolutely true."

"If we didn't suspect it to be true," said Aurora. "You wouldn't be sitting here. You see, every religious movement attracts individuals making grandiose claims, and every business conglomerate attracts those who would seek to profit from unlikely co-ventures. As you can imagine we get so many of these people knocking on our door that we have a whole office dedicated to vetting them. When they came to check you out they found, to their surprise, a fair bit of evidence that you were bona fide."

"Good," I said. "So where do you want to go?"

Star Baba smiled.

"Neptune." he said.

"*Neptune?*" cried Buster.

Chapter thirty eight

I jumped at Buster's yell. His surprise was too revealing and this was not good for business. I needed to talk to him before we went on.

"Do you mind if I speak with Professor Ames in private?" I said.

"By all means." replied Aurora. "There's a conference room through those doors. Take all the time you need."

God knows what kind of bizarre conferences had occurred in the anonymous room the Infinite Pantheon people directed us to. The first thing I did was check the place for video cameras. The fact that I couldn't see any obvious signs of surveillance didn't mean the place wasn't bugged. I'd certainly bug the place if I was them. I motioned Buster to be quiet and spoke to him just above a whisper.

"How far away is Neptune, Buster?"

"Depends on the time of year. About two and three quarter billion miles."

That Buster knew this offhand without Google was impressive, as was the distance.

"That's pretty far. How long would the car take to get there, flat out?"

"About five and a half hours, each way. It's a shame they don't want to go to Mars."

"It's not a shame, it's bloody brilliant. A trip that far, with the amount of money these people have. We're going to score bigtime on this one, Buster."

"Enough to stop sneaking around and go legit?"

"Definitely," I said. "I think we should ask them for this much." Just in case they were listening I took out a notepad and pen and wrote 'Ten Million'

"Ten million!" said Buster.

"Shhh!"

"Sorry. Do you think they'll pay that?"

"Probably not, but that's where we'll start. If they won't pay that we'll go back and forth a bit but I don't think we should go lower than this, and please don't say it out loud."

On the notepad I wrote 'Three million.'

"Sounds good to me." said Buster.

"Fine. Just let me do the negotiation."

"I will watch the master at work."

We walked back into the big room. Star Baba and Aurora were still sitting on the antique chairs.

"Professor Ames and I were just discussing logistics and such," I said breezily. "What exactly do you plan to do once you get to Neptune? You realise it would be impossible to land on the planet, don't you?"

"That's all right," said Star Baba. "We won't be needing to land there. Orbit is fine."

"So what will you be doing in orbit?"

"That doesn't concern you," said Aurora. "We're only paying you to get us there."

"You're not going to kill yourselves are you?" said Buster.

I was mortified. I know Buster can be a bit tactless but this really was too much. He may have just cocked up the whole deal. Luckily after a moment of tense silence the two cultists chuckled.

"I know what you're thinking," said Star Baba. "And I understand your reasons for thinking it. We don't hold those kind of beliefs. To kill ourselves would be to kill a part of the consciousness of God. Such an action would be unthinkable."

"Good," said Buster "Because we wouldn't want you to make a mess in our car."

"Can we get down to business?" I said. I wanted to get off this track before Buster screwed things up properly.

"Certainly," said Star Baba. "I assume you'd like to inform us of your charge for this trip."

"That's right. Now, our pricing scheme is this: We charge one hundred thousand to go into low Earth orbit. The Moon is five hundred thousand. Inner planets are five million for orbit with a supplement of one and a half million if you want to land. Anything outside the asteroids is ten million, that includes Jupiter, Saturn, Uranus and Neptune. We don't land on gas giants but we could land on one of their moons for the one and a half mil supplement."

Buster gave me a sideways look. I knew what he was thinking: *'When did you think up this pricing scheme?'* I had worked it out that morning on the back of an envelope but hadn't shared it with him. In my experience people are more likely to pay for something if it looks like part of a fixed tariff. It makes it look less like you're just pulling numbers out of the air, which of course I was. Aurora nodded thoughtfully.

"I assume those numbers are in pounds sterling?"

"They are. Payment in full in advance."

"Any other conditions?" she asked.

"Yes, we'll provide the vehicle and pilot it but you have to provide a secure take-off and landing venue. We'll need a level field and four hot-air balloons."

"Hot air balloons?" asked Star Baba.

"Yes, not to lift the craft but to provide cover from ground-based radar. We'll need the balloons to be aloft for our return as well."

"Ten million pounds is a lot of money." said Aurora.

"Not for a passage to Neptune it isn't. It wouldn't even pay for the instruments on a robot probe if you went to NASA."

"We'll accept it on these conditions," she replied. "One, anything either of you see or hear on the trip is confidential. I'm talking about activities of the CIP as carried out by myself and Star Baba."

"Agreed." I said. I was really curious as to what they would be getting up to now.

"Two, any photos or video of Neptune gathered on this trip, either by us or you, remain the sole property of the CIP."

"OK."

"And three, you must give us a demonstration of the capabilities of your craft before the trip commences."

"What kind of demonstration? We're not giving you a free trip into orbit."

"We're not asking for that. Just enough to show that you're not confidence tricksters or frauds."

"But I thought you've had us checked out already," said Buster.

"For ten million pounds," said Aurora "We are not risking

the possibility of an error in our own vetting procedures."

"All right, fair enough," I sighed. "Buster, will you please go downstairs and give a demonstration to our friends here? Nothing above the rooftops OK?"

Buster smiled in reply, stood up and left the grand room by the doors we had come in.

"Where is he going?" asked Star Baba.

"You wanted a demonstration, he's going to give you a demonstration." I replied, walking to the windows that overlooked the courtyard. "You might want to come over here and watch."

The two of them walked over to the window. Below us we saw Buster exiting the building and using his magnet to zip open the driver's side door of the Space car.

"Why is he getting into your car?" asked Aurora.

"That's not a car, that's our spaceship."

"What?"

I didn't need to elaborate. The car rose silently into the air like the very first time we realised it could fly. I heard Star Baba gasp quietly as it rose level with our window. Buster waved at us cheerfully through the windscreen, then did something typically foolhardy. He dropped down, turned the car's nose up until it hung there vertically, then flipped it end over end several times, finishing with it upside down. He waved at us again, this time through the side window. I turned to face my prospective passengers.

"Is that enough of a demo?"

"We've got a deal." said Star Baba.

This time we shook hands on it.

Chapter thirty nine

"This is more like it, eh?" said Buster as we barreled up the M1 towards the Midlands. "No more sneaking about looking for Balloon festivals and old RAF strips."

He was right in that respect. We'd left the hinge car behind in favour of a state of the art car transporter, one that we'd hired from a company that services race car teams. The Space car was in the back, covered by a tarp and firmly belted down to prevent it blowing off in the wind. There was a storage chest behind the driving compartment into which we'd packed the inflatable slide but it was only for backup. Where we were going it looked like we wouldn't need it, for we were going to the CIP headquarters.

No more sneaking about, as Buster had said. The CIP had hundreds of acres of private land and had specially hired in four hot air balloons to be piloted by their own people. It was the bespoke spaceport we'd been hankering after all this time and best of all for Buster, it wasn't in New Mexico. I still wasn't happy, though.

"What's the problem, Philip? You've been moping ever since the service station. Didn't the transfer go through?"

He was referring to our payment from Star Baba and his crew. It certainly had gone through, all ten million of it. I had checked the balance at the cash machine and the sight of all those zeroes ought to have had me dancing a jig right there outside WH Smiths but once again I felt we'd been outplayed.

"No, we have the money," I said. "But they didn't even try to knock us down on the price. That can only mean that we could have got away with more."

"Oh come on! You said you'd be prepared to go down to three million. Compared to that, ten million is a great result."

"It's an even better result for them. We should never have agreed to give them the rights to the pictures and data and stuff. Those alone are probably worth ten mil. I bet that's why they didn't bother negotiating."

"Hey, we didn't get into this game to take photos of Neptune. Let them take that action and we'll finally start making Space cars. You're going to be rich, isn't that what you always wanted?"

"I've been rich already. Money has a habit of coming to visit me for a while and then buggering off."

"You keep referring to your old glory days," said Buster. "But you never told me exactly what you did to get that money or how you came to lose it. It wasn't the Karaoke Piano thing, was it?"

"Oh, God no. It was much cleverer than that. It was my medical studio."

"Medical studio? I can't imagine what those two words are doing together. Come on, tell us the story."

We still had a fair way to go so to pass the time I told Buster all about my 'first million'. It started when I went to the dentist for a root canal. Like any normal person I'd been ignoring the checkup reminder notes he'd been sending me and only went when something actually went wrong with my teeth. He diagnosed root problems and booked me in for the treatment, which was a lengthy job. While my mouth was propped open and he was doing all the drilling we had one of those one-and-a-half-sided conversations that dentists specialize in.

Now this dentist fancied himself as a bit of a TV star and had even appeared as a pundit on the news channels from time to time whenever a tooth-related story came up and they needed an expert to chip in. He'd got a taste for the limelight and once you're on the address book of a TV company they tend to keep coming back, so when they needed to film a dentist filling a cavity for some special report they dispatched a TV crew to his place to get the footage.

Anyway, the dentist was telling me all about this and bitching that the TV crew had so much camera kit they were getting in the way and knocking over his equipment while he was trying to work, plus they tried to get him to do the work at arm's length so they could get the camera in there for the close-up shot. The last straw came when their lights blew a fuse and nearly screwed up some guy's mouth when a high speed drill suddenly stopped. *Serves you right for trying to be a TV star* I thought, *when what you should be doing is working on peoples teeth.* Anyway, he finished the canal and I paid and that was that.

Until, that is, I happened to have a chat with a doctor friend of mine who was moaning about some medical TV drama he'd seen which was obviously inaccurate in its portrayal of the equipment they use in surgery. Obvious to him, of course. Most of us non-doctors wouldn't be able to tell one way or another. I tried to explain to him that these shows were shot in TV studios and the equipment was all just props selected for how good they looked rather than how accurate a reflection they were of current medical facilities. He just fobbed me off -he was a bit drunk at the time- but it got me thinking.

If TV studios aren't kitted out like proper surgeries, and if proper surgeries don't have the right facilities for filming, wouldn't there be a gap in the market for a studio that was both properly equipped for filming *and* carrying out genuine medical procedures? I did some research and the idea still seemed to fly so I got together a consortium of doctors and we fixed up an old TV studio that was situated conveniently close to a teaching hospital.

It was expensive as hell, of course. Just cleaning out all the generations of grime, gaffer tape and gaffer's sweat was a job in itself. Studios are bloody filthy- I tell you those film crews are animals. Luckily the doctors had a ton of dough and good connections so we got a lot of the medical equipment cheap from bankrupt private hospitals.

When we finally got the ball rolling we found two different but very lucrative classes of customer looking to hire the facility. One was film productions whose directors were sick of their own doctors bitching about lack of realism in the movies so were going for the ultra-realistic look. The other was doctors who wanted to promote themselves by having their operations professionally filmed without the film crew getting in the way.

We were doing very nicely and quickly getting a reputation as the go-to place for shooting medical dramas or actual operations when a third revenue stream opened up that pulled down the serious dough. Rich patients, it turned out, had an insatiable need to have their operations filmed for their own records. Either they wanted to collect evidence in case they needed to sue the Doctor later on or else they were just paranoid about being under anaesthetic without knowing what was being done to them, or maybe they were just curious. Whatever it was, they paid through the nose for the privilege and the money flowed out of their noses right into my pocket.

Here's how it all went wrong: A silly mix-up in the bookings led to a very famous Hollywood actor performing a genuine operation on a real patient whom he believed to be another actor kitted out with prosthetic skin and fake organs. I can't name the actor because of the terms of the subsequent lawsuit but he'd been method acting and researching the procedure so thoroughly that miraculously he'd done an OK job on the guy. The patient hadn't even minded that much at first, being a bit starstruck that such an A-lister had done the work on him but when his lawyers got hold of the footage it was all over for us. The doctors got cold feet, the insurers refused to cover us and the whole venture went tits-up. Within a month I was broke again.

"All I had to show for it was hundreds of hours of operations on tape," I told Buster. "I tried to sell them as training videos but there were rights issues. Plus all anyone wanted to see was the A-lister taking out that guy's appendix and that tape was sealed by the courts."

"Seems like most of your ventures end up in the courts." said Buster.

"You should pop down to the courts sometime," I replied. "I used to go when I'd have an afternoon to kill. I'd sit in the public gallery and watch people's lives and businesses go down the toilet. It's very entertaining if you're not the one in the dock. It's an education as well. You can learn a lot from other people's mistakes. Cheap, too. I'd usually go when I was piss-broke and couldn't even afford a ticket to the cinema."

"Did you see any good murder trials?"

"I was never into that. Plus they were hard to get seats for. They tended to attract a right bunch of weirdos, guys like Sparky. I'd go for the insolvency cases, the bankruptcy hearings, lawsuits and suchlike. I'd been on the receiving end of those trials often enough that I knew what was going on."

"Did anyone ever attend your own court cases for their amusement?" asked Buster.

"Plenty. Bloody ghouls, feeding on other people's misery."

"But you..."

"Yeah, I know, I'm a hypocrite. Still, you throw a rock in one of those courtrooms you'll hit ten hypocrites. And if you do, throw it hard, as they say."

"Look, they're turning off." said Buster.

He was right. The Bentley containing Star Baba and Aurora which we had been following was exiting the motorway ahead of us. They hadn't given us the address of their headquarters but instead had told us to follow them up there. I didn't know if that was a security thing as I'd still be able to get a fix on where we were with the Sat-nav. Maybe they didn't want us writing the address down where it could be discovered.

The Bentley went round a roundabout and turned off at a small country road that snaked through fields and woods for another six or seven miles, coming to a halt at a boxy stone gatehouse. The gates to the property were imposing- at least ten feet high and topped with spikes. They opened automatically and we followed the Bentley up an immaculate gravel path that wound past a stand of tall yew trees and round a corner revealed the house in all its majesty.

Majesty was the appropriate word. It looked like the kind of place that royalty might own- either royalty or an extremely well funded multinational. Even from a distance I could tell it was well maintained. Its stone frontage was pale brown and gleamed in the sun. There must have been sixty windows on this side alone. As we approached I saw several figures step out from the covered porch at the front. Four of them were dressed in flowing turquoise robes and the fifth in a conservative black suit.

We drew up behind the Bentley and saw the four figures in blue surround the car. They were women, all astonishingly beautiful. They opened the Bentley's doors and when Star Baba got out they took turns embracing him before escorting him into the house, followed by Aurora.

"Wow," I said. "See how the other half lives."

"Other half of what?" replied Buster. "We're nowhere near the world this lot come from."

The man in the black suit, who had the bearing of a Butler, came up to my side of the transporter. I wound the window down.

"Follow the path round to the back and unload there, please." he said, then disappeared into the mansion. I shifted the vehicle into gear and took us round the path. The back of the house, if anything, was even more impressive than the front. Here we could see not only a multitude more rooms in the building but outbuildings, balconies and gardens, which were laid out in a symmetrical, classic style. Little topiary hedges lined the grounds, cut into cubes, spheres and narrow pyramids. A wide thoroughfare led directly from the back of the house to the end of the landscaped gardens some distance off.

"Check it out." said Buster, pointing toward the field at the end of the gardens. There, laid out in an exact square, were four white hot air balloons, all inflated and ready to go.

"Now that's more like it," I said. "I was worried for a moment one of those balloons would have a big '76' on it."

We got out and started unhooking the car from the back of the transporter. Neither of us had much experience in working these things so it took us a few minutes to get the ramp unfolded from the back. I toyed with the idea of just flying the car off the back of the transporter but decided against it. No point in messing about, I thought. There'll be plenty of flying later on.

The butler joined us just as Buster was reversing the car down the ramp and onto the ground. He was carrying a tray piled high with sandwiches and cold bottles of water, which he placed on a nearby stone plinth.

"Conveniences are through the door behind you," he said. "May I request that you remain here until Sir and Madam are ready?"

"Yeah, sure, no worries," I said. "Do you know when that will be?"

"In about an hour. They are preparing for the ceremony."

"Ceremony?" said Buster, cracking open a bottle of water. "What's that?"

"I'm afraid I can't tell you. We would also appreciate it if you remain in your car until you are directed to the ceremony site."

"Yeah, whatever." Replied Buster in a casual tone. I could tell that he wasn't really comfortable though. When the butler had gone he came up to me and spoke in a low voice.

"What the hell are these freaks up to?" he said.

"Relax, they're just doing their thing. Go to the toilet, sorry, the 'convenience'. We've got a long trip ahead. I'll check the kit."

Buster went off and I laid out our equipment on the car bonnet. Sat-navs, two of them. One calibrated for interplanetary trips, one for regular Earthbound use, energy drinks, power bars, the marine radar, batteries, a pair of binoculars, a world atlas, a camera, the child tracker, the iPod and speaker, wet wipes and a big Tupperware box for any toilet emergencies which I sincerely hoped wouldn't be needed. Talking of which, I used the 'convenience' myself when Buster came back.

We then sat in the car and waited for the show to start.

"Did you check the kit?" asked Buster.

"Yeah. It's all there. Everything I could think of, anyway. It's hard to think of eventualities when you're about to travel further from Earth than anyone's ever been. How about you?".

Buster smiled enigmatically

"I took a few precautions before we left. You know, just in case things went wrong."

"Like?"

"Well for one thing, if our passengers turn nasty or go batshit crazy up there, I brought this."

Buster opened his bag and withdrew a terrifying twelve-inch knife.

"Jesus Christ!" I yelled. "Put that away!"

He ran his thumb along the serrations that went half way up the blade and nodded approvingly.

"It's just in case." he said.

"What else did you bring, a gun?"

"Don't be ridiculous. If I shot a gun in here it would either decompress the whole car or the bullet would bounce around until it killed all of us." He put the knife back in his bag. "Like I said, I took a few precautions. Hey, look."

He pointed to the wide stone staircase that led from the back of the house to the garden. A line of turquoise robed men and women came down the stairs, carrying what looked like baskets.

"Wow," said Buster. "Those women are hot. Do you think when we get back Star Baba would introduce us to a couple of them?"

"Something tells me it wouldn't work out," I said. "Oh my God, are they actually scattering rose petals? How quaint."

The procession carried on down the wide avenue toward the hot air balloons. There must have been at least a hundred of the acolytes, walking two abreast and sprinkling the petals between them as they went.

"Oh, look there's our passengers," I said, as Star Baba and Aurora made their way down the steps. "Mr and Mrs. Pantheon themselves, all decked out in their white robes."

"Bernhard Giddins." said Buster

"What?"

"That's his real name, Bernhard Giddins."

"I can see why he changed it. You can't run a cult with a name like that. How about Aurora?"

"Aurora is her real name. Aurora Cohen. I looked them up on the Cultbusters website."

I jumped as the butler knocked on my window. He in turn jumped a bit when I unzipped the door to talk to him.

"Yes?"

"It's time," he said. "Follow on at the end of the procession and wait in the centre of the field at the end, between the Balloons."

"OK. Can you give this to one of the Balloon crews?" I handed him the child tracker transmitter, switching it on as I did so.

"What is it?"

"It's a tracking device. It's so we can find our way back."

He gave me an odd look and took the item. I eased the car onto the path behind the last of the blue robed people and crawled after them at a walking pace. It was certainly the grandest drive I had ever made. The gravel and rose petals crunched below us as we made our stately way towards the four hot air balloons, the columns of people forming two blue lines ahead of us and our passengers standing out as white specks half way along.

When the procession reached the take-off field the two columns split left and right and the Community of the Infinite Pantheon lined the perimeter of the field, leaving Aurora and Star Baba standing in the exact centre. I inched the car forward and stopped just behind them. The car's soundproofing prevented us from hearing what was going on but by the looks of it the blue robed people were all singing, their arms interlocked.

"What do you think they're up to?" I said.

Buster muttered something under his breath. I only caught the words 'Wicker Man'. I imagined he was even more keen to get this trip started than I was. Finally Star Baba raised his hands and spoke to the multitude, looking every bit the high priest. I busied myself getting the Sat-navs and the Radar all hooked up and ready. Buster had devised a metal frame that bolted to the top of the dashboard and could be used to hold the devices steady. After what said he'd said about the Sat-nav falling off the windscreen we weren't taking any chances.

It looked as if the ceremonies were coming to an end. To my satisfaction I saw the Butler dart over to each of the Balloon crews, presumably giving them the go-ahead and passing the tracker to the first one he spoke to. One less thing I had to worry about. Star Baba and Aurora walked to each of the passenger doors and Buster and I unzipped them. As they opened we caught the sound of some kind of chant the devout were intoning but it was quickly silenced by the doors zipping shut.

I looked over my shoulders at the two figures in white behind me. Their faces were different to how we'd seen them last in their London pad. The accolade they had received from their followers seemed to light them up with a rapturous glow, giving them the bearing of people who had been told some wonderful truth, or whose asses had been thoroughly kissed.

"All right?" I said.

"Wonderful," replied Star Baba. "Let us begin the journey."

Chapter forty

With a gesture through the window from Aurora the butler withdrew a whistle from his pocket and blew it. Simultaneously all four balloons cast off their moorings and rose into the sky. I turned around, unlocked the steering wheel and pulled back, lifting the car to the level of the balloons' giant gas envelopes and keeping pace with their steady ascent. My last view of the ground was of all the blue robed cultists dashing into the centre of the field and gesticulating wildly, the butler a little black dot in the middle of the crowd.

"The voyage begins," announced Star Baba. "From the Yoni of Earth to the eye of God, we…"

"Yeah, just a minute," interrupted Buster. "Can you both take two of these, please?" He held out four little gelatin capsules. They were half purple and half dark green.

"What are they?" asked Aurora.

"Immodium," replied Buster. "They're for diarrhoea."

"We don't have diarrhoea." Said Star Baba.

"Doesn't matter," said Buster. "They stop you shitting for at least six hours, and we've got a twelve hour trip ahead. I'm not taking any chances."

"We would not presume to pollute our bodies with chemicals." Said Aurora haughtily.

"If it's pollution you're worried about," Buster retorted. "The last lot polluted this craft before we even got back from Mars and that's not happening again. Go on, take them."

"We will control ourselves." Said Star Baba.

"And as Captain, sir. I am controlling this ship," I cut in. "And for health and safety reasons I will control it right back to the landing field if you don't do what Professor Ames asks. I don't suppose a fifteen minute voyage would impress your friends in the blue robes, would it?"

I had no idea Buster was going to spring this on us but I was glad he'd thought of it. It must have been one of these precautions he'd been on about. Threatening to turn back was a gamble and I really hoped our passengers would see sense. If the trip ended now we'd probably have to refund them and I'd sooner have them fill the whole car with shite before I did that. Luckily the words 'Health and Safety', the magic phrase that allowed people to get away with the most unsafe and unhealthy practices, did the trick. Grudgingly Star Baba reached out and took the capsules, passing two to Aurora. I gave them a bottle of water to wash them down.

"You too." said Buster, handing me two more.

"How many of those did you bring?"

"Enough to bung up the whole Starship Enterprise," said Buster, swallowing two capsules himself. "I got the idea from those guys who broke the speed record crossing the Atlantic. They saved weight on their powerboat by not installing a toilet and just taking pills."

"How long did it take them?"

"Four and a half days."

"Do you have any other unpleasant surprises for us?" asked Aurora acidly.

"No, hopefully not," said Buster. "Unless we crash into an asteroid or something."

"Which we won't," I said emphatically, seeing the alarm on the faces of our passengers. "We have a system in place to prevent that." I patted the marine radar. I was lying, of course. At the speed we'd be going, chances were we'd never see an asteroid until it vaporised us.

The car kept rising, keeping level with the balloons although by now the balloons had broken formation and were drifting apart. I hoped they were still creating enough radar noise to cover us.

"Buster, how long before we can leave our escort?"

"Depends on how high they're going to get. I think they're going to top out pretty soon. Those crews don't have breathing apparatus."

I looked down. There was no altimeter in the car. I don't think one would have worked in the driving compartment anyway as we were so insulated from the outside but the ground looked pretty far down. I could just make out the estate we'd taken off from below, though it was the size of a postage stamp. Above us there was only a thin layer of high-altitude cloud.

"Tell you what," said Buster "let's get above that cloud and then shoot for orbit."

I kept the car level as possible and rose slowly above the Balloons. Soon they were just four white blobs below us.

"Can you test the tracker device, please Buster?" I was trying to keep communication between us nice and professional sounding for the benefit of our passengers. Buster plugged the child tracker into his phone and switched it on. After a minute it displayed a map of the landscape below us and featured two dots, one green and one red. The green one was our present position and the red one was the child tracker in one of the balloons.

"Child Tracker online, Captain" said Buster. I know he was trying to sound professional as well but I wished he hadn't referred to it by its full name. Luckily neither of the two behind us seemed to notice. They were staring out of the windows, mesmerised. Just you wait for the next bit, I thought to myself. As soon as we broke through the wispy high altitude cloud things were starting to look promising for the next stage of ascent. The sky was darkening and the horizon was just beginning to curve. Stratosphere, I thought.

"OK," I announced. "Is everyone strapped in? We're about to make the jump to orbit."

"Ready." said Buster.

"Yes." said Star Baba. I looked back at him. He and Aurora had put their seatbelts on and were holding hands, looking nervous. Let's make this as quick and painless as possible, I thought. I tipped the nose of the car up and after a second, hit the gas. As usual there was no feeling of acceleration, no Gs at all. The sky, which was all we could see through the windscreen, faded from blue to star-studded black within two seconds with roar like a wave crashing on a beach and receding. There were two gasps from behind me.

"We have now entered low Earth orbit." said Buster, switching on the 'planetary' Sat-nav. I reached beside me and fumbled for the iPod. Might as well have some music while the Sat-nav warmed up. The familiar sound of Vangelis filled the car. I was determined to get someone to like this music in Space, and with Star Baba I had finally found an appreciative ear. Unfortunately he liked it a bit too much and was inspired to deliver a sermon so florid it would have made Carl Sagan himself shiver.

"O majesty of the heavens, Abeleth and Osiris, Wodin and Yaweh! The Pantheon exists, it extends! The eye of God sees itself! We are the missive of Gaia, its lingan becomes whole and brings us unto itself full circle!"

He went on like that for ages. It was full of references to every deity and demigod yet invented by mankind and a few I think he'd cooked up himself. Even after I cut the music, even when Aurora started looking tired of the whole carry-on, Star Baba held forth on the cosmos, the Gods and his own starring role in the scheme of things.

Buster casually handed me his phone. On the screen was typed 'SHAME THE IMMODIUM DOESN'T STOP SHIT COMING FROM MOUTH'. I exhaled sharply in the beginning of a laugh that I disguised as a cough. This, by the way, was how we'd arranged to communicate covertly in front of our passengers. There was no divider between the front and back so we'd simply type messages on a phone and casually hand it back and forth. With all the other equipment we'd be operating it probably wouldn't be noticed.

Talking of which, it looked like Buster finally had the radio signatures of the Sun, Jupiter and the mysterious Russian 'buzzer' located in the modified Sat-nav which was showing us to be on Threadneedle street, right outside the Bank of England. Buster had spent the last couple of days working on the unit, loading the latest coordinates for Earth, Neptune and the other planets. I'd asked him to calibrate it with the Earth at the Bank of England, not Shoreditch. It just seemed more relevant considering the amount of money we'd be making on this trip.

Buster scrolled through the list of favourite locations he'd already entered into the Sat-nav and selected a branch of 'Superdrug' in Epping High street. The Sat-nav calculated a route there, though it wouldn't be the A104 we'd be seeing out of the window, nor would we end up at a Superdrug, but Neptune. Finally he changed the Sat-nav to 'rambler' mode, which displayed the direct as-the-crow-flies arrow to our destination for me to follow.

I shifted the steering until the arrow showed dead ahead and floored the accelerator. The Earth receded behind us at an astonishing rate, as if shot out of our exhaust. If Star Baba had been expecting the streaming starscape so beloved of the movies he'd have been disappointed but at least we weren't being pressed horribly back in our seats. I don't know how those astronauts can deal with that kind of nonsense. Obviously it was something they'd managed to sort out in the future.

I made sure I was pressing as hard as I could on the accelerator until I felt a kind of click underfoot and withdrew my foot. The pedal stayed fixed to the floor. I'd discovered this feature while we'd been parked waiting for the procession to start. It was the car's top-speed cruise control to stop you having to lean on the gas pedal the whole way. Once down, I'd only have to touch the pedal again to release it.

Once the Earth had disappeared behind us the only indication that we were moving at all was the movement of Sun, which over the next half hour slowly drifted from our left to directly behind us, getting smaller over time. For the first time since we'd joined that pre-flight procession I relaxed. Better still, Star Baba seemed to have talked himself out at last and was gazing distractedly out of the window.

"Right everyone," I said in my best captain of the ship voice. "We are on our way to Neptune. Flight time is about five hours and twenty five minutes. I hope you brought something to read because there won't be much to see out of the windows."

"Will we be passing Jupiter or Saturn?" asked Aurora.

"Buster?"

"'fraid not," said Buster. "They aren't lined up with Neptune, nor have they been since the late nineteen seventies."

"When will they be lined up again?"

"2854"

"Sorry, folks," I said, turning round to address Aurora. "Though feel free to book a trip to any of those planets in the future. They're a lot closer than Neptune."

"Yeah, why'd you want to go to Neptune anyway?" chipped in Buster. "It's bloody miles away. Jupiter and Saturn are the big showstoppers, surely? Even Uranus is worth going to for novelty value but Neptune? It's a ball of blue ice billions of miles away."

"I think you'd need to know a little more of our beliefs to understand that," replied Star Baba haughtily. "You see, we are Pantheists which means we believe the entire universe is the body of a single Deity. Every tree, every person, this car, Neptune, everything is just another part of God."

Buster considered this for a moment.

"What part of God is Uranus?" he asked as innocently as he could. I stepped in, fearing a rift in client/provider relations. After all, these were extremely rich people and possible repeat customers.

"I've got to say I greatly admire your beliefs," I blathered. "If everything is just part of God it's a bit like saying we've all got free will. You can lead whatever life you like because you're just part of God just like everyone else. Whatever you do it's all part of God's plan, You're just another cog in the machine, right? It's almost the same as saying there *is* no God."

"Erm, Philip," Said Aurora, "You haven't really grasped what we're about, but that's fine. Naturally there is secret knowledge and certain elaborations that are not privy to anyone but full members of the Community, so I don't expect you to get it in one go."

"But you haven't answered the question," said Buster. "Why Neptune?"

"It's none of your concern!" snapped Star Baba. "All you need to do is get us there and bring us back."

"Look, your business is your business and I respect that," I said, trying to smooth things over. "But speaking as the Captain, can I just have your word that you won't get up to anything that will endanger this craft or anyone in it?"

"You have our word," Said Aurora. "We're going to take

some pictures, do some incantations, meditate and then go home. An hour, maximum."

"Fine, that's all I wanted to know." I checked the Sat-nav bearing. The arrow was still pointing straight ahead. "Why don't you all lie back and get some rest? Buster, you're on driving shift in two hours."

Everyone, to my satisfaction, settled down in their seats and stopped talking. I was glad of the quiet and put my headphones on for a bit of music to pass the time. I was done with Vangelis and tried a bit of Sparky's 'Planets' by Holst. Neptune, of course. The music was ethereal, transcendent even. A little too relaxing though. I almost found myself nodding off and as I was supposed to be driving the car I ought to be at least conscious. All I had to do was make sure the arrow on the Sat-nav stayed at twelve o'clock and the pedal was fixed to the floor so there wasn't a great deal else to do except keep my hands off the wheel.

I stole a glance at the others. Star Baba was sitting back with his eyes closed. Aurora's eyes were open but she seemed to be mesmerised by the stars all around us. Buster was asleep. I checked the marine radar. Nothing. I considered switching on the HUD but decided against experimenting with the workings of the car whilst we were in deep Space.

Despite the fact that we were shooting through the cosmos at three quarters the speed of light I was quickly getting bored out of my head. Once or twice I thought of engaging Aurora in conversation but the only thing I could think of to say was 'What's a nice Jewish girl like you doing in a Space like this?' which was a bit weak. I hate talkative cabbies and decided to exercise some speak-when-you're-spoken-to discretion.

Eventually, through a combination of listening to music and fantasising about the ten million pounds waiting for me back on Earth I passed the time until the end of my driving shift. Buster was still asleep.

"Buster." I said, shaking his shoulder gently. He gave a sudden jerk and looked around him blearily.

"Where are we?"

"Middle of nowhere. Come on, it's your shift."

Two grown men clambering over each other in a confined space is never a pretty sight and I hoped I'd spared our passengers the sight of space captain's arse crack.

"Excuse me, how much longer before we get there?" came Star Baba's voice from the back. I checked the Sat-nav. It showed us in Wanstead, about half way between the City and Epping.

"Just over two and a half hours." I said. "Would you like a sandwich?"

"We have our own food, thank you."

The mention of food got me hungry myself. I dug out a sandwich from the bag and ate it. Buster didn't want one. I took one last look back at the Sun. It was about the size of my little fingernail and it didn't hurt to look at it but that may have been the car's eye protection thing. Confident that Buster would know what he was doing I closed my eyes and had a nap.

Chapter forty one

I awoke from very odd dreams to a wailing noise coming from the back. Star Baba and Aurora were having a bit of a sing-song.

> *Under mountains, over seas*
>
> *Through the planets, Gods are we.*
>
> *Our bodies form the cells divine*
>
> *Of one great being, its thoughts are mine.*
>
> *From Earth to Space and in between*
>
> *In every place existence seen.*
>
> *The eye of God, its view is ours*
>
> *We see the worlds, we are the stars.*
>
> *Kama hua Sh'tainu Brahn*
>
> *Alau v'min Sh'tainu Tah*
>
> *Kama hua Sh'tainu Brahn*
>
> *Alau v'min Sh'tainu Tah*
>
> *Aaaaaaaaaaaaaaah.*

You may be wondering how I could possibly remember every word of this song having just woken up. It was easy because over the next fifteen minutes they sang the song another twenty times. Buster looked tense, sitting rigidly upright and gripping the steering wheel. He passed me the phone. 'THEY HAVE BEEN AT IT FOR AN HOUR PLEASE MAKE THEM STOP OR I WILL BRING MR. KNIFE INTO PLAY.'

By now I had enough of an idea of what would snap them

out of it.

"Holy Jesus!" I shouted, pointing out of the window. The singing stopped immediately as the two of them followed my finger. Naturally there was nothing out there to point at except stars.

"What is it?" cried Star Baba.

"Nothing," I said. "I thought I saw a shooting star. So Professor Ames, how close are we?"

"Epping high street, so we're pretty close. Couple of minutes."

"*Under Mountains, Over seas...*" began Star Baba.

"I'm sorry, but you'll have to hold off on the singing for now," I interrupted. "We're entering a critical stage of the trip and will need full concentration."

Star Baba kept quiet but I could see it was hard for him. Both our passengers were getting excited and jumpy, swiveling round in their seats and looking out of every window. By now the sun was really small, only big enough to be called a disc and not just a bright point of light.

"We're here." said Buster, releasing the gas pedal.

I looked out of the windscreen but saw nothing.

"What do you mean, we're here?" I said. Buster tapped the Sat-nav. It showed our position next to a little chequered flag.

"Superdrug, Epping High street. This is it."

"Where is Neptune?" asked Aurora.

I struggled to keep a professional tone but it wasn't easy. The prospect of not being able to find Neptune after five and a half hours of trekking through space was so horrible that I hadn't even considered it.

"It must be round here somewhere." muttered Buster.

"We're not looking for your keys behind the sofa, Buster," I said. "This is a planet as wide as four earths next to each other."

"I'll try the radar."

Buster adjusted the radar to its maximum range but something was interfering with it. Little flecks of snow appeared and disappeared, making the screen sparkle. Buster turned the wheel and hit the gas.

"What are you doing?" I asked him.

"I'm going around in a circle. Keep a lookout for a big blue planet."

The stars slowly turned about the car as Buster made his circle. On the Sat-nav we went over to the rear of Superdrug and then back to the high street, making circuits of Epping town centre that grew gradually wider each time we went round. The interference on the marine radar rose and fell.

"Hang on, Buster. Does Neptune emit radio waves?"

"Bloody right it does, tons of them."

"Then go back to where you were a minute ago."

"Can you be more specific? A minute ago I was a hundred thousand miles away."

"Er... the north end of Epping high street."

Buster turned round and following the Sat-nav, headed back to where I had said. The noise on the radar grew steadily as we went.

"There," I said. "The further you go in this direction the

more interference there is on the radar. That must mean you're getting closer to its source, and out here that has to be Neptune, right?"

"Good thinking, Philip. You're showing quite an aptitude for astro-navigation."

I don't know about that, but when there's ten million on the table I'd try my hand at brain surgery if I had to. The radar interference grew until it was blanketing the screen. Whatever was ahead, it was powerful. Suddenly some of the stars dead ahead went out, followed by more surrounding them until a black patch was established and growing bigger by the second.

"Buster..."

'I see it,'

Buster brought the car to a halt when the black disc in front of us was just big enough to fill the windscreen.

"We're in the shadow. Can you take us round?" I asked him.

Slowly he manoeuvred the car round the planet. The first thing we saw was the sun rising over the left hand side of the vast black disk which then became a dark blue crescent as we moved round to its sunny side.

'Sunny Side' though, turned out to be a bit of an exaggeration. Although recognisably blue, Neptune in the flesh is a lot darker and dimmer than the pictures would have you believe. I could make out some little white clouds but that was it. In fact it looked a lot like the upper atmosphere of Earth.

"It's so...dark." Said Star Baba, rapt.

"The photos must be long exposures," replied Buster. "Remember, we only get one nine hundredth the light that Earth does."

If they ask for their money back because Neptune's not bright enough they can shove it, I thought. In fact the sight of the vast planet filled me with a sense of peace. Not because of some kind of mystical quality of the place but due to the fact that we'd fulfilled our contract: we'd got them to Neptune and they'd have a hard time denying it. Our ten million was now safe.

My sanity, on the other hand, was taking a beating. The singing and chanting on the way here turned out to have been just a warm-up. Aurora's estimation of 'an hour' may have been correct but possibly due to the theory of relativity it felt like ten hours. Buster, to my surprise, was bobbing his head along with the singing, looking fairly cheerful. They hadn't converted him though; on closer inspection I saw he was wearing ear bud headphones. Although it went against the terms of our agreement I made a note of some of the mumbo-jumbo:

Star Baba: "The darkness heals and we heal the darkness. Awake, awake! Lord open your eye divine and sense the message within from thine own neurons. My Lingam is the astral vapour."

Aurora: "My Yoni the nebulae divine."

Star Baba: "The Pantheon will be extended."

Aurora: "The Extension shall be mine."

Eventually they finished their incantations and pulled out a couple of cameras to take pictures of Neptune. For an outfit with as much money as them I was pretty shocked at the crappiness of the equipment they were using. They had a nasty looking Olympus that looked about right for taking snaps at a friend's wedding and a camcorder that I swear was loaded with tape of all things.

"So what was the meaning of all the, er, prayers and songs you were singing all the way out here at Neptune?" I asked.

"We believe that Neptune is the sentinel of our solar system," said Star Baba. "It is first planet to be reached by visitors from other stars on their way to Earth. For this reason it contains the eye of God."

"Really?" Now he mentioned it there had been a fair few references to God's eyes. Star Baba withdrew a folded piece of paper from his robe. He unfolded it and showed me a photo of Neptune, one of the few taken by Voyager. He pointed to a dark spot on the surface.

"The eye of God." he said.

"That's the great dark spot," said Buster. "It's a storm. Or rather was a storm. It's not there any more."

"It is the eye of God," said Aurora emphatically. "And its closing is the cause of the tribulation that has come down on Humankind in recent years."

"We will open the Lord's eye once more," continued Star Baba "So that he may watch over and protect us."

"Protect us from what?" asked Buster. "If God is everything then why does he need to protect us from himself?"

"Please." Said Star Baba in a pained voice. "It is not easy to explain these concepts to the uninitiated. We must meditate now."

Buster was about to argue the point further but I gave him a look that shut him up.

"Right you are. Meditation, then home, right?" I said to our passengers.

They nodded and settled back in their seats, holding hands. They looked contented, blissful even. What a strange bunch of people, I thought. Coming all this way to re-open the eye of God so he can look out for mankind. What a strange situation all round. I looked over at Buster, He was typing something on the phone, which he then passed to me. 'HAD AN IDEA. WAIT TILL THEY'RE ASLEEP AND NIP OFF TO TRITON.'

I typed 'WHAT IS TRITON?"

'MOON.' He typed back.

I motioned for him to wait, then stole a look at the two behind me. They looked as if they'd both passed out. I leaned over to Buster and kept my voice low just in case.

"OK, why do you want to go to Triton?"

"I was thinking, didn't those two make us agree that any pictures taken of Neptune are their property?"

"Yeah, and I'm beginning to regret it."

"The contract never mentioned Neptune's moons, right?"

A smile crept up my face.

"You're right. It was just for Neptune. But so what? The big planet's the big draw, isn't it?"

"On the contrary," said Buster. "Out here with the gas giants the moons are where it's at. They're much more suited for putting bases on. Anyway, Triton's very cool. It's the only moon to go round its planet backwards and it has ice volcanoes. The only pictures of it were taken by Voyager and they weren't exactly hi-res. Anyway, if we get a bunch of new pictures from new angles they'll be worth a bundle. You're the businessman, I don't know why you haven't already thought of it. And when are we going to be round Neptune again?"

He was right. There was no reason why we couldn't make a little side action on this trip. In any case the Pantheists were sound asleep. They'd never know we'd been to Triton.

"Do you know where it is?"

Buster patted the Sat-nav.

"I took the liberty of pre-loading it with Triton. It's up the high street a little."

I was uneasy about this.

"Didn't that thing send us to empty space just an hour ago?"

"Yeah, but if we keep the radar on we should find it. We certainly can't get lost with the big planet sitting right there. Worst that could happen is we don't find Triton and have to go home."

I knew that Buster wouldn't rest until he'd tooled around Neptune looking for a big ice cube. Still, no harm in trying. I put my seatbelt on and gave him the nod. He fiddled with the Sat-nav until it gave him an arrow to follow and grabbed the steering wheel. Neptune slowly moved around to the right of the car and began to rotate as we headed round to its dark side. I shivered as we went into the planet's shadow. Suddenly the icy cold of space seemed to be getting to me. Feeling sleepy again I lay back and closed my eyes, letting Buster go about the business of finding a moon that went around the wrong way.

"Philip!"

I felt someone shaking my shoulder.

"Philip!" hissed Buster. I felt groggy, as if I'd been woken in the middle of the night.

"Mnn," I mumbled, rubbing my eyes. "You found Triton?"

"No, I found trouble."

"What, aliens?"

"Worse."

"What?"

"We're out of gas."

Chapter forty two

I was still half asleep and irritated, but only 'bloody hell, now we'll have to go get some more gas' irritated. The full implications of the car not being able to get us back to Earth took a bit longer to hit me, and they hit me hard. This couldn't be happening. There'd have to be a solution. There'd have to. Keep calm. I looked behind me at the others. They were both still asleep.

"OK, Buster. Talk me through this. What exactly happened?"

"Well, I couldn't find Triton. Looked everywhere but there was too much interference on the radar. So I had the bright idea of trying the car's Head Up Display. Well, it worked, up to a point. It labeled Neptune and the stars and even showed lines leading to the other planets and stuff. The layout's much easier to read in Space. We should have used it on the way up."

"OK, So why did it only work up to a point?"

"Because after a few seconds this happened."

Buster turned the knob that controlled the HUD. Nothing came on the screen except the words 'CHARGE OUT' in big red spidery letters. Below it was a flashing red rectangle with an unmistakable lightning bolt icon inside it.

"Have you tried switching the car off, then on again?" I asked.

"Several times. I've jiggled the accelerator, the steering wheel, looked for a hand crank, everything. The car's not moving. Probably going to Neptune at three quarters light speed was pushing it a bit. We should have stuck to Glasgow."

"You mean we're stranded out here with these two?"

"Look on the bright side," said Buster. "We won't be suffering for long. Do you feel cold at all? Tired?"

Now that he mentioned it I had felt chilly, just before I'd passed out while he'd been looking for Triton.

"The air's not heating or circulating any more," explained Buster. "Not only that, we're using up the Oxygen. I reckon Star and Aurora are unconscious already."

"How long does that give us?"

"All four of us? About two hours. But if they die quickly we'd have four hours each."

"Yeah, and if I kill all three of you I'd have eight hours. Just find a way to get this started, will you?"

Buster shook his head.

"There is no way. We don't even know how it's powered."

"Great."

"There is a way out of this car, though."

"What?"

"We assemble a cube and crawl through it back to my place."

"Very funny." I said dejectedly.

"No, I'm serious. That year you thought I wasn't doing anything, I was experimenting like crazy with four dimensional cubes. I was trying to work out how to crawl into one and out of another at the same time. You know, like a transmitter and a receiver. Bit like that film 'The Fly'."

"I didn't see that film, Buster. I really hope it has a happy ending," I said. "So how did the experiments go?"

"Well, I completely failed to make the thing work properly."

"Oh, wonderful."

I didn't know how many ups and downs I could take. My hopes were rising and being dashed with every one of Buster's statements.

"But that was because I realised that you can't be in two places at once in the same reality," he went on. "That's what's stopping you from leaving one space, say a car in orbit around Neptune, and entering another space, say, back at my lab. But get this: You can't move between spaces in the same reality but you can move to a different space in another reality. A sort of diagonal movement."

"Hang on," I said. "So if we had one of your cubes, we could get back to Earth, but only Earth in a different reality?"

"Yes. It might be almost like ours but it might also be Hitler-won-the-war."

"Good enough for me. Shame we don't have one of your cubes with us."

"But we do."

"What?"

Buster gave a wry smile.

"One of those precautions I was talking about. I didn't know if it was going to work but I thought I should set up a sort of 'Escape hatch'. Before I left my place this morning I switched on all the mirrors and lights in the big cube, you know, the one we got the car out of. It's been running there in my lab ever since we left. Ideally that's where we'll come out."

"Buster, you're a genius. But where's our end of the tunnel? Where's our escape hatch?"

"It's in the boot."

"This thing has a boot?"

"Yeah, I discovered it just yesterday, Had to rig up an opener but it works a treat. All you have to do is place it on the boot from the outside and it opens the whole thing up."

"The outside?" I asked, pointing out of the window at the vacuum of Space. "As in out there?"

"Ah. Hmm."

"So the one thing that could save us is in a place that would kill us if we tried to get to it?" I said.

"Errrr."

"Do you at least have the opener?"

"Yeah, it's in here."

Buster drew from his bag a lithe, bendy length of thick cable, wound all around in copper wire. On closer inspection the cable was a section of garden hose. At one end were four square 9 volt batteries taped together. This thing, this home made contraption was going to save our lives. It wasn't going to be easy, though.

"Here's what we're going to do," I said. "To get that escape hatch cube of yours out of the boot we aren't going to get it from the outside, we're going to have to tunnel through the car to get to it. I don't suppose you have a tool box stashed down there?"

"No, but I've got this." Replied Buster, holding up his giant knife.

"That's a start."

"And these." he added, bringing another three knives out of his bag. Not one of them was shorter than eight inches.

"Who goes to Neptune with four giant knives?" I asked incredulously.

"Always travel with my knives," muttered Buster.

"OK, Assuming the way into the boot is behind the back seats, our first job is to get these two out of the way. We're going to have to get them into the front."

If switching seats earlier had been difficult, moving two semi-comatose people from the back of the car to the front was nearly impossible. There just wasn't enough room to get ourselves out of the way and get them into the front seats. We tried every way we could but Star Baba kept getting caught up in the gap between the front seats. The voluminous robes he was wearing didn't help. I was just about to suggest taking their clothes off when something happened that made the whole operation suddenly possible. The gravity cut out.

It must have been something to do with the car's dwindling power supply. I was in the back trying to hold Aurora's arms out so Buster could grab them when my stomach lurched and her hair was all suddenly in my face. I heard Buster say 'Woah!' and Aurora shot up to the ceiling, hitting it with a bump. Although her hair kept getting in the way she was floppy enough to be bundled up against the windscreen while Buster got into the back. Then we floated Star Baba up front using the same method and secured them both with the front seat belts.

Once we had the back of the car to ourselves we got to work. I looked all around the rear seat but couldn't find any release catch that would enable us to get the whole thing off in one piece so we each took a knife and dug into the springy cushioning. It was a tricky job in zero G. I had to brace myself against the front seat to get some purchase with the knife and keep from launching myself across the car. As we carved chunks out of the seats the air filled up with thousands of tiny tube-like fibres. Buster said something about the seat fabric looking like it was part of the air filtration system but I was done with analysing the workings of the car. I just wanted out. The work warmed us up which was good because the air was becoming noticeably colder.

Finally we got to a thick barrier layer of some kind of black plastic. It was tougher getting through this but two of Buster's knives were serrated up to the tip which helped us saw a big hole in it. When we pulled the plastic away we came to a smooth white wall. It was the familiar material of the car's bodywork. Buster took his electric boot-opening hose and laid it against the surface in a roughly oval shape. When he connected the batteries a dark rim slowly spread from the outside of the oval to the centre. Buster reached out to the darkness and his hand disappeared as it went in. The black shape was a hole in the bodywork.

"Keep the opener in place," he said. "I don't want to lose an arm."

I held the cable up to the body of the car as best I could while Buster rummaged around inside. Finally his face lit up and he withdrew his arm, holding a triangular piece of mirror.

"I hope there's more than that." I said.

"There's *lots* more."

Over the next few minutes Buster withdrew about thirty more mirrors in a variety of different shapes. Some were plain squares, some L shaped and many small triangles. In addition there were metres of wiring, little LEDS and some old electronics from a disco light controller. I tried to keep the bits in some kind of order but in zero gravity they were floating all over the place. By the time Buster had emptied the boot the air was crowded with mirrors and wires. They hung in the air rotating slowly and reflecting each other and everything else, looking like a slow motion explosion in an IKEA factory. How Buster was going to put this lot together I had no idea. It would be easier to arrange a swarm of bees into straight lines.

Good for me that Buster was so bloody-minded when faced

with an impossible task. Good for all of us. He hunted out each piece and picked it from the air in a studious manner, carefully examining it before attaching it to another. When I wasn't watching him I looked out at Neptune. It was getting harder to see out because the windows were misting up with a thick layer of frost. Time was running out.

Slowly the cube took shape. As it grew, the space for the rest of us diminished until I was obliged to get into the front with our unconscious passengers. Bits of stuffing from the mutilated back seats kept getting caught in my mouth and once I inhaled some which triggered a choking attack. I thought I was going to faint after that- the lack of Oxygen probably. I checked on Aurora and Star Baba. They were still breathing but out cold. That was OK by me. The last thing we needed now was for them to wake up and start asking questions. In a way they were doing us a favour. They'd put themselves in such a state they were hardly using up the air at all.

I shivered, not feeling very good at all. The car was starting to feel like the unpressurised hold of a Boeing 747. Before too long it would feel like the outside of a spacecraft. Buster, to his credit, showed no signs of discomfort or lethargy at all. He beavered away at his cube until, about half an hour later, it was all assembled.

This was a different cube, one that I'd never seen before. It was much more delicate than the first sheet metal one or the big one we'd got the car out of. It was made of thin mirrors, lights and almost nothing else. The opening facing us was barely two feet wide. It would be a squeeze.

"This is the stripped down model," said Buster, reading my thoughts. "The escape hatch. I had to slim it down to fit all the parts in the boot. 'Scuse me."

He swung round to hover beside me, working the control box connected to the cube by a thin wire. Without any fanfare the lights in the box clicked on and once again the interior was full of shifting points of light. It was still an impressive sight- more impressive even than the actual Universe outside our frosted over windows. By now it was getting hard to talk without one's teeth chattering. It was also getting hard to breathe. I was starting to feel sleepy- a bad sign. Whether it was oxygen starvation or hypothermia I knew it was a sleep I wouldn't wake up from.

"Let's g-go." I said.

"OK, here's how we're going to do it," announced Buster. "I'll go first so I can find the way. You hang on to my trouser cuffs with one hand and pull the others behind you."

"How can I do that? The box is only narrow enough for us to go single file."

"We'll tie them together, end to end."

It took several agonising minutes to hitch Star Baba's feet to Aurora's shoulders with strips torn off their robes. We had just managed to make the two of them look like a long ragged salami when I heard a sound come from Aurora. I leaned over to her face, It was deathly pale and her lips were tinged with blue. Nevertheless they were moving.

"What did you say, Aurora?"

Her voice was insubstantial, as if the words were being carried from far away by a cold wind.

"Leave us..." she said.

"What?"

"Leave us here. The Eye of God will..." The words petered out.

"What did she say?" said Buster.

"She wants us to leave them here."

"Fine, cut the robes loose and we'll go."

"We can't leave them here, they'll die."

"Isn't that what they want?" protested Buster. "At one with the universe and the dark spot of Neptune and all that? What made you so moral all of a sudden?"

"It's not a question of morality. The contract was for a return trip to Neptune. They can't go changing the terms of the agreement now, their brains have been scrambled by lack of oxygen. If we come back without them the rest of their brigade will think we've killed them or something, which is what we *will* be doing if we leave them here. We might even have to forfeit the money."

"Well, if we…"

"Buster, can we argue about this later? I've got a headache and an earache and I feel like I'm going to pass out any m-minute. Just lead the way and I'll hang on to you and the others."

Buster shrugged and lined himself up with the entrance to the cube. I held onto his trouser cuffs with one hand and grabbed a fold of Star Baba's robe with another. The car's interior light dimmed and went off as the last trace of power ran out. The light from the cube was the only thing left to see.

"One more thing before we go," said Buster. "If we get separated, head for the smell of lavender."

"What do you m-m-mean?"

"I set up an air freshener in front of the big cube and an electric fan blowing air into it. Smells travel through the portal better than anything. It's how I'm going to find the way back."

"Lavender?"

"Lavender. Let's go."

Chapter forty three

Buster launched himself toward the cube and I floated after him, pulling on Star Baba as I went with Aurora taking up the rear. I had one final glimpse of the wrecked interior of the car and entered the cube myself.

Ahead of me all I could see were the soles of Buster's shoes but on all sides I saw reflections of myself hanging on to the white ragged forms of Star Baba and Aurora. An image of our whole procession passed us going the other way. Suddenly the mirrors moved and we found ourselves in a vast chamber of twinkling lights.

Buster paused, then twisted and moved along a new axis. I caught a smell. It wasn't lavender, more scorched raspberry. It triggered a memory of the time my mother burned a strudel in the oven. Buster turned again, pulling us round to the left. A whole procession of smells charged through my sinuses, from jet fuel to Coca Cola to cut grass. All around I could see floating squares that joined up with each other and then drifted apart. A shockingly putrid odour like a rotting corpse hit me right in the face. Instinctively I put my hand up to my nose and let go of Star Baba. He and Aurora span away into the depths of the chamber. I tried to call out to Buster but the rotting smell was too powerful to overcome.

Suddenly Buster pulled himself into another direction. I nearly lost my grip on his trousers but my momentary panic was quelled by the welcome scent of lavender. Buster must have smelled it too because he made for its source- a square that looked like all the others but one that he had somehow identified as the source of the smell. The square grew bigger and bigger but just before we reached it Buster realised it was the reflection of a square and dodged round in a ninety degree angle that took us right through the actual square and dropped us in a heap on a dusty, hard surface.

I lay there for a minute with my eyes closed, gulping air and checking my body to see if any part of me had been left behind in the cosmic causeway. Apart from pins and needles all over my skin I felt OK and risked opening my eyes to see where we were. It was Buster's lab, looking pretty much the same as usual, ie. absolute chaos.

"You can let go of my trousers now." said Buster.

Fifteen minutes later Buster and I were standing in front of the big cube, sipping cups of tea. He hadn't switched it off yet in case the Pantheists would be able to find their way out themselves.

"It's my fault," I said. "I lost my grip on Star Baba. God knows where they are now."

"Look on the bright side," replied Buster. "Wherever they went, it's better than where they were. They might have fetched up on an Earth where everyone is a Pantheist and they'll feel right at home."

"Well which Earth is this, do you think?" I asked.

"Close enough to where we started. I mean, this is my place, these are my mugs. If there's any difference between this Universe and the one we just left I haven't seen it."

I decided to reserve judgment on that. Outside there might be posters of Hitler everywhere for all we knew. I cast my eyes around the room. For all its clutter it was good to be here. The smell of lavender helped. Then my eyes fell on something that stopped me cold.

"Buster, did you say you left a lavender-scented air freshener by the cube?"

"Yeah, one of those cheap plastic ones. Why?"

"Look."

I pointed at the thing that had stopped me. It was beside the cube and naturally it smelled of lavender because it was lavender. A big bunch of actual, natural lavender.

"Hmm," said Buster, wandering over and picking out a stem to examine it. "OK, it's not exactly like the universe we left. You might find a couple of things different here and there. Close enough though. It just proves the point I was making about not being able to travel between two points in the same reality. It's interesting, because…"

I slammed the cup of tea down so hard some of it splashed out and burned the skin between my thumb and forefinger.

"The money!" I yelled, and ran for the door.

I was half way down the alley outside before Buster caught up with me.

"What… money?" he gasped as he followed me out of the alley and down the street.

"The money they paid us to go to Neptune! What if we never made the trip in this universe? No trip, no money! I've got to find a cash machine!"

There was one round the next corner. I let out a long sigh of relief when I saw all the zeroes on the end of my balance but then got a nasty shock when I saw the front end of the number.

"There's only five million here!"

Buster shrugged.

"Maybe in this Universe you don't negotiate so well." he suggested.

"We just lost five million pounds!" I complained. "This Universe sucks!"

"Philip, you didn't lose five million, you made five million.

Be happy with what you've got. Better that then being dead in a car orbiting Neptune."

"Shit, we lost the car as well. Thanks for reminding me."

Buster grinned.

"I'll call you a cab." he said.

Chapter forty four

"There's someone to see you, Mr. Benson." came Annabel's voice over the squawk box. I pressed down the 'speak' button to reply.

"Is it my ten o'clock?" I asked.

I was lying. Annabel knew as well as I did that I didn't have a ten o'clock, but it sounded more impressive to whoever was waiting outside my office that I had a busy schedule and could just about fit them in. It meant that they were already indebted to me before they even came through the door. It was a basic business tactic and it gave me a great deal of satisfaction not to be answering my own phone or opening my own door any more.

I'd moved up, you see. It had only been a month since we'd got back from Neptune and I'd got over the loss of half the money I'd earned. It sometimes gave me a twinge of regret but with five million in my back pocket I'd set myself up pretty nicely. I'd wasted no time in buying a 99 year lease on a suite of offices and set about furnishing it with cheap but flashy furniture from one of the many local businesses that had gone bankrupt. The squawk box was antiquated but I'd always wanted one. They don't make them any more but I found one, ironically, in the same re-use shed at the recycle centre that Buster and I had been to all those months ago.

Except that it hadn't been the same re-use shed. Not really. This was a different universe, an almost identical reality to the one we had left when we'd escaped from the car and gone through Buster's cube. It was very nearly the same, though. I was pleased to find my door key still worked and my stuff was all still where I'd left it. I had to get used to the lavender though. The stuff was everywhere. It grew wild in the cracks of the pavements, it adorned most of the restaurant tables I'd sat at, Annabel had even put a vase of it in the outer office until I'd told her to get rid of it.

No wonder Buster had found this reality, it stinks of lavender everywhere. On the plus side none of my new suits had been attacked by moths.

The only other thing that was different in Lavender World was the absence of The Community of the Infinite Pantheon. We'd Googled it and there was no sign of it at all. We'd also Googled Star Baba and Aurora Cohen but that had also turned up nothing. I tried Googling 'CIP' but it was too wide a term. I gave up on the search after the Cipriani Hotel in Venice.

I was happy enough to be done with them, to be honest. Now I could get on with running Bensonite Inc., a company that so far had a nice office and a healthy source of funds but not a lot else. That would come in time, I assured myself. After much coaxing I had managed to persuade Buster to relocate his laboratory to the cellar of the office building, into which he was now busy hauling all his old tools and equipment. In a week or so I fully expected it to look like the disaster area his old lab had been.

"No, it's not your ten o'clock Mr. Benson. I'll just ask him to wait until you've got a minute". Good old Annabel. Not old at all but young and quick on the uptake too. She'd adjusted to my ways within a week of starting work here. Possibly her last boss had been a part-time fraud like me. I spent the next two minutes examining my finger nails before hitting the button on the squawk box again.

"OK, send him in." I said.

The smug feeling that came from playing the big Boss evaporated when I saw who my visitor was. This may be Lavender World but the close cropped grey hair, the suit and the flinty eyes of Mr. Dennett were exactly the same as the last time we had met, amongst trays of wheatgrass in my old office above the juice bar. I pulled myself together and put on my best fake smile.

"Mr. Dennett! Have a seat." I said, gesturing to the chair in front of my desk. It was a leather one that looked more comfortable than it really was and was a couple of inches lower than mine. I had picked it out specially. He sat down and leveled those piercing eyes at me, then around the office.

"Nice office," he said. "Better than the last place."

"Well, I've come up in the world."

"Have you? And where have you come up from exactly?"

Careful, I told myself. Don't tell him anything and don't let him intimidate you.

"Are you with the Police, Mr. Dennett?"

He shook his head.

"Security agency?, any Government body?"

Another shake of the head.

"Then," I announced. "I don't have to tell you anything. What's your business? I'm a very busy man as you can see."

He cast his eyes around the room again and back on my empty desk. We both knew I was lying but he didn't challenge me on it.

"Mr. Benson," he said. "I work for the security department of a very large corporation. We check into the activities and backgrounds of other companies and individuals that we do business with. Just to make sure everyone's on the level. You understand."

"Fair enough. But I've never done business with you."

"Have you not?"

"We had that one meeting a couple of months ago where you made some vague threats and that was it."

"Really? Does the name Connaught Industrial Products

mean anything to you?"

"Nope."

"CIP?"

That brought me up short. Of course I'd heard the acronym CIP before but it had stood for something very different then.

"Go on." I said.

"Two months ago one of your agents, introducing himself as David, met our CEO at a function and told him about a flying car you were in possession of. A flying car that had orbital flight capability. Ring a bell?"

David. He meant Davo. It was hard for me to process the timeline but it all sounded very familiar so far. I remembered Star Baba having told us that they'd already vetted us at our first meeting. Dennett was evidently part of the vetting team.

"Your CEO," I said carefully. "What was his name again?"

"You ought to know that. It's Bernhard Giddins."

"And is his wife's name Aurora by any chance?"

Dennett bored those eyes into me again.

"Now why would you be interested in his wife?" he said.

"Well, I…" I didn't know what to say. I needed more information from this guy. Thankfully he obliged me.

"Exactly one month ago Bernhard Giddins and his wife Aurora disappeared. The last thing they did before they went was authorise a transfer of five million pounds to yourself. He said they were going on a trip, then the next day they went to his country residence and weren't seen again for twenty seven days."

My mind was spinning. I tried to hide it by looking down

at my fingernails again.

"Mr. Benson, I need to know what you did with our chairman and his wife. I need to know where you went and what happened to them."

I snapped out of my guilty reverie. Sod this guy I told myself, but be polite.

"I'm sorry Mr. Dennett but I'm bound by a non-disclosure contract. I can't speak about this to you."

"Well, you can listen to me," he said. "Something very odd happened to Mr. Giddins and his wife and I know you're mixed up in it."

"Hang on. You said he disappeared a month ago and he wasn't seen for twenty seven days. That's not a month."

"That's because we found them three days ago."

I sat up in my seat. Dennett went on.

"We found him and his wife in a psychiatric hospital. They had been picked up by the Police wearing filthy white rags wandering the streets and babbling nonsense. The Police couldn't ID them so they were being held pending a court order. We picked them up through their fingerprints. We have contacts on the Police force."

I sat back and resisted the urge to smile. So they had made it back after all. They'd come back to a Universe where their business empire was still here but their cult had disappeared. Two crazy people don't make a cult, they make an entry in the mental health statistics.

"What, er, kind of nonsense were they babbling?"

"Just garbage, nonsense. Not even words."

"*Kama hua Sh'tainu Brahn?*"

Dennett shot forward in his chair.

"That's it! How did you know that?"

"Like I said, Mr. Dennett, I'm constrained by the terms…"

"Screw the terms!" Dennett cried. "What happened to our Chairman? He won't even answer to his own name any more!"

I couldn't resist.

"Star Baba?"

"Yes!" Dennett was really getting upset now and I was relishing every minute of it. "He's insisting on being called Star Baba, he's going on about God's eyes and the Universe non-stop and he won't stop chanting that bloody nonsense of his. His wife too." Dennett looked at me with a new suspicion in his eyes. "Did you give them LSD?"

I decided to torture him again with the disclosure thing.

"I'm sorry, but I can't tell you…"

"But it doesn't make *sense*!" he whined. "We found them after twenty seven days in a mental hospital but they'd been there for a whole *five months*. How can that *be*?"

My fun with this man came to an abrupt end.

"Hang on, where and when exactly were they picked up by the Police?"

"The Police records state that they were found in late February this year wandering the streets in a state of complete disorientation. They had no ID and were half crazy, talking that gibberish you just repeated. What did you *do* with them?"

"Where were they found? The exact location?"

Dennett pulled a piece of paper from his inside pocket and

unfolded it.

"It doesn't say the name of the street, it just says Park Royal."

"Park *Royal*?" now it was my turn to get worked up. "Park Royal, last February?"

"Yes."

I sprang to my feet and grabbed my jacket from the back of my chair.

"I'm sorry Mr. Dennett. I have to curtail this meeting. I have an urgent appointment."

He got up slowly from his chair. Obviously this meeting hadn't satisfied his need for answers. All his steely confidence seemed to have left him.

"Can I ask you one more thing?" he said plaintively.

"What's that?"

"Is there any chance of a job here with you?"

"With Bensonite Inc? Don't you have a nice little thing going at CIP?"

"Not any more, I don't. Not with Star Baba in charge. He's turned the whole company upside down. The board are going nuts. They're thinking of removing him and having him sectioned under the mental health act. Guess who's the scapegoat? The guy who vetted the people who did this to him. In other words, me. *You* did this to me. You owe me."

"Leave your CV with Annabel," I said, hustling out of the door. "I'll have a look at it later."

I took the lift down to the basement. Buster was there, arc welding some pipes into an abstract jumble. He stopped when he saw me and lifted his mask.

"They've found Star Baba."

"And Aurora?"

"Her too."

"Good for them. How are they?"

"Barking mad. Even more so than before by all accounts."

Buster chuckled and went to pull his mask down again. I stopped him.

"Do you want to know where and when they found them?"

"OK."

"In Park Royal. Last February."

"Oh."

"Remember what happened then?"

"Yeah, that's when we got the car. Sounds like they found their way out via the big cube but I don't remember seeing them at the time. Do you?"

I thought back to that dark night when the big cube was up and running. I was so excited to be doing the experiment I suppose it was possible they had sneaked out the back of it unnoticed.

"Screw it, Buster, do you know what this means? You've invented *time travel*!"

He considered this for a few moments, then shrugged again.

"It's a bit crap though," he said. "If the only time and place you can go is where you've already been and set up an exit cube then there's not much point to it. Tell you what, I'll give it a bit of thought once I've finished this."

"What is it?"

"A shelf for my tools. Always wanted one of those."

Ben Slotover

EPILOGUE

Three months later they announced a new space probe that would be going to Neptune. It would be the first one to go there since Voyager 2 in the 1980s and there was much fanfare made over the fact that it wouldn't just be going there but coming back as well. Ostensibly its purpose was to study the planet and collect samples of its rings to bring back to Earth. I had a close look at the diagram of the probe in the free newspaper I'd found on the Underground. Call me paranoid but the supposed 'ring dust collector', a shielded scoop measuring about three metres by two by two was exactly the right size and shape to fit a car into.

After a bit of research I found out that the probe was being developed by the astrophysics department of Birmingham University. Buster said that the university department was a well-known front for M.I.18, a secret Military Intelligence technical department previously thought defunct. Don't worry about it, he told me. It'll take years to get there and years to get back and there's nothing that can connect that car with us except the handful of insane and/or drugged up passengers whose testimony would be highly questionable.

But I am worried. Not about them finding us through Star Baba or A to B Spacelines or even Mr.76. I'm worried because I've lost my driving license. The last time I can remember having it was when I shoved it down the side of the driver's seat before our very first flight. If they get that car back and take it apart... well, let's just say I'll have a lot of questions to answer.

Author's note

The great dark spot of Neptune was discovered by the Voyager 2 space probe in 1989 and had disappeared by 1994. Soon afterward another dark spot appeared in Neptune's northern hemisphere. This is known as the Northern Great Dark Spot (NGDS). The spots are believed to be giant swirling holes in Neptune's methane atmosphere featuring winds of up to 1500 miles per hour, the fastest in the Solar System.

Ben Slotover was born in London in 1971. He went to school in London and aside from four years spent at Trinity College Dublin and the occasional holiday he has lived in London all his life. He has worked in the media production industry and made several short films as well as written for Channel Four and the BBC. He has been one of the organisers of the London film club Exploding Cinema since 1998, drove a car for the 2012 Paralympics and is married with three children.

Made in the USA
Charleston, SC
14 March 2014